CW01668442

FALLING FOR MY BROTHER'S BEST FRIEND

PIPER RAYNE

This book is a work of fiction. Names, characters, places and incidents either are products of the author's imagination or are used fictitiously. Any resemblance to actual events or locales or persons, living or dead, is entirely coincidental.

© 2019 by Piper Rayne

All rights reserved, including the right to reproduce this book or portions thereof in any form whatsoever.

Cover Design: By Hang Le

Line Editor: Joy Editing

Line Editor: My Brother's Editor

Proofreader: Shawna Gavas, Behind The Writer

ABOUT FALLING FOR MY BROTHER'S BEST FRIEND

Let's say you're an independent, self-sufficient woman who runs the family company and you find yourself falling for your little brother's best friend. Now, more than ever, you need to count all the reasons why you need to abandon falling.

Abandon Falling #1 – He's a womanizer. Hasn't had a serious relationship a day in his life and changes women more often than he changes his sheets.
Abandon Falling #2 – He's never serious. He cracks one-liners, mostly at your expense.
Abandon Falling #3 – When things go wrong, he seems unfazed and always remains in control. It's *so* annoying.
Abandon Falling #4 – He has tattoos. Lots of them. Everywhere. Not to mention, he owns a tattoo parlor. (Damn it! Why doesn't that sound like a bad thing anymore?)
Abandon Falling #5 – There's a growing list of how different you two are. You can't get along for fifteen minutes —a lifetime together would land one of you in prison.

Keep repeating those reasons and drown yourself in work. Pretend you don't notice his good qualities or how enticing he looks without a shirt, and do not, I repeat, do not agree to live with the man while your place is being repaired from flood damage.

Trust me, even the strongest of us can only forego temptation for so long.

Falling for my *Brother's Best Friend*

The Baileys

Austin Bailey - 33 years old
(Biology Teacher/Baseball Coach)
Savannah Bailey - 31 years old
(Runs Bailey Timber Corp)
Brooklyn Bailey - 28 years old
(Runs Essential Oil Company)
Rome Bailey - 26 years old
(Chef)
Denver Bailey - 26 years old
(Bush Pilot)
Juno Bailey - 25 years old
(Matchmaker)
Kingston Bailey - 22 years old
(Smokejumper)
Phoenix Bailey - 21 years old
(Student)
Sedona Bailey - 21 years old
(Student)

ONE

Savannah

Early Wednesday morning, I tiptoe down the hall wearing a towel wrapped around my body, slide into my bedroom, and slowly close the door. Once it clicks shut, I release the breath I'm holding, hoping I was quiet enough not to wake Liam.

Getting ready while trying not to make any noise is harder than dragging Grandma Dori out of Lucky's Tavern on dart night. I've managed to avoid Liam these past few days by being out of the house before he wakes up, and I don't plan on running into him today.

Slowly sliding hangers over the metal bar, I select my most loose-fitting outfit from the closet. After Austin's wedding on Saturday—with the heat index the highest it's been in three summers—I'm bloated. Once I'm dressed, I comb through my long blonde hair, hoping it air dries enough to throw up in some sort of updo before I leave.

I make my bed, hang the damp towel on a hook on the

back of the door, then grab matching heels and close my closet. I turn to leave, but before I do, I walk back over to the bed and slide my hand along the comforter to smooth out a wrinkle.

I grip the door handle and turn it slowly, halting at the sound of movement in the hall. I hear a groan and the sound of someone using the washroom down the hall without the door closed. My shoulders sag in relief. *Denver.*

I sneak a peek as he walks out of the bathroom, still half asleep in a pair of boxers, scratching his junk.

Just what every sister wants to see.

He walks back into his room and shuts the door.

I slide out of my room and tiptoe down the hall as fast as I can, carrying my heels down the stairs into the kitchen area. I place my shoes with my computer bag and purse on the table by the front door, setting my keys down quietly so I can quickly grab something to eat from the kitchen and get the hell outta Dodge.

As I open the fridge door to grab a yogurt, shivers race up my spine with the sound of the front door opening and closing. He's already up, not fast asleep in his room as I'd hoped. I close the fridge door and turn around.

"Aaaahhhh!" I jump back, startled to find his big body already leaning against the counter with his arms crossed.

Damn him.

"Good morning, Savannah," Liam says with a cocky smirk.

"Stop it." I peel back the lid of my yogurt, eyeing the spoon drawer he's currently blocking.

This is exactly why I was trying to sneak out. Liam Kelly is my brother's best friend, very often the bane of my existence, and unfortunately too hot for my own good. He's also my landlord for the foreseeable future since my insurance company's contractor is taking his sweet-ass time fixing my place after the flood.

"What?" he asks.

"You and that look."

"What look?"

I want to scream at him for making this uncomfortable. How many people hook up at weddings? It's a common occurrence, so there's nothing special about us messing around after Austin and Holly's wedding reception.

"The look that says you just caught your prey," I say.

"And you think you're my prey?"

"No." I glance at the drawer again.

He follows my vision, his smirk only widening further. His T-shirt is sweaty and clinging to his muscles, which means he woke up earlier and left to work out. But he always keeps his door open when he's not in his bedroom and it was definitely closed when I left my room to come down here. Did he set me up in order to talk about what happened Saturday night?

I glance at the fast food straw on the counter, next to an empty fry container. Denver. But that straw might work for my yogurt.

"Do you *want* to be my prey?" he asks.

"No. Why would I?"

"You seemed to enjoy it the other night."

I inhale a sharp breath. "That was a mistake. A *drunken* mistake."

"I wasn't drunk."

I step toward the drawer and jut out my hip. He could be a gentleman and step aside, but he doesn't.

"I don't think you were drunk either," he says.

I stare into his bright blue eyes then let my gaze drift down his tattoo-covered arms that aren't hidden by his Smokin' Guns Tattoo Shop T-shirt. I remember when he shot those T-shirts out of a handheld cannon blaster at the last Founder's Day Parade. They were a hit, as is everything he does in Lake Starlight. Young and old, people love him.

"It doesn't matter whether I was or wasn't. It changes nothing. We're not—"

"Spare me the lecture, I have it memorized." He pushes off the counter, the blue of his eyes lighting with humor. "The fact remains that you couldn't resist me."

Liam Kelly couldn't be any fuller of himself. Yes, he's hot, but if he thinks I'm going to sleep with him just to be tossed aside like one of his Smokin' Guns groupies, he's wrong.

I open the drawer, grab a spoon, and slam it closed. I whip around to face him. "What do you want from me?"

He opens the paper that was sitting on the counter and takes a seat on a breakfast stool. "Nothing, Savannah. That's your problem. You always think everyone wants something from you."

He's got to be kidding me.

"Because everyone does. Everyone always wants or needs something from me. Ever since I was nineteen, it's been Bailey Timber or Austin or Grandma Dori or this town. You wanna see the list of people who depend on me?" My phone dings in my purse as though it's agreeing with me. I don't need to look at the message to know that it will be *someone* who needs *something*.

He continues to read the paper, cool and collected, while annoyance grates at me as if I'm a chunk of cheese.

He has no idea what it's like to have all the responsibilities of the second oldest Bailey. The one who was chosen to take over the family business. I can't even remember who I was before my parents died.

After a minute of me staring daggers into the side of his head, he says, "I said I don't want anything."

"And you're lying." I shove a spoonful of yogurt into my mouth.

He lowers the paper. "You're right. I'm lying. I'd like you to admit that you weren't drunk on Saturday."

I throw my hands in the air. "Seriously? What does it matter to you?"

The paper falls from his hands and he leans back. I soak him in once again, pushing back the memories of what it felt like to have his hands all over me.

He says, "It'd be nice to see you be honest with yourself for once."

"Why? So you'll feel better? Are you looking to up the caliber of woman in your bed from giggling girl to sophisticated woman?" I heap another spoonful of yogurt into my mouth.

He narrows his eyes. "You know what Saturday was. Tell me you didn't enjoy it."

I clean off the spoon and put it in the dishwasher before throwing away my yogurt container. "What was it then? If you remember, I ran out of the room."

I'm starting a fight I can't win. We didn't fall into bed while stripping off each other's clothes in a drunken haze. We had a heavy make-out session like horny teenagers. His words of praise for my body have repeated in my head ever since, but I can't live in some fairyland where I'm the one woman who could make him change his ways.

"If I have to tell you, then you're not worth it."

His words cut deep, as he meant them to. Rarely does Liam say anything without thinking it through. That's where he differs from my brothers. The three of them may be best friends, but Denver and Rome say whatever, whenever without thinking of the consequences. Liam though, he chooses his words wisely and with purpose.

My phone dings again and I sigh. "Fine. I need to get to work." I slide on my heels and swing my bags over my shoulder, digging my cell phone out of my purse.

"You gotta bear all that weight, right? I mean, the success of everything rests on you." His back is to me. He's stripped off his T-shirt and is digging through the fridge.

I stand in place, staring at him. My shoulders fall, my bitchy attitude faltering. I hate that we're like this. "You just don't understand... I mean, the company and the family. Grandma Dor—"

"Don't worry, Sav. I'm a big boy." He raises his hand, his back still toward me. "Have a great day."

Defeat consumes me. I wish I could break the distance, place my hands on his hips and cast a trail of kisses up his back, taste the saltiness of his skin and trace his intricate tattoos with my tongue. Instead, I spin on my heel and slam the door behind me.

My phone dings again.

"For the love of God, who wants something now?" I yell, thankful Liam lives miles from neighbors.

But my anger dissipates when I open the text message thread with my sister and see a picture of her and Wyatt inside a chapel in Las Vegas, their left hands raised. In full Brooklyn fashion, she writes *Guess What?* Followed by another text.

Brooklyn: *Time to plan a reception, Maid of Honor. YAY!*

I stare at the phone before looking back at the house one more time. Liam would be the best kind of distraction to make me forget that I'm going to die alone after watching all my siblings get their happily ever afters.

TWO

Liam

The door shuts behind Savannah, and I slam the fridge door out of pure frustration.

"Whoa, what did the ketchup do to you?" Denver walks into the kitchen wearing only his boxers, his hair poking out in a million different directions.

This is the first I've seen him since the wedding. I have to assume he was holed up in bed with someone all day and night after the wedding. My friend is awesome, but he needs to get his shit together.

"Coffee?" I change the subject, noticing Savannah's to-go coffee mug sitting by the pot. "Don't make me throw this at you" is inscribed in a girly script on the side. Juno never lets an opportunity to razz her sister pass, and Sav's past birthday was no exception.

"Definitely." His head hits the table.

I fill our coffee mugs and sit next to him with the paper. "First you go missing at the wedding, then you don't return until late last night?"

He picks up his head to give me his classic I-got-some smirk.

"Who was it?" I ask.

"A repeat."

I run the guest list through my mind, but it's still hard to narrow the options down because it was the first Bailey wedding and practically the entire town was in attendance. Then a tiny brunette pops to mind. "Mindy?"

His smile grows and he sips his coffee. "She still loves it when I—"

I hold my hand in the air. "We're not sixteen, desperate, and horny anymore."

"You're not horny?"

I cock an eyebrow.

"Don't shoot me that look. I get that you respect that Savannah is living here, but your dry spell has been going on since before she moved in." He sips his coffee.

How do I tell him my dry spell is by choice, not necessity, and that it's only been thirty-six hours since a woman was in my bed? And that woman was his sister.

Savannah is like an itch on my back I can't reach. I'm not exactly happy with myself for still being pissed off that she ran out of my bedroom on Saturday night when we were making out. We were seconds away from quenching the thirst we both have for one another. Savannah may be in denial, but I know that whatever is brewing between us isn't going away.

"The tattoo shop is busy, and I don't have time." I stand to dump out the rest of my coffee. Might as well shower and head to the shop to do the books since we don't open until later.

"It's funny." He meets me at the sink. "I was thinking, when I was at Mindy's house—"

"You slept with her at her parents' house?" Last I heard, Mindy had moved to Vancouver.

"She stays above the garage." He shrugs and leaves his mug in the sink while I put mine in the dishwasher.

"Did you sit down with her parents for breakfast?"

"No," he scoffs. "We stayed in bed. Stop trying to make me forget my original thought."

"It's so easy though." I pluck his cup from the sink and add it to the dishwasher because we both know he won't.

"Har-har. So you and Savannah...? Buzz Wheel reported about you two."

Of course Buzz Wheel had something on Savannah and me leaving Austin's wedding together. I hate that online gossip blog. "I drove her home."

"Good. Not that I'm a dick of a best friend who'd say you can't date my sister, but I was hoping this whole dry spell wasn't because you had the hots for her."

"You're delusional. I gotta shower." I head for the stairs.

"Are you dodging me?" he calls.

"I answered the question," I say before I shut my door.

Once I'm secluded, I push his words out of my head but my bed being front and center only reminds me of her. The way her body slid against mine. The softness of her skin. The flowery smell of her hair. Her swollen lips and lust-drunk eyes. Somehow or another, I gotta shake her out of my system.

After stripping down, I head to my bathroom and brush my teeth while I wait for the shower to warm up.

Denver might think he'd be okay with me messing around with his sister, but he's a classic after-the-fact-opinion guy. And this is one area where he'd definitely have an opinion about it after the fact. Especially since his sister thinks I'm not good enough for her.

WANNA KNOW WHAT SUCKS? When you've got woman issues and you can't go to your two best friends because they're the twin brothers of the girl you can't get out of your head.

I enter Smokin' Guns and lock the doors, keeping the blinds shut so no one bothers me. I'm still pissed off after my confrontation with Savannah this morning and could use some alone time. In my office in the back, I'm only alone with my music for a few minutes before the door chime rings.

"Liam!" Rhys calls. He rounds the corner of the office before I can tell him where I am. Being my right-hand man, he knows what I do every Monday. "What's up?"

He leans his shoulder on the doorframe, crossing his arms. Rhys is unique for a tattoo artist because the man doesn't have a drop of ink on him. He looks like a skateboarder, with his beat-up Vans and endless supply of worn-out jeans and T-shirts.

"Not much." I drop my pen on my desk and slide out my chair. "How was your weekend back home?"

"Good. Seattle is changing. Not sure it's a good thing."

Rhys is a transplant. No one knows much about him other than that he showed up at my shop one day, asking if I was looking for any artists. He keeps a quiet life with his dog on the outskirts of town. We've gone camping and fishing a few times. Compared to Denver and Rome, he's mellow as hell.

"How?"

He shrugs. "Just different, I guess. Lots of new condos going up. People being pushed out to the 'burbs because they can't afford rent in the city anymore. But tat places are lighting up every block. Maybe you should do a branch?" He smiles because anyone who really knows me knows Lake Starlight is my home and I have no plans to make Smokin' Guns some kind of franchise.

"Maybe you should open a shop?" I raise an eyebrow.

He guffaws. He's gun shy, which I get. Especially not having any tats himself. Some people would say he's not a true artist because he doesn't understand what it's like to get one. Lucky for him, I'm not one of those people. He's a skilled artist and that's all that really matters as far as I'm concerned.

"I like you branching out better."

I chuckle. "Why are you here so early?"

"I was gonna sketch out some ideas I have."

"And your place?"

He shrugs again. He's a man of few words. "How was the wedding?"

Okay, I can take a hint. He's not up for talking about himself. "It was great."

"Great not good, huh? Did you finally get laid?" He laughs.

"None of your damn business."

He nods and pushes off the doorframe.

But Rhys is someone I can trust, and I need to talk to someone before I go apeshit crazy. "Hey, Rhys?"

He turns around, his smirk saying everything I need to know. Rumors are already spreading, even with how careful we were when we left the wedding together.

"What's the word?" I ask.

"Nothing. I just know you and Savannah Bailey in a room together can be either hot or cold. You forget I was here for the blackbird tattoo."

I had tunnel vision the night she came in, asking me for

something to remember her parents by. It still surprises me when I look back on it—that she trusted me to permanently mark her skin. "Truth?"

He walks back to the doorframe and leans against it in the same position he was in previously. "Always."

"I took her home and we messed around and now I can't get her out of my head, and since we live together, I spend most of my time out of my own house or in my barn." I sound too vulnerable and way too much like a chick.

Rhys loses his smirk. "You need to decide right now if you're going to pursue her. Either you go after her with everything you got, or you walk away."

"You make it sound so easy." I run a hand through my dark hair then pull on my neck, wishing the knots in my muscles would vanish.

"Believe me, I get that it's not. But you can't be in limbo like you have been. It's not healthy, man. If it's not gonna ever happen, you need to move on with your life." He crosses his arms, and I wonder what brought him here. He sure sounds as if he's speaking from experience.

"She's my best friends' sister."

"Exactly."

"Meaning I can't very well separate myself from her forever."

"You won't, not can't." He pins me with a stare as if to say, "tell me I'm wrong."

"What do you want me to do? Kick her out of my house and date other women?"

He touches his nose as though I got the answer right.

"I can't kick her out. Her grandma would hunt me down and strip me of my balls. Have you ever met Grandma Dori?"

He chuckles. "Then do the one thing you can. Date

around. Work her out of your system. I get the situation isn't ideal, what with you two living together, but if she's the one putting out the Heisman arm, you can't be expected to play priest in your own house."

I debate his words. Maybe he's right. I've been so hell-bent on not disrespecting Savannah, maybe I went about this wrong.

"The only other thing you could do is convince her to sleep with you. I mean, you don't do serious relationships, right?"

His question throws me into a tailspin at first. I've never had a serious girlfriend, but I'm not against having one. I've just never found someone I could imagine infiltrating my life. I've lived on my own since I was eighteen, so she'd have to be amazing for that to happen.

I can't say the thought of just sleeping with Savannah hasn't occurred to me before though. "I'm not sure her brothers would be okay with me doing a fuck-and-chuck with their sister." I raise an eyebrow.

"Do they have to know?"

"I guess not. Maybe you're right."

He pushes off the wall again, cocky smirk in place. "I usually am."

"Is that why you ran all the way up here to Alaska? To prove you were right about something?"

"Nah. I just got tired of the view." He goes to the front desk everyone gravitates toward to draw for some reason.

I press play on my phone and "Call You Mine" by the Chainsmokers comes on through the Bluetooth speaker.

Rhys comes back and grabs my phone. "Listen to this a few hundred times and you'll start to believe it."

"Get Lucky" by Daft Punk plays. He pats my shoulder and leaves the room.

Maybe he was a therapist before he came to Lake Starlight. Either way, I'm going to do what he says. Either I try to sleep with her, or I date random women until Savannah Bailey is so far out of my mind, I can barely remember what she looks like half-clothed.

THREE

Savannah

"You're cranky today." Juno sits across from me at Lucky's Tavern, sipping her new favorite drink—Malibu and Coke.

She drinks something different every time I'm here with her. My only saving grace is that Colton hasn't joined us yet. And by yet, I mean I anticipate him walking through the door at any moment.

"I'm not cranky." I sip my wine. Damn Holly. The girl only supplies us with white wine, so now I know all the different kinds. I'm currently torn between Riesling and Moscato as my favorite.

"You are cranky, and I think it has something to do with the guy over at the pool table."

I don't bother to look. "Well, our brother pisses me off on the regular."

"Denver especially," she agrees without pushing me to look at who he's with. I see Liam enough. I saw him this morning, this evening before I came here, and I'll see him before I go to bed. That's enough for me. "Maybe it's not the guy but the girl at the pool table with him that's making you cranky?" She taps her finger against her lips as if it's something she has to contemplate.

"I don't really care. As long as I don't have to hear her moaning my brother's name at night."

"I don't think it's going to be Denver's name you hear." She puts her red lips around the straw of her drink, sucking the coconut-flavored liquid into her mouth while her eyes zero in on what's happening behind me.

I glance over my shoulder. Liam's attention is on a girl in a short skirt, sitting at the bar table next to the pool table. Denver's playing wingman with her friend. I want to roll my eyes but school my features at the last second.

"So I was thinking... let me set you up," Juno says. "I'm between clients right now and I want a tough project."

I purse my lips. "I'm a tough project?"

"You aren't exactly Mary Poppins."

I tilt my head. "Was Mary Poppins really that nice? She was strict."

"It's a phrase, Sav."

I place my wine down and crack my neck when the girl by the pool tables laughs so loudly, my eardrums hurt. I think they might be bleeding as a result of her cackle. "I have no time to date. I have to plan Brooklyn's reception. When are they coming home again?" I twist the stem of my wine glass with my fingers.

"She said they're home tomorrow, since it was spur of the moment. I'm not surprised she eloped after he-who-shall-not-be-named stood her up the first time around. And you know I can help with the reception too."

I nod. "Wyatt's parents are flying in and we're doing it in two weeks."

Only Brooklyn would think that's feasible. She better mean small when she says it. Not like Austin and Holly's "small" wedding. They would've been better to invite the entire town of Lake Starlight.

"At least you'll be able to check it off your to-do list quickly."

I roll my eyes.

"Come on. You need some fun in the meantime. I know I can find you a good guy. It's what I do."

I glance over my shoulder again. The girl's tits are practically pressed against Liam's chest. His legs are widened with a pool stick in one hand and his beer in the other. Liam is obviously moving on from last weekend, as I knew he would.

I sigh. Truth is, I could probably use a distraction while I'm forced to watch Liam showboat around town—at least until I can move out of his place. "If you think you can find someone I'd like, go for it. But the man has to be able to handle the fact that I'm a business owner. I work a lot of hours, and I won't be made to feel guilty over it. I have family obligations."

I stop stating my wants when she laughs, her Malibu dripping down her lips. I swear to God, if she sprays me with that drink because she can't hold in her laughter...

"Got it, sis. So pretty much you want a guy who understands that you're a workaholic and accepts that dates will be canceled due to your hectic schedule?"

"Exactly." I bring my wine glass to my lips.

"And you don't think you're a tough case," she deadpans.

"Where do you find people who want to use a matchmaker anyway?" I ask.

She shrugs, never one to let out her secrets. Juno truly

believes she got handed the gift of matchmaking through our genetic ancestry. The other eight of us have either struggled or are currently struggling to find our Mr. or Miss Right, but Juno—

"Hey, ladies," Colton says, sliding into the booth. Juno's best friend smiles at me, raising his hand to Nate at the bar.

"Colton, how's the internship going?" I sip my wine and straighten in my seat as though anything Colton is going to say is the most fascinating thing I'll hear all night. Anything to distract me from the shrill laughter coming from the pool table area.

"Good. You know Dr. Murray. Stickler for the rules. Mrs. Klein came in with her cat today..."

Colton's boring story about being a vet intern turns into background noise as Liam's deep voice sends a shiver up my spine. He's razzing Denver about playing another round. One last game before they head out.

Head out? As in back to our house, er, his house? I inwardly reprimand myself and make a mental reminder to drill a new asshole into my contractors tomorrow. My entire focus is off. Even at work. Living with Liam is not an option anymore. But if I leave, then I'm admitting defeat. I can already see his cocky smirk as he helps me load my last box into my vehicle.

Screw him.

"Couples?" The woman's voice is as grating as Janice's from *Friends*. I can't be the only person annoyed by it.

"Perfect," Denver says. "Can I pick my partner?"

As Colton makes eye contact with me, I shake my head and smile, pretending I'm still paying attention. It's great that Juno's so enthralled with his vet stories, but since I'm not much of an animal person, they don't really excite me.

"And then the cat pisses and Mr. Dweedle's dog, the German Shepherd..."

Seriously, I can't sit here anymore. My body is full of nervous energy and I just want to move around.

"Who wants to be my partner?" Denver yells.

Without thinking, I stand. "I'm in."

"What? Sav?" Juno whines, but I have no control of my body as I make my way over.

Liam's wearing his classic smile as he tips back his bottle of beer. For a moment, I think I've fallen into some trap he's set, but this is him. Drinking, messing around with my brother, and picking up women. It's the Liam I haven't witnessed since I moved in a few weeks ago, but it's classic Liam Kelly.

"Perfect." Denver points at me with a big smile.

The girl on the bar stool looks me up and down and whispers something to the one who currently has her fingers resting inside the waistband of Liam's jeans. I eye her hand and shift my gaze to my brother.

"Who's this?" the girl who seems to be interested in my brother asks. She must be from a few towns over.

Denver turns back toward her. "She's my big sister. This is Savannah." There's pride in his tone.

"You haven't picked up a pool stick for a decade," Liam reminds me. One good thing about looking at Liam now is he's stepped away from the girl and her hand is on her fruity drink instead of halfway to his junk.

"It's like riding a bike."

We used to have a pool table at my parents', which is now Austin and Holly's house. Everyone hung out at our home when we were younger. Dad would come downstairs and challenge the guys, which only made them better players as they grew older. Mom would feed everyone snacks. We were *the* house. Most of our friends would sit and talk with our parents before ever finding whatever sibling they were there to see.

"Let me grab you a pool stick," Denver says.

"Sav can just pull the stick out of her ass and use that one," Liam says with a bite to his tone.

"Another?" Nate asks before I can respond.

"Sure." I have a feeling I'm going to need more wine to get through this.

Nate picks up the empty beer bottles and heads back to the bar.

"I thought we were having a conversation?" Juno says as she and Colton join us, taking a seat at the bar-height table next to the two women.

I shrug. "Well, I wanted to play pool."

"Since when?" Juno asks.

"Exactly." Liam leans some of his weight on the pool cue in his hands, looking at us over the top of the stick. I wish he'd slip and the cue would slide up his nose.

"How come you aren't playing?" Juno asks the woman into Denver. She's not shy. How can you be when you set people up for a living?

The woman smiles politely while flipping her hair. "It's not my thing."

"And where are you from?" If they were from Lake Starlight, we'd know them.

The good thing is I won't have to dig up any information about Liam's date tonight. Juno will do it for me.

"Sunrise Bay."

"Nice, and you're here with Denver and Liam?"

"We came for a change of scenery. Met them here."

Juno nods and slides her stool closer to the woman. "So you're single?"

"Yep." She nods enthusiastically and reminds me of a bobblehead doll.

I let Juno get to know Denver's "date" while I chalk the tip of my pool cue. "What are the stakes?"

Denver looks at Liam and shrugs.

"We could do household chores, but if I win, Denver will leave all that on you," Liam says.

"Deal." Denver laughs.

"How about we kiss our partner for every ball we sink?" the woman next to Liam says.

I stare blankly at her.

Liam wraps his arm around her waist, pulling her closer but stares at me over her head. "What do you say, Sav?"

"I say I'm not kissing my brother."

"Let's just do shots for the losers." Denver finishes racking the balls and slides them to the line, then twirls the holder in his hands as he removes it.

"Fine." There's no way this girl has a shot at beating Denver and me.

Liam grabs a cue ball from the holder and puts it on the opposite side of the table. "Which one of you wants to go first?"

"Sav can," Denver says.

I go around Denver, overhearing Juno giving her card to the woman here for Denver. I laugh on the inside because Juno has no shame.

"Ready?" Liam eyes me as the stick slides back and forth through his fingers. Cocky bastard.

"Yep."

His eyes never leave mine as he hits the cue ball. It rolls back almost to where he hit it from. I might as well just tell him he's got first shot, but I don't play that way.

I align my ball and watch the tip of my stick leave a blue

circle on the cue ball. It slowly comes back but doesn't come as close as Liam's.

"I guess that means I win," he whispers in my ear.

"Not yet." I narrow my eyes and walk around to the other side of the table.

"I have this guy in Sunrise Bay. He's a fisherman and he's super nice and—"

Denver finally pays his date—or hook-up or whatever she is—some attention. "Juno!"

"What?" Juno looks over all doe-eyed like.

Colton laughs from behind her.

Denver's gaze shifts to Colton and back to Juno. "She's here with me."

"She said she didn't come here with you."

Denver blows out a breath and shakes his head as if he can't believe her. "I just bought her a drink."

Juno stands, holds up her hands, and goes back to her table with Colton. "Okay, sorry," she says to Denver then turns to the woman. "Call me tomorrow."

The woman looks as if she's trying to figure out Juno's words.

I bite my lip to stop from laughing.

"Thank you," Denver says, sidling up next to the woman and blocking Juno from talking to her anymore.

Juno's and my eyes catch, and we both smile because we know she's just a hookup. That's what Denver and Liam and our other brother Rome (before he became a father) are known for.

The crash of balls pulls my gaze to the table where Liam's setting up his next shot.

I forgot. It wasn't just my brothers my dad taught in our basement... Liam was always there too.

FOUR

Liam

"You sure you want another game?" I ask Savannah. She's plastered from the shots she's taken.

"Yep, because my dad might've taught you, but he taught me too." She loses her balance and her finger jabs me in the shoulder instead of the chest.

A small part of me likes her like this. Not the drunk and incoherent part, but the part where she's not worried about Bailey Timber or one of her eight siblings or Grandma Dori or any of the million things that seem to be running through her brain at any given moment. She's in the moment and just wants to beat me and yeah, I do love when I'm the center of her attention.

Darlene or Marlene or maybe it's Carly, sidles up next to me every time Savannah gets too close. I'd like to ditch her, but I'm an asshole who's trying to get Savannah jealous. Make her believe she's missing out.

"Come on. Let's go back to your place." The girl's fingers dig into the waistband of my jeans in the back.

"Oh, you want to go to Liam's?" Savannah says, and I grab her arm to keep her steady before her shot ends up on the felt of the pool table.

Darlene or Marlene—hell, let's go with Bar Chick at this point—shoots me a questioning look. "What is it with the two of you?"

Savannah waggles her eyebrows at me, turns around, and downs the shot, holding onto the table as if it's a railing above a cliff, keeping her from falling into the crashing waves below.

"She's my buddy's sister."

Savannah whips back around, another strand of blonde hair falling loose from her ponytail. "Is that all?"

The conversation between Juno, Colton, Denver, and his hookup halts, and an awkward silence paints the room.

"Isn't it?" I ask Savannah, baiting her to answer the question herself.

"Yes." She smiles sweetly at Bar Chick. "He's all yours."

Bar Chick comes closer and my body stiffens, heat brewing in my veins.

"So another game?" Sav sets her empty shot glass on the table and slides her hands down the pool stick.

Bar Chick tried to turn me on with that move two games ago. Savannah's getting the reaction out of my dick that Bar Chick wanted. Apparently dating another chick isn't the way to work Savannah out of my system. Maybe Rhys's Plan B is the way to go, but I definitely won't be sleeping with her tonight. Not in her condition.

"I'm tired," Denver whines, his hand venturing up the woman's thigh.

"Yeah, we're out," Juno says, standing.

Colton pulls out his wallet and heads over to the bar to

pay Nate for their drinks. Remind me again why those two aren't a couple.

"What? I'm finally out and ready for some fun." Savannah does a little twirl before hanging on to the table and clutching her stomach. "Whoa..."

"Come on, Sav, I'll get you home." Juno comes to her side. Her gaze lands on me and there's accusation there.

What the hell? I was over here minding my own business before they joined us.

"This isn't my fault," I say.

Juno nods and inhales a deep breath.

"Liam can see me home," Savannah says, her gaze skirting over my body.

Huh, alcohol really does make you truthful. I've said a helluva lot of lies while I've been drunk, but from the smoldering look Savannah's shooting me, I have to believe it's a truth serum for her.

"Sav, he has Marlene to see home," Juno whispers but not so quietly that I can't hear.

Savannah's head turns to who I now know is Marlene. Thank you, Juno. "Oh."

Marlene places her pool stick on the table and wraps both hands around my waist. She's so tiny, not like Savannah. "Come on."

I scour Savannah's face for any sign not to take this invitation. But she smiles and entwines her arm through her sister's. "I'll spend the night at your place so Liam can have alone time with Marlene." She spits the word 'Marlene' as if it has a foul taste.

I don't even blink. We both know I want to put her over my shoulder and carry her out of here to my bed again. Instead she's going to play like the idea of me with someone else doesn't even register on her scale of things to be annoyed about. Anyone who knows the woman knows that she can find a way to be annoyed about *anything*.

"Thanks. I appreciate it." I dislodge Marlene from me but take her hand. "Better luck next time," I whisper in Savannah's ear before I walk out of Lucky's with Marlene at my side.

"Finally. Is she, like, an ex or something? Because she totally wanted you. I mean, have some respect, I saw you first." Marlene gets me against the brick wall, her hand already over the bulge in my pants.

But that bulge isn't because of or for her.

I put my hand over hers to stop her. I'm not going to lead this girl on, no matter what I'll let Savannah believe. "No. She saw me first."

Truth is, I saw *her* first—*so* many years ago.

Lucky's Tavern's door opens, and Savannah stumbles out between Juno and Colton. Juno barely has a handle on her sister. Colton's doing all the heavy lifting. Savannah glances over and catches us, her eyes falling to where my hand is over Marlene's—which is over my junk. *Fuck.*

"I'm gonna be sick." She bends over the tree at the edge of the sidewalk and throws up.

Colton's eyes shut and his head falls back.

Denver comes out right after. "Party foul, Sav!" He laughs, just as drunk as his sister, but I'm not worried about Denver. He can handle himself. He smirks at me, thinking I'm about to get busy with Marlene. "Don't mind us."

"You okay, Sav?" Juno asks.

Lucky's door opens, and Nate comes out with a bottle of water for her because she's probably the entertainment for the rest of Lucky's Tavern's patrons right now. Pictures are probably being snapped and she'll likely be on Buzz Wheel before the night ends.

"Denver, get Marlene an Uber." I give Marlene a smile that I hope communicates regret and push away from the wall.

I swoop Savannah up in my arms. Her head falls over my bent elbow while her arms hang loosely at her sides.

"She can come to my place. No need to upend your night." Juno follows me to my car.

Since we won all the games, I only had one beer tonight, so I'm fine to drive. "No, I got her. Just make sure Denver doesn't come back to my house with those two." I nod behind me.

Colton opens the passenger door, and I lay Savannah in the front seat. She mumbles something as I strap her seat-belt into place.

"Just don't throw up again," I say.

"Thanks, Nate." Juno holds the water bottle out for me.

I take it before rounding my car and sliding in. One last glance at Savannah in my passenger seat, and I turn the key in the ignition and get her away from this situation which could damage her reputation. After all, it's what she lives for in Lake Starlight.

FIVE

Savannah

My head pounds as I roll over, finding myself wrapped in navy sheets. I glance over, expecting to see my alarm clock, but there's no clock. Just a drawing of an intricate Celtic image.

Liam's masculine smell surrounds me, and I search the room for him but come up empty. It doesn't even look as though he slept in the bed with me last night.

I sit up and hold my head. "What happened last night?"

I try to answer for myself, but I can't recall anything after the second game of pool.

Shifting my legs over the side of the bed, I stand, and the cool breeze from the fan spurs me to see what I'm wearing. I'm in my bra and panties—not even my good ones. Just a plain cotton bra with a pink bow in between, like it's a trainer and I'm eleven. My panties cover my entire lower abdomen. Fantastic. I grab the sheet to cover myself.

The door downstairs opens and closes, alerting me that I need to get my ass moving. With Liam's sheet wrapped around me, I tiptoe down the hall to my room in what feels a lot like the walk of shame—just without the prior benefits.

Once I throw on a pair of shorts and a T-shirt, I return his sheet to his room, still finding it vacant. After making the bed, I search the entire house for him. He's nowhere to be found. Then my eye catches the green barn outside, the door slightly ajar.

He's always so secretive about what he does in there.

I walk out of the house, trying to ignore my pounding head, and up the brick path, but as I'm about to open the barn door, Liam steps out and shuts the door. Sometimes I think he's got superpowers. Either that, or a video monitoring system.

"Morning," he says. "Did you get the aspirin and water on the kitchen counter?"

I shake my head. "What happened?" My voice sounds rougher than normal.

He heads down the path toward the house, so I follow. He's still wearing the jeans and T-shirt he had on last night, except they're more wrinkled now.

"You got drunk."

"And how did I end up in your bed?" I ask with no shortage of attitude.

He stops at the door to the kitchen and turns around, almost making me run right into him. "You put yourself there."

"I did?" My eyes dip down to look at the perfectly lined bricks that Liam most likely laid himself. "I don't remember that."

"Probably because if you were sober, the last place you would've put yourself is in my bed." He stuffs his hands into his pockets.

I want to ask if he joined me. How I ended up half

naked. But it's too embarrassing. I'd rather fly blind than get the answers from him.

"Thank you. I apologize if I inconvenienced you last night." I slide by him, having to step on the grass to dodge the chance of my body touching his.

He grabs my arm lightly, stopping me. I shift my weight, trying to slide out of his grasp, but he won't let go, so I stop, staring into his blue eyes.

"I slept on the couch." He moves a few inches closer. "You stripped yourself down." Closer still. "And you never inconvenience me."

"But you were with that girl. What happened?"

He winces, but his smirk is on full display shortly after. "We just used the couch instead."

My body goes cold and all my muscles seize. "Oh."

"Jesus, do you really think I'd do that?" He releases my arm and walks back to the barn.

"It isn't that out of the realm of possibility," I holler at his retreating back.

He stops, his head hanging low. I watch his back rise and fall as it often does when he's exasperated with me. "I didn't want her. The woman I want in my bed was already in it." He doesn't turn around to face me.

"Liam?" What's he going to do? Give some declaration as to why we should sleep together? "You should have gone home with her."

My heart rate picks up speed with each degree he turns until he's facing me. "Is that what you want?"

"I don't see how it can be any other way."

His tongue skates over his bottom lip. "You can honestly stand there and deny that you want me to pick you up and carry you into my room?"

I step forward, wanting to touch him, but I stop myself.

Liam is the type of guy who if I give him an inch, he'll go the mile to win me over. He loves a challenge, and that's all I am to him. The first woman who hasn't stripped down and laid herself willingly on his bed. Well, shit, I have done that, he just had the decency not to take advantage of me.

"Why didn't you do that last night if you think that's what I want?"

"You were drunk." He pierces me with a stare that makes me feel as though he can see deep inside me, to all the uncertainty and insecurities lurking there.

"You've taken drunk girls to bed before. Why not me?"

His eyes narrow and he shakes his head as though I'm not speaking English. "You passed out. Even when you stripped yourself down, you weren't in any frame of mind to take to bed."

"Thanks, I suppose."

He blows out a breath and his demeanor does a one-eighty, his usual smirk shining brightly. "You're welcome, I guess." I roll my eyes, and he crosses his arms. "It was nice to see you let yourself go."

"Wish I could remember what it felt like, but the night's a blur." A nervous giggle slips out of me.

"Maybe you should let that side of you out of your cage more often."

"If only." Even I can hear the wistful note in my voice.

His eyebrows raise in question.

"What do you want from me, Liam?"

"What do you think I want from you, Savannah?"

"I think you want me to be the naïve girl from before my parents' accident. But I'm the one who runs Bailey Timber now. I'm the matriarch of the Bailey family—after Dori, of course. There are expectations. I can't just hop on the back of a motorcycle and party every night."

He soaks in what I said before he speaks. "You have no idea what I want from you. And I saw that girl last night."

I throw my hands in the air. "Because I was drunk! But that's an exception for me."

"If you keep telling yourself that, you'll believe it."

"Stop it." I jab a finger in his direction. "This is who I am now."

"Fine. I didn't ask you to change everything about yourself."

He doesn't see what I do when I look in the mirror. He searches for traces of that girl who flirted with him when she shouldn't have. The one who drew his attention because she was the older sister of his best friends. The one shiny red apple in a pile of bruised and rotten ones. That's what he's attracted to, not the version who's thinking spreadsheets and quarterly reports and what I need to do to make sure all my younger siblings are okay.

"Let's agree to disagree. I'll check with my contractor today so that I can get out of your way. When there's more space, this whole thing"—I wiggle a finger between us—"will go away."

He slow claps, and I narrow my eyes. "Bravo, Sav, you always have a game plan."

"Stop it!"

He laughs and shakes his head. "Go. I'm sure someone needs you somewhere."

He disappears into the barn, leaving me shaken.

THAT EVENING, I'm at Northern Lights Retirement Residence for my weekly knitting class. Originally, I thought knitting would be fun. Keep me from obsessing over my to-do list and only think about the stitching. But I think I'm too neurotic to enjoy the art, and my instructor, Ethel, agrees.

"You're not doing it right." Ethel leans over my shoulder, taking the knitting needles and showing me for the millionth time how to get the stitch looser. "Better."

Grandma Dori rolls her eyes. She's on her phone with her feet on the coffee table. "Buzz Wheel said you threw up on a tree last night. I don't think I need to tell you that's not how a Bailey should act." She doesn't make eye contact with me.

"Agreed, but let's remember all the stupid shit Rome and Denver have pulled."

"They get the pass. They're boys, and they don't run Bailey Timber." She sets her phone down. She's not a knitter, so she grabs her pack of cards and shuffles.

"So I'm just supposed to always be on?" Damn it, I dropped a stitch and now I have to go back and fix it.

"I didn't say that, but in my experience, when someone gets so drunk they're throwing up, they have issues they're not dealing with." She cocks her gray eyebrow my way. I should suggest she get them waxed or threaded, but I don't because I'm a polite granddaughter.

"I don't have any issues," I mumble.

"How's living with Liam going?"

"Fine. My contractor said that it'll be another month. I think I'm going to move in with Juno. It's fire season, so Kingston's not around much. I can move into his room."

She shakes her head. "That won't do."

"Savannah, I know you're a little high-strung, but loosen up. Your stitches are going to be too tight." Ethel hits the tops of my hands because I'm holding the needles so tightly my hands hurt.

"You don't have to hit me," I say, but Ethel presses her hearing aid.

"There she goes again, answering the phone." Grandma Dori shakes her head. "It's so rude."

"And you're one for manners?"

She stops setting up her game of solitaire to give me a look. "I am not rude. I may be direct, but that isn't the same as rude."

I hold up my hands. "My mistake."

"Anyway, back to you moving out of Liam's house. I don't suggest it."

"And why's that?" I knit a stitch and smile as I get the hang of it a little more.

"Because you two have been chosen to plan the fundraiser for the library extension."

The needles clink as I drop them in my lap. "What?"

She continues to deal her solitaire game without granting me a glance. "It makes sense. Everyone in Lake Starlight loves Liam, and all the business owners downtown really look up to him. And one of us Baileys has to do it of course."

"Why a Bailey and why me? I have Brooklyn's reception on my plate already, on top of everything else I do."

"Well, Phoenix is interning at Bailey Timber this summer, so she'll help you there, which should give you more time for the fundraising, and Brooklyn's reception is right around the corner. The charity gala isn't for two months. I raised your father while doing all the same things you do."

My eyes bore into the side of her head. She's taken it too far this time. But I can't disrespect her and say my grandfather was running the company that I currently am. She thinks she's pulling one over on me but being the Thelma to her Louise all these years has granted me inside knowledge of what her true intention is. "You're meddling and trying to get us together."

"Believe me, I know better than to meddle with you. This is the most logical thing. That's all. You'll keep it organized and neat, and Liam will add his creative flair and secure all the items for the silent auction."

"Why don't *you* do it with Liam?"

She taps the side of her head while laying down a card. "My memory. I'd probably screw it up."

Her memory is more than fine.

"I smell a scheme," I say, reaching for my phone.

"If you'd rather, Rachel Quinlan volunteered. I could always tell the board I was mistaken, and she and Liam could work together to make it happen. I'm sure they'd get on."

She leaves the bait hanging there like a fat juicy worm, hoping I snag it like a starving fish. Rachel is the only girl I ever saw Liam go on more than one date with. In fact, they may have dated that first year I was away at college before I got called back to Lake Starlight because of my parents' deaths. She's the one he took to his senior prom.

I shouldn't care, but damn it, I do. "It's fine. You're right. A Bailey should do it."

She smiles at her cards. "Glad you're in agreement. Do me a favor and set up a meeting with him tomorrow at the office. I'll be in at ten thirty, after my cataract surgery."

"Excuse me?"

She stops dealing cards to herself. "What did you not catch, dear?"

"Your cataract surgery is tomorrow? Who's taking you? You can't drive."

"Phoenix is. Since she returned from Los Angeles, I told

her she's my helper for the summer. No way is she going to be sitting around the house Instachatting or whatever. If she's not going to try to make it in LA, she needs to figure out what her next path is."

"Okay, for a moment I thought—"

"No, I'm not going to drive after cataract surgery. Who do you think I am?" She acts as if I'm stupid for thinking she would, but the sheriff is about to revoke her license if he catches her driving out of town again.

"Dori Bailey, that's who."

She pats my knee. "Just set the meeting, dear."

"Great job, Savannah, but right here." Ethel points at an area that looks a bit wonky.

I have no idea what she's talking about. I'm over this knitting thing. "What kind of spinster am I going to be? I hate cats, and I can't knit."

Ethel rounds the couch and sits next to me, patting my knee. "We'll get you there, don't worry."

It's good to have goals, I guess.

SIX

Liam

I pocket my cell phone and open the door of Bailey Timber Corporation. The four-story lumber building is still impressive, even after being here so many times. Mr. Bailey is the one who worked with an architect when we were growing up to build the larger office. Bailey Timber had outgrown the small building near the production building.

I step up to the receptionist and I'm about to say who I'm here for, but she slides a name tag over the top of the desk.

"Here you go, Mr. Kelly. Ms. Bailey is expecting you. Do you know where her office is?" The woman is in her mid-twenties and she's cute. Her smile says she might think I'm cute too.

"Don't even think about it, Carrie, he's in love with my sister." Phoenix pops out of nowhere. "Liam." She raises her eyebrows.

I grin at her. "I heard you were sticking around."

She shrugs, her long dark hair a stark contrast from her older sister's. "LA didn't pan out yet, but I won't be here for long."

"Heading to New York with Sedona?"

"No way. I hate that place. Besides, Broadway isn't my calling. Stardom is." It's not the first time I've noticed that her eyes light with fire when she talks about her singing aspirations. "I love Hollywood, but it's so expensive."

I put my arm around Phoenix because she's like a kid sister to me. "Fall-back plan?"

"*Uuugh*! You sound like Savannah. What's wrong with pursuing your dream?"

She presses the elevator button for the top floor, where all the executives are. I remember Denver, Rome, and I riding our bikes over here to get money from their dad back when we were twelve.

"Because there're little things called rent, bills, food. Those necessities you need to survive in life."

After politely waiting for everyone to file out, we step into the elevator. "I know, I know. Austin keeps reminding me of how me moving in with him and Holly has increased those costs for them."

"Why don't you move in with Juno for the summer while Kingston's off smoke jumping?"

"Last I heard, Savannah had dibs there."

I whip my head in her direction. "What?"

She covers her mouth as if she spilled a secret. She can spare me the drama. "Oh sorry, I figured you knew." Her shoulder hikes up in a shrug, but her smirk is in place. "She must have wanted to surprise you."

The elevator dings and I follow Phoenix down the hallway.

"So you're into the older woman thing, huh? And the

older sister of your best friends at that." Only Phoenix would ask me point blank. That's her style. She's a lot like her grandmother that way.

"What are we, thirteen?"

She nudges me with her arm, stopping us in front of a corner office with Dori Bailey etched in the foggy glass door. "I can keep a secret."

"None of you Baileys can keep a secret, and there's nothing to tell. Savannah and I run cold together."

"Except when you run hot. Like the night of Holly and Austin's wedding?" She leans forward as though she wants in on the gossip Buzz Wheel is reporting.

"You can put your notepad down, detective. There's nothing to tell."

I knock on the glass because Phoenix's dark eyes are still trying to figure out the situation between her oldest sister and myself.

"Come in," Dori says, and Phoenix opens the door.

Low and behold, there's my soon-to-be ex-roommate, sitting on the couch with a pen between her teeth and her fingers pecking at the keys on her laptop. That's how I find her most days. Saturday and Sunday included.

"*Liam*!" Dori rises from behind her desk, an oversized pair of dark glasses on, and heads toward me.

There was a time when Grandma Dori scared me—back when we were young and Denver and Rome were constantly testing limits, which usually meant they came off as entitled little shits. I was the third amigo, so my reputation is similar to theirs. The only difference being that I'm not a Bailey.

"Dori." I kiss her cheek and hug her. "I haven't been to the office in ages. Good to know not much has changed."

Phoenix interrupts our hello. "Am I staying or going?"

"Going," Savannah says at the same time Dori says, "Staying."

Phoenix sits next to Savannah, putting her feet on the table. Savannah knocks Phoenix's legs off, but Phoenix does it again. Looks as if Phoenix presses Savannah's buttons as well as I do these days.

"This is where you offer to get everyone drinks." Savannah shuts her laptop and twists her hair into a bun before sticking the pen in to hold it.

"It's just Liam," Phoenix says, her feet remaining on the coffee table.

"We're not at our house," she says.

"You mean *my* house."

"I mean Austin and Holly's house." Savannah gives her a stern look, but Phoenix remains seated.

"Did you know they're taking down the flower wallpaper in the half bath?" Phoenix asks.

"Really?" Savannah and I say in unison. She looks at me.

"I liked it," I say with a shrug.

"It was ugly," Savannah adds.

"But it was unique," I say.

Savannah reluctantly nods. It's the first thing we've seen eye-to-eye on in a long time.

Since Austin and his new wife took over the family home, they've been making changes to make it their own. While I know everyone supports them doing so, it's also got to be hard to see some of the last reminders of their parents disappear forever.

"Phoenix, go get Liam a drink," Dori interrupts. "What would you like, dear?"

Phoenix stands as if she's been asked to clean toilets. "What do you want?"

"Phoenix, this is good practice for you," Savannah says.

"Water is good," I answer, and Phoenix leaves. There's an awkward silence for a beat, so I decide to fill it by whispering to Savannah, "I put your coffee mug in the dishwasher."

I take Phoenix's spot next to Savannah and ignore how her body shifts slightly away from me until she hits the arm of the couch.

"Excuse me?"

"I'm sure it's been bothering you, so I figured I'd give you one less thing to obsess about today." I lean back, resting my ankle on my knee. One loose strand of golden hair is falling down her neck, directing my attention to what I know is a sensitive spot. How easy it would be to run a small circle over her delicate skin and wrap her hair around my finger.

Phoenix pops her head back in the office. "Liam, do you take cream or sugar?"

"I said I'd take a water." An annoyed huff sounds from Savannah as her gaze shoots to Dori.

"Give her a break. She's out of her comfort zone." Dori sits in the chair next to us, and I get the feeling her gaze is shifting between us. I can't see anything through those glasses, but I'm smart enough to know not to ask why she has them on. "What are you guys whispering about?"

"Liam was so kindly telling me how he put my coffee mug in the dishwasher." Savannah takes the pen from the bun she created, letting her long blonde hair fall over her back.

My gaze is transfixed on the movement of the silky strands, and I remember how I wove my fingers through them that one night. I hear Dori saying my name and shift my attention to her, but her knowing smile says she liked the way I was looking at her granddaughter.

The granddaughter, not so much though.

"You know how Savannah is. Neurotic to the tenth degree," I say.

Savannah's eyes narrow to the smallest slits, and the door opens again with Phoenix's entrance.

"Here you go." She drops a bottle of water fresh from the fridge in front of me and plops down in the chair on the other side of me before slipping off her shoes and putting her feet on the table again.

Dori sighs. If Savannah could take her eyes off me, she'd give the scathing look normally reserved for me to her sister.

"Thanks, Phoenix." I crack open the bottle and offer it to Savannah, whose head rears back as if I offered her monkey brains. "No?"

"No," she confirms.

"You looked hot." I shrug.

She rolls her eyes and focuses on her grandmother in order to get our meeting started.

"So, Liam, we brought you in today because we'd like you to be part of the committee for the Bailey yearly charity event. You know there are plans for an addition to the library to expand the children's section. I don't have to tell you how near and dear that is to me, and I can only trust certain people with this endeavor."

I'd do just about anything for the Baileys. They're my second family, but this couldn't come at a worse time. Not only is the tattoo shop busy, but Wyatt asked me to be his pseudo best man for the reception. Plus, it means more alone time with Savannah.

"I'll do it," Phoenix volunteers.

I think she's only considering the entertainment portion

of the event. The girl would throw a huge party and generate no money.

"That's okay, sweetie, you're needed here." Dori smiles at her, but everyone in the room, probably including Phoenix, knows why Dori isn't taking her up on her offer.

"How big is the committee?" I ask.

"Just you and Savannah." Dori grins at her granddaughter like "come on, it'll be fun."

Savannah's clearly not on board, which I suspect has more to do with me than the work the event will entail.

"What are you thinking? Silent auction? Do we want a dinner or a lunch? How formal will this be?"

This isn't my first time helping with charity planning. My mom was the go-to helper until she moved away. I can't blame her. When your best friends die, you tend to want to escape.

"I trust that you and Savannah can plan an amazing event that will get the funds needed for the library extension. I think we should keep this upscale though. Let's do a theme dinner with a silent auction, but we need specialty items. Big ticket items. Unique items."

I nod. "I can go around to the local businesses, recruiting."

Dori points at me. "That's where I knew you'd excel. Savannah can handle the where and when as well as the decorations."

"You think I can't handle deciding on white or ivory linens?" Phoenix interrupts, turning Dori's attention her way.

While Dori politely turns Phoenix down once again, I turn my gaze to Savannah. She's looking at where her fingers twist in her lap.

"You're game for this? I'm shocked."

She side-glances at me but responds to her hands instead of me. "I don't have a choice."

"You always have a choice."

She raises her head and turns to me fully, giving me the scathing look I'm becoming immune to. "You don't understand."

"Tell me again what I don't understand." Before she can release that annoyed breath, I continue. "Oh right, how much pressure you're under? How it can only ever be you who makes things happen? Someone might think you were the president with how often you use your responsibilities as an excuse to avoid things that scare you."

She gives me a bland look and turns to look at her grandmother. "Are we done? I have calls to return."

Dori's head swivels in Savannah's direction. "If you two think you can take it from here, we can be. I know you might be limited with what you can accomplish until after Brooklyn and Wyatt's reception, but I wanted to get it on your calendar, Liam."

Savannah puts her hair back up in the bun, stands, and pulls her laptop to her chest. "I'm good. Liam?"

I raise my eyebrows. "I'm good. We can always discuss this more over dinner at home."

"Good point." Dori smiles at me. "You living with Liam will make this all the more convenient."

Savannah stops at the door. I baited her. Right about now, she's figured out that I know she was going to sneak off to try to get away from me. She peeks over her shoulder, and I raise my eyebrows in challenge. This is her chance. Stand up to her grandmother and tell her that she can't stay with me anymore.

"Tomorrow? I'll pick up Wok For U?" I ask.

"Sounds great." She walks out of the office.

"That went better than expected." Dori stands. "Thank you, Liam. I didn't know who I was going to hand this over to. Austin is too busy and Rome, well..."

She doesn't bother mentioning Denver. We all know he can't handle anything like this.

I stand and kiss her cheek. "Happy to do it."

Her wrinkled hand touches my cheek and she stares into my eyes. At least I assume she is since she still has those ridiculous glasses on. "You've really grown into an amazing man. A little too many tattoos, but your heart is pure gold."

I chuckle. "Thank you."

"You're totally kissing up to him." Phoenix stands. "I think I would've planned a kickass party."

"That's the problem, you see it as a party. We're not doing keg stands and Jell-O shots." I hug Phoenix goodbye. "Thanks for the water, kiddo."

She rolls her eyes like the twenty-year-old that she is. "Grandma Dori, can I get off early?"

"Why?"

"I told Juno I'd help her interview guys for some girl she's trying to set up."

"Sure, but you can't leave early every day."

"I can give you a lift," I offer. "I'm headed over to Brooklyn and Wyatt's place. I'll drop you at Juno's on the way."

Both their gazes widen.

"Why are you going there?" Dori asks.

I tilt my head and look at her. "Wyatt needs my help with the event tent for the reception."

"Oh."

Phoenix laughs and Dori shoots her a warning look, but Phoenix pays no attention.

"What am I missing?" I ask, unease building in my gut.

"Nothing, dear, you go and have fun with Wyatt." Dori pats my shoulder.

I wrap my arm around Phoenix's shoulders, escorting her out of the office.

"Phoenix," Dori says.

They share a look before Phoenix nods.

We step out of the office and I immediately dig in. "So what was that about?"

"Savannah has a date. She's getting ready over at Brooklyn's so that he wouldn't have to pick her up at your house."

I nod, a little happier that Wyatt thinks I'm his on-call handyman. Not that I mind—especially today, because nothing gives me more satisfaction than watching Savannah squirm.

SEVEN

Savannah

I barely escape my meeting with enough time to hightail it over to Brooklyn's in time to get ready for my date. Juno is already antsy that I'm going to bail, and I don't need her calling Brook and finding out I'm late.

I park in front of what I think of as the Whitmore Estate, because this giant-ass farmhouse in the middle of Alaska is an out-of-place monstrosity. But that's what you get from a millionaire trust fund baby, I guess.

I walk up the gravel walkway—they haven't gotten a chance to pave it yet—and two men unloading something large and white from a box truck draw my attention. At the door, I ring the doorbell.

"Sav?" Wyatt comes out from around back of the house. He's all sweaty in his track pants and T-shirt.

"Do you still run the resort?" I ask.

He smiles and runs his hand through his dark hair. "You know the chickens your sister bought are a full-time job."

I return his smile. "You should make Brooklyn do it."

He agrees, but from his expression, I can see that will never happen.

"Where is she anyway?" I ask, eager to get inside and get ready to be picked up because I want this date done and over with. Yes, I know, not the best mindset to go into this with, but it's the truth.

"She went into town to grab more plants. She's trying to build a garden. She said she'd be back by now though."

"Sick of heading over to Holly and Austin's every time she needs to make essential oils?" I ask, unsure if I should open the door and go in or not.

Wyatt steps up onto the grand porch. "She caught them screwing the other day when she went by to pick some things from her old garden."

I cringe, imagining myself in that scenario. "Seems like a regular occurrence for the newlyweds."

"Yeah. I heard they're trying."

I ignore the pang pulling at my heart. I may never "be trying" because what am I going to do? Run a business with a baby hanging off my right breast? No other Bailey is interested in working at Bailey Timber, and Grandma Dori spends less and less time there as it is. I'm the one and only Bailey who can keep the family company, and thereby our legacy, going. Not to mention the problem of finding someone who will accept me for me, falling in love, and getting married first.

"I heard the same," I say. I watch the men round the box truck again and realize it's a tent they're carrying. "That for the reception?"

He glances back as if he doesn't remember. "Yeah. So much for a small ceremony."

"No such thing when you marry a Bailey."

"My only saving grace is that half of Manhattan won't be here."

"True."

I can't imagine what it would've been like if they'd invited half of the upper east side to attend. Wyatt's family owns hotel chains around the world and I'm sure his father would've loved nothing more than a swanky Manhattan wedding. As a businesswoman, I have a lot of respect for Wyatt for striking out on his own and purchasing the failing resort in Lake Starlight and turning it around. As a sister, I have even more respect for all the love and support he's shown my sister since she was left at the altar right before they met.

"Anyway, I'm done talking wedding shit. It's the reason we eloped. What are you doing here? Brooklyn mentioned you'd be coming by, but she didn't say why." He eyes the bag hanging off my shoulder.

"Well..."

As I'm about to tell him the embarrassing fact that I allowed my matchmaking sister to set me up, Brooklyn's tires sound on the gravel drive before coming to a stop. She opens the trunk of her fancy SUV and grabs a bin of plants and flowers. Wyatt jogs down the steps and grabs them from her.

"Thanks, babe." Brooklyn smiles at me. "Sorry I'm late. The nursery had some new plants in I couldn't resist checking out." She waves it off like it's not a big deal that she wasn't on time. "Can I do your makeup?"

She's forgotten the plants and is on to the next task at hand, but that's Brooklyn.

"I can do my own makeup."

"Is this a trial for the reception or something?" Wyatt

drops the big crate full of stuff for Brooklyn to plant on the side on the lawn.

"No. Savannah's got a date." Brooklyn's proud tone makes my cheeks heat.

"Oh..." Wyatt's eyes drill into Brooklyn as though he's trying to convey something to her, but she's too busy opening the door for me. "Brook?"

We both turn our attention back to him on the porch, but before he has a chance to say anything, a familiar muscle car comes roaring down the driveway.

"Why is Liam here?" I ask through clenched teeth.

Wyatt runs his hand through his hair and shifts his weight. "I asked him to help with the tent set-up."

"Why?" Brooklyn screeches.

My eyes are trained on Liam, who has yet to get out of his car. He didn't mention any of this earlier at the office.

"I just told you. I love that you think I can do everything, but you forget people were paid to do this crap for me my entire life. I just showed up to the events." Wyatt's frustrated tone says they've had conversations behind my back about Liam and me.

"It's fine," I say to stop the newlywed couple from arguing.

"Are you sure?" Brooklyn's hand lands on my arm. I look at it then up at her concerned gaze.

Liam steps out of his car, looking just as gorgeous as he did at my office. His casual look of jeans and a T-shirt works for him. No other man in Lake Starlight makes a shirt stretch across his shoulders like Liam does. Then again, no one has the sex appeal of Liam, but I'd never tell him that.

"It's fine. Whatever you guys heard, you're wrong."

"Buz—"

Wyatt shoots a look at Brooklyn to shut up. No one

wants to be reminded they're in that stupid Lake Starlight gossip blog.

"Let's go get ready. Hey, Liam!" Brooklyn waves.

I'm sure he noticed my SUV in the driveway and it's no surprise that I'm here, but he hasn't looked our way. After Brooklyn's boisterous hello, his attention falls to us on the front porch. My body ignites with heat as his smile shifts to his smirk, resembling that day in the bar when I stood up to play pool as Denver's teammate. Like he's cornered me.

"Brooklyn. Wyatt." He raises his hand in greeting and sets his gaze on me, dropping his hand. "Sav."

The use of my nickname reminds me of the times when we're alone together. How my shortened name drips off his tongue like ice cream from a cone on a hot day, and I react like that drip, free-falling to the ground.

"Hey. Nice of you to help Wyatt."

Brooklyn's foot is tapping on the porch, her hand still on the doorknob. When she opens the door, Gizmo jets out of the house and leaps off the first step, thinking he's a German Shepherd. He's a husky and Corgi mix, so his short legs don't go far, and he falls down each step like a ball, but before he drops to the gravel driveway, Liam swoops him up in his arms.

"I think my ovaries just exploded," Brooklyn whispers.

Wyatt cocks an eyebrow at her. "Ease up."

"What? Come on, he caught our little guy." Brooklyn pushes past Wyatt and me and scoops up her little furball when Liam steps onto the porch, towering over her.

My eyes veer to his tattooed arms for a moment.

"Gizmo, you can't go running like that no matter how much you love Liam." Brooklyn pets under the dog's chin and carries him into the house. She shoots me a look.

"See you guys later." I step toward the front door.

"A word?" Liam's brooding voice booms at my back.

Brooklyn whips around, probably giving Gizmo whiplash. His eyes bulge out of his head, but he sees Liam and his tongue falls out of his mouth. I get it, little guy. I totally get it.

"With who? We can go over your speech later," Brooklyn says, looking panicked.

Liam's confused gaze shifts from all of us and lands on me. "Savannah. We're planning the charity event for the library together and I need to talk to her for a sec."

"You are?" Brooklyn's surprised tone is to be expected.

"Grandma Dori," I answer.

"Always the meddler. I'll go get a head start, Liam. Come down when you're ready." Wyatt thumbs behind him toward the back yard.

"First, can I have a word with you?" Brooklyn asks Wyatt.

I shake my head as poor Wyatt's eyes are already filling with questions as to why he's being pulled into the house. I set my bag by the door and walk down a few steps in case Brooklyn puts a glass to the front door.

"What's up?" I force casual into my voice though I feel anything but right now. Liam can be the strong silent type at times, and I don't feel like staring at each other for an eternity while I wait for him to spit out whatever it is he has to say.

"So... a date?" His arms cross, and he leans back on the railing.

I totally ignore the way that position makes his biceps and his pecs pop. "Yes. A date."

"It's funny, don't you think?" He tilts his head.

"What's funny about it?"

"That you get sick the night I have a woman who wants

to sleep with me, yet here you are, trying to hide the fact that you're going on a date." His arms clench tighter, his muscles stretching the thin fabric of his shirt.

"You could've gone home with her."

"And taken her where? You took my bed." His lips tip up like he loves the memory of the night I had an out-of-body experience and forced myself into his bed.

"I was drunk."

"That's the second time."

I throw my hands in the air. "What do you want from me?"

"If you're going to date, why hide it?"

"I'm not hiding it."

He tilts his head again, this time with the same expression my father gave me when I told him they weren't my cigarettes in junior year.

A deep sigh rolls out of my chest. "It's uncomfortable."

"Why? We're friends. I'm best friends with your brothers. It's not like anything is going on with us."

Those blue eyes bore into mine. Testing. Taunting. Almost demanding I admit to something just to prove he's right. But we both know I'm just a conquest to Liam.

"Exactly. So excuse me so I can go get ready." I take a step up the stairs.

"Can't wait to meet him."

I swivel back around, but he's right there and my hands land on his biceps. His eyes dip down and I retract my hands.

"Too hot to touch?"

Anger and annoyance hijack my body. "Just worry about the tent."

"You forget how good I am with my hands already?" He

brushes his knuckles down my arm and shivers follow his touch. "Maybe you need a reminder?"

I pluck his hand off my skin. "Just stay out of the way."

"I once told your dad I'd always look out for you Bailey girls."

"Well, I release you of any obligation when it comes to this Bailey girl." I point at my chest. "I can handle myself."

I stomp up the stairs, grab my bag, and swing open the door.

"I'm not sure you know what kind of man is good for you, so I'll be quick. A quick hello and a handshake with the guy in question won't hurt."

I give him a death glare that should keep him away, but his laughter says he's going to ambush this date. I wish I cared a bit more.

I growl and slam the door.

"You're lucky I don't write Buzz Wheel myself," Brooklyn says, obviously eavesdropping on our conversation. "Sounds like you guys could have a daily feature."

EIGHT

Liam

Savannah reacted exactly as I assumed. She's uncomfortable that I'm here and that I'll be standing witness as she climbs into another man's car. She'll be thinking for the entire night about how pissed off she is at me. I should probably feel bad for potentially ruining her night, but somehow I can't find it in me.

I slide my palms over one another, jumping off the porch of the Whitmores' house and shaking my head. This house will never be complete, but I gotta hand it to Wyatt. He's determined to do it himself.

Wyatt and the tent delivery guys are spreading out the tent when I reach the backyard. The view of the lake behind their house distracts me. It's clear and blue and I'm a little pissed I didn't find this piece of property when I built my house years ago. Not that I don't love the seclusion I have, but the lake here reminds me a little of one on the Bailey family property, where we used to hang out growing up.

"Sorry," Wyatt mumbles as I jump in to help secure one of the poles.

"For what?"

He shoots me a look like I should know. I do know. Everyone in this town seems to think there's some hidden relationship between Savannah and me. But the truth is, I think I'm infatuated with a woman who may no longer exist.

"It's fine. I'm good. Let's just get this tent up."

He nods, burying his head in the work of getting a tent up to celebrate his recent marriage to the love of his life. I'd be lying if I didn't admit that I'm jealous to some degree.

When we finish the tent, I tear off my shirt because it's drenched in sweat. I wipe the sweat dripping off my forehead and head out to see how the chicken coop I helped Wyatt build is holding up. Watching the chickens wander around with no clear direction, I debate whether I should leave.

Why am I still here? I should've run away the minute the tent was up. Let her stay in denial and go on a date with some guy who has no idea who she really is. But a small amount of hope still lives inside me and flares to life every time we find ourselves at a crossroad.

"Here you go." Wyatt hands me a water.

I slide my hand down the condensation before running the coolness over my forehead. "Thanks."

"Savannah's date just pulled up."

I nod. '*Stay here. Just fucking stay out here. Don't bother with it,*' I say to myself for the umpteenth time, but sometimes I'm not good at listening to my inner warnings. That's how I ended up in jail with Rome and Denver for pranking the school on senior day. It was a shitty idea from the start, but hey, it was fun.

"Good decision to stay out here."

Wyatt's words spur me into action.

"Would you?" I ask.

He's quiet for a minute. Wyatt and I shoot the shit all the time. It's probably why he picked me over any of the Bailey boys to be his best man. I probably shouldn't involve him in this, but he's not blood-related to Savannah.

"I'm not sure what you and Savannah are, so I don't know what to say," he says.

I down half the bottle of water. "That's a bullshit answer."

"It was kind of a bullshit question."

I cock my head and question him from the corner of my eye. But the guy is right. What the hell am I doing? I don't accept defeat this easily. I pat his back and head toward the house. "Thanks."

It's not until the chill of the air conditioning hits my skin that I remember I'm shirtless. By then I'm standing in their kitchen, Brooklyn's wide eyes taking me in. Some guy in khakis and a polo shirt is looking at me with a quizzical expression.

"Um..." Brooklyn's essential oil bottle slips from her hands, but she grabs it before it shatters on the floor. "Lose your shirt?"

I hold it up.

"Maybe put it on?" she says, but I'm way too busy throwing mental daggers at the guy standing with his hands in his pockets because I know who he is.

Out of all the men Juno could've picked, this douchebag is the one she thinks is the right fit for her sister?

"Liam Kelly?" Brent Jacobs looks me up and down. "Still doing your own tattoos?"

A condescending laugh slips out. "Still working for Daddy?"

The door behind me opens, and Brooklyn's shocked gaze focuses behind me. I assume Wyatt is there.

"If you mean do I run the show now, then yes," Brent says.

Brooklyn places the vial of essential oils on the table. "You two know one another?"

Wyatt rounds me. "Want me to grab you a new shirt?"

"Nah, I'm out of here soon anyway. Thanks though."

"You sure? Because the air is on and—" Brooklyn's words freeze when Wyatt's huff echoes through the quiet room.

"I'll grab you a shirt," Wyatt says.

"I can do it." Brooklyn puts her hand on Wyatt's arm before he has a chance to leave the room. She walks out—off to warn Savannah, I'm sure.

"Using a matchmaking service to get your dates now?" I ask, leaning against the counter, crossing my arms.

"I wasn't going to pass up a date with Savannah Bailey. Besides, we have a lot in common."

"Which is what exactly?" The air might be on in here, but jerk-off is stoking my anger and my skin feels as if it's burning.

Wyatt comes next to me, mimicking my stance. I cock my eyebrow but focus my attention on Brent.

"We both run huge companies."

"And?"

Brent rocks back on his heels, and my eyes fall to his stupid loafers. He looks as if he's stepped out of a Tommy Hilfiger ad. "Am I going out with *you*? What's with the third degree?"

I shrug. "I'm close with the Baileys."

"Oh, that's right." A Cheshire Cat grin pulls up the corners of his mouth. "Am I stepping on your toes?"

Wyatt chokes on his water but recovers quickly after I give him a scathing look.

I hold up my hands. "Not at all. Savannah's not mine. If she was, you wouldn't be here."

"Then what's with the protective act?"

"I'm friends with her brothers."

"And I'm her brother-in-law," Wyatt pipes in with an attitude as if to say, "take that."

I cock my eyebrow at him again.

"The baseball players?" Brent nods in understanding.

Whereas all the Bailey boys played baseball, I played football. So did Brent. For the opposing town's team. The team who beat Lake Starlight at the state championship my senior year. We were rivals then and now.

"That's them."

"I'm assuming they're in jail by now?" Brent sneers.

I eye the hallway. No sign of Savannah yet. "No."

"Why would you say that?" Wyatt asks, which shifts Brent's attention to him.

"They were juvenile delinquents. Started more fights than they could finish. Lucky for them they had Liam on their side."

"Bullshit," I say.

Brent's sneer moves my way before settling back on Wyatt. "They did a senior prank that landed all of them in jail. They're misfits."

I push off the counter, but I'm blinded by a shirt landing on my head.

"Here. Put that on."

I grab the shirt Brooklyn so nicely threw at my face. It

reads, "Sorry, girls, I'm taken." I look at Wyatt. "She seriously got you this and you wear it?"

"Hell no. I've never worn it," he says.

I call bullshit, because Wyatt loves to please Brooklyn. It might only be in the house, but he's worn it.

"Couldn't have found a better one?" I pull it on over my head.

"Sorry, I was in a hurry." She turns to Brent. "She'll be right down. An important call came in. Would you like a drink?"

Brent pulls out a chair. "Sure, whatever is fine."

"A light beer?"

"Perfect."

"I'll take one too." I raise my hand.

"You can take yours to go," she says, pushing it into my stomach.

"And me?" Wyatt asks.

"You can get it yourself." She hands a beer to Brent, taking a seat at their kitchen table. "So how does Liam know you and I don't?"

Wyatt shakes his head, walking past me to the fridge.

Brent's challenging eyes land on me first before returning to Brooklyn. "It was the state championship in our senior year. Kelly choked and I didn't. Head over to Sunrise Bay High School and you'll find the state trophy."

I roll my eyes. Wyatt stands next to me, cracking open his beer and eyeing me to say, 'what a fucking douche.' Yeah, he is.

"You act like it's a defining moment in your life," Wyatt says.

"My high school still looks at me like I'm a god. Can't say the same about Kelly."

Brooklyn glances over her shoulder, her eyes narrowing in question. I say nothing.

"Everyone loves Liam. I don't remember this. Why don't I remember this?" she asks me.

"You were in college."

Her gaze falls back to Brent. "That was high school. What do you do now?"

"Polish the state trophy every week?" Wyatt asks.

I bust out laughing, almost spitting out my beer. Never would I think a guy like Wyatt, so composed and professional, would call someone out like that.

Brent now realizes I'm not the only one in this room who isn't his fan.

Brooklyn stands and holds up her finger. "I'll go check on Savannah."

"Thank you, we have reservations," Brent says.

"Where?" Wyatt asks.

"I scored a chef's table at Fazio's. You know the one by the Portage Glacier?" He's practically puffing out his chest in pride. Idiot.

"That's cool. If you don't look at the Yelp reviews." I shrug, tossing back some of my beer. I have no idea what the Yelp reviews say, nor would I care, but guys like Brent care what people think. I guess that's another way he and Savannah are similar.

"Whatever, Yelp sucks." He sips his beer.

"I figured a man like you couldn't really think for himself."

Brent's eyes zero in on my biceps for a split second before the legs of his chair skid along the floor and his hands press on the table to rise. Wyatt and I push off the counter.

"Here she is." Brooklyn walks in with her arm out behind her, gesturing to Savannah.

I swallow the lump in my throat. Her hair is down and in waves instead of her usual stick-straight look. Her high heels only accentuate her long legs, and the tight dress she's wearing ends too far up her thigh. Fuck Brent Jacobs.

"Savannah?" Brent asks as though he doesn't know who she is.

He works one town over. Everyone knows Savannah Bailey. Her picture ends up in the newspaper for every charity event.

"Brent?"

They shake hands.

Asshole.

I'm not sure at what point all eyes turn in my direction, but they're all zeroed in on me with a look that says, 'What the fuck is wrong with you?'

"Did I say that out loud?" I ask.

No one answers, but Savannah shakes her head. "Who's the lucky girl?"

I look down and mentally kick myself in the balls because I forgot the crap shirt I was wearing. Like always, I recover quickly. "Jealous?"

"Come on, Savannah. Nice to meet you, Brooklyn. Beautiful home." Just like the jack-off he is, Brent puts his hand on the small of Savannah's back to escort her down the short hallway between the kitchen and foyer and doesn't say goodbye to Wyatt or me.

"You too, Brent. Have fun, you guys." Brooklyn follows them.

I decide it's impolite of me to stay in the kitchen, so I set my half-empty beer on the counter and head toward the front door to say a proper goodbye as well. "I should go too."

Savannah stops at the door with Brent. The idiot doesn't even take the clue to open the door for her. Wanting to piss her off a little more, I slide by them and open the door for the two of them with a dramatic wave as though she's the queen and I'm the noble attendant.

"Thanks," she grinds out and steps onto the porch.

I take my time committing to memory how she looks.

"Yeah, thanks."

Brent sneers, and I release the screen door. It hits the entitled fucker right in the nose. Whoops.

"Asshole," he mumbles.

"Liam!" Savannah's scathing gaze flies to mine.

I hold up my hands and cringe. "It slipped."

Brent grabs his nose, cursing under his breath.

"See you guys later." I wave, barreling down the stairs, but stop at the last one. "I almost forgot, Wyatt."

Savannah is one stair down and stops when I do. God forbid her body touch mine. I strip off the T-shirt and toss it to Wyatt. Savannah's gaze follows the planes of my abdomen, her eyes filling with desire.

"Thanks for the T-shirt." This could be the stupidest move ever. Get her horny and send her on a date with someone who isn't me, but I trust that I know Savannah better than anyone. "Sav?"

Her gaze shoots up from where my jeans hang low on my hips after a hard day's work. "Yeah?"

"I'll wait up for you."

Her face flushes and she swallows so loudly. I'm positive they can hear her in downtown Lake Starlight.

"Okay," she croaks.

I hold my smile until I turn around and make my way toward my car. Damn, I love making her speechless.

NINE

Liam

My gaze darts to the microwave clock—again.

Midnight.

Fuck, I did the wrong thing. I shouldn't have stripped off my shirt. I shouldn't have challenged her and sent her off with another man. What the hell was I thinking?

I throw myself on the couch and click on the TV with the remote to try to find something to distract me.

Denver barrels down the stairs, dressed in a pair of jeans and a T-shirt. Nothing suggests he's going out except for the fact that his unruly hair is styled. "I'm heading to Lucky's. Wanna come?"

"Nah."

He opens the fridge and grabs a beer, then sits on the couch before cracking it open. "Come on. I'm so sick of doing stuff by myself. Rome is busy all the damn time."

I tip back my own beer. "He does have two kids and a restaurant to run."

"Still. I only have Juno and Colton, and neither of them

look at anyone but each other. I have no wingman anymore."

I chuckle. "You've always done well on your own."

"Agreed, but you know chicks always come in packs, or pairs at the very least."

"Maybe you'll find a new girl in town, like Austin did."

He's shaking his head before I finish my thought. "No, that was one of those damn once-in-a-millennium Hallmark movie moments."

I don't argue with him, though I'm not sure Hallmark starts their movies with a bang in a Jeep behind a bar.

There was a time I thought maybe Savannah and I would get our Hallmark moment. But the fact is that she's five years older than me and I've been infatuated with her since I was thirteen. Add in the fact that I'm her brothers' best friend, and I used to worry that she'd never actually notice me. I've yearned for her from afar for so long, but her eyes have opened and it's worse than ever now because she's purposely dodging me. The other side of the coin is that now I can't jeopardize my relationship with the Baileys. They're my family too.

"Well, good luck. Maybe you'll find a stray cat."

He downs his beer. "On second thought, I'll just chill here."

Hell no he won't, because as soon as his sister returns from her shitty date, I plan on cornering her. Laying what's going on between us on the table. Rip my shirt open and let her drool fall to the floor. I'm going to proposition her outright because I'm losing my ever-loving mind.

"Nah, there's nothing on television and I'm going to head to bed soon." I put my empty beer bottle on the table and sit up as though I'm going to do exactly that.

"Really? You're turning into an old man." He stands.

A good sign. Now he just has to walk toward the door.

"I'm just beat. Hours are killing me."

"Why aren't you at the shop tonight?"

His question is a good one. I should be at the shop, but my mind is so spun, I couldn't work on people. I had no appointments, and Rhys was there for any walk-ins.

"Like I said, I'm tired. I shouldn't ink when I'm not in the right frame of mind."

He stares at me for a long time but nods and places his empty beer on the coffee table.

I won't razz him about not throwing it away as long as he gets the hell out of here.

He stops at the door. "Oh."

Fuck. Just go already.

"Yeah?" I act as though I have nothing better to do than to talk to him.

"After Brook's reception, I'm heading a survival excursion, so I won't be around. Chip was supposed to go, but he asked me to cover."

My forehead wrinkles. "He good?"

Chip is pretty much Denver's mentor. He's the one who gives him majority of his bush pilot business, who taught him how to survive in the wild, and who Denver looked up to after his parents died. Usually Denver goes along with Chip—not that Denver can't handle himself alone. When his plane went down a couple years ago and he got that music producer out of the bush with a broken leg, it proved he can handle himself.

He shrugs. "I think there's something going on that he's not telling me. Just asked if I'd be willing to take on some tours for him."

"Huh."

"Yeah. I'm hoping to find out more before I head out, but you know Chip."

By that, he means tight-lipped about everything. Not that I blame him. No one wants all their dirty laundry fanned out for everyone to see.

"I hope everything's okay."

His lips form a thin line and he pushes a hand through his hair before opening the door. "Me too. See you, old man."

He laughs and walks out of the house, shutting the door before I tell him to go to hell. I glance at the clock. Though it felt like forever to get him out the door, in reality, it only took ten measly minutes. It's gonna be a long night.

I click off the TV, throw mine and Denver's beer bottles in the recycling, and head to the barn. I'll kill some time in there while I wait for Savannah to return home.

I'M in the kitchen at seven the next morning, pouring my coffee, when I hear a car pull into the driveway, followed by a door shutting. The next thing I know, a key is in the lock. Denver returned home alone at two-thirty, saying that Lucky's sucked, so it's Savannah for sure. The cup of coffee I had earlier sours in my gut.

The door opens and I debate not turning around, but who am I kidding—I want to see the condition she's in.

I'm not sure what I expected, but her hair is thrown into the same messy bun she wears when she returns from work most days. Her dress isn't too wrinkled, which hopefully means it wasn't balled up in the corner of Brent's bedroom. It's not ripped, so at least they weren't having the kind of sex where clothes can't come off fast enough. But she's not wearing a bra. Her hard nipples are on display through the tight dress, and my jaw clenches with the thought that she may have had sex with him. It should put such distaste in my mouth that the desire coursing through my body vanishes, but all the want I have for her is still there.

"You're up early for a Saturday." She sets her keys in the dish by the front door, but keeps her purse hanging off her arm. It probably holds her underwear.

My fists clench at my sides. "I told you I'd wait up for you."

Her gaze falls to the floor. "I thought that was some sort of power move. Brooklyn told me you know Brent."

"I do know him, so believe me when I say I had my reasons for waiting up."

"He's not a bad guy." She heads toward the kitchen.

I'm surprised at how civil we're being. "I beg to differ."

She reaches for her mug, but even on her tiptoes, she can't reach it. I cage her in the corner of the counter and reach above her. She doesn't smell as though she's been up all night having sex. Putting the cup on the counter, I grab the pot of coffee to our right and pour her a cup.

"Did you just sniff me?"

"I want to make sure you don't smell like him." I inhale her special scent one more time before stepping back. I need to stop torturing myself.

"And if I did?" She turns but stays in the corner.

All I can think about is having her nipples in my mouth. My tongue twirling the stiff peaks until she moans my name. "I'd be disappointed that you fell for a jackass."

She stares at me. "He was a perfect gentleman."

"Really?"

I could probably write the *Idiots Guide to Savannah Bailey's Expressions*. It comes from years of watching her.

Years of looking at her first to decipher her reaction. I can pinpoint a hidden scowl by the arch of her eyebrows. Or when she's trying to disguise being affected by something from the way her jaw flexes.

Right now, I can tell she didn't completely fall for Brent, but she's not going to tell me because that would mean I was right. In Savannah's world, only she's allowed to be right.

"Yes, and if you'll excuse me, I have to get ready to help Brooklyn with some reception stuff." She takes her coffee and her purse and heads toward the stairs.

"Are you gonna see him again?" I sit at the breakfast bar and straighten the morning paper in front of me.

Her feet stop walking, and she hovers near the stairs. "Maybe."

"Good to know you're still lying to yourself."

She whips around, and a splash of her coffee spills on my hardwood. "Shit."

She returns to the breakfast island and puts her coffee and purse on the granite counter. When her purse flops to the side, there's the evidence I need—her bra is barely able to stay contained in the small purse.

I close my eyes to rein in my anger—anger I may or may not have any right to—but it's building too fast for me to stop it. If I stick around here, we're going to end up in a screaming match that will wake Denver, and whatever this is between us will blow up in our faces. And then Dori will interfere—more than she already tries to.

I round the breakfast island. "I can't believe you'd fuck him." The words are out of my mouth before I can stop them.

She freezes right before pulling a paper towel off the rack. "What?"

"I can't believe you'd fuck that egotistical jackass and strong-arm me. What gives? Is it the suit and the money?"

She tears off a paper towel. Forcefully. I glance over my shoulder to make sure Denver isn't there.

"Who said I fucked him?"

The word fuck rolling off her tongue does something to my dick, but I beg it to stay out of this fight. I tilt my head and huff. "I'm not an idiot. You walk in here braless the next morning. I'd bet my house your panties are in there too."

She bumps her shoulder into me to get to the spill and gets down on all fours to clean it. It's like a form of torture, watching that and knowing I can't have her. "You should go to your room and stop talking. Now."

"I'm sure you'd like that. To not be responsible for what you're doing."

She stands, the dirty paper towel hanging from her hand. "And what am I doing, Liam?"

"You're a fucking tease. You come home with me, make out with me for hours. Let me commit your body to memory, and then the next morning, you pretend it only happened because you were drunk. Now you're dating some douche and letting a guy like Brent stick his dick in you."

She looks over her shoulder because my voice is rising the longer I talk.

Stepping up close, to my surprise, she doesn't poke me in the chest. She waits to make sure I'm listening. "Don't you ever talk to me like that. What happened between us was a mistake. And if I did sleep with Brent, I was acting like every woman you bring home, and you have the nerve to judge me? Just because you weren't the one I chose to fuck? Stop acting like I broke your heart because I wouldn't sleep with you."

My heart is pounding like a tribal drum and I can feel heat rising up my neck. "What the hell are you talking about?"

"I get that I'm a conquest. The uptight older sister who you think your dick will unravel. And then once you've had me, you can move on to greener pastures and put a check-mark next to my name."

"You're delusional." I grab her hips and push her against the counter, driving my half-hard dick into her pelvis as I lean in close. "This doesn't affect you at all?"

She laughs and rolls her eyes. "Just because I'm attracted to you doesn't mean anything. You're hot. I never said you weren't."

"So let's work this out. Come upstairs with me."

She huffs and looks across the room before bringing her vision back to me. "No."

"What are you afraid of?" I hover over her, my hands sliding down her backside.

"What the hell is wrong with you two?" Denver appears at the bottom of the stairs, rubbing his eyes from just waking up.

I step back.

Savannah turns around, acting as if she's picking up her coffee. "Nothing."

"Why are you arguing?" he asks while yawning.

"I spilled some coffee on Liam's precious hardwood floors." Savannah heads to the stairs, our eyes testing one another over Denver, who still hasn't fully opened his eyes. "You look like shit by the way."

"Thanks." He stretches his arms over his head and takes in his sister's appearance. "Looks like you finally got laid. Hopefully it improves your mood."

Denver steps into the kitchen and grabs a cup before he pours himself a coffee.

"You're all a bunch of assholes." Savannah disappears upstairs.

"Sometimes I wonder what happened to her. Why is she so high-strung when the rest of us are pretty chill?"

I sit back down with the paper. "Give her a break. A lot was thrown at her at a young age."

Denver contemplates my words for a moment, then he nods and sips his coffee. I should thank him for interrupting us. I was about to do something I'd regret after she had sex with Brent Jacobs last night.

Maybe it's time to give up the fight.

TEN

Savannah

It's been almost a week since my date with Brent, and I've dodged Liam all week. Eventually I'll have to meet with him about the charity auction, spend time alone with him. I'm not sure I can control myself. I can't shake the feeling of having him pressed against me in the kitchen, and my mind has wandered with daydreams of what would've happened if Denver hadn't interrupted us.

The excuse of Brooklyn and Wyatt's reception helped, but after tonight, I'll have to figure out how to turn off this attraction I have to him. The flirtatiousness between us has gone on long enough and seems to be turning into something caustic. Our biting words always felt like some kind of fucked up foreplay. But lately, everything feels more serious and more destructive.

Phoenix walks up as I arrange the presents on the table so they don't topple over. "Sav, you have to do something about this deejay."

"What?" I say over the music.

"The tracks he's playing are horrible, and the way he goes in and out of songs is choppy."

I shrug. "The deejay wasn't my department."

I pick up a big box. My guess is a blender from the shape and weight of it.

"Brooklyn and Wyatt are too busy talking, but look." Phoenix swivels me around by my shoulders. "No one is on the dance floor."

Phoenix is right. No one's on the makeshift dance floor under the twinkle lights I helped hang. Dinner is over. This is when guests should be enjoying themselves.

"Fine. I'll say something as soon as I finish this."

"I'll finish." Phoenix takes the box from me. "The deejay is a 9-1-1 level catastrophe, Sav." She lightly pushes me toward the dance floor.

I make it halfway across the floor and exhale a deep breath when Dori stops me. "The deejay has nothing prepared. He said he only has the songs Brooklyn okay'd. I told him I wanted to do the chicken dance and he said that the bride said no. I told him my granddaughter wouldn't say no because she knows I love that song."

I bet Brooklyn did indeed tell the deejay no chicken dance. At Austin's wedding, Dori wiggled her ass down into a crouched position and it took all four Bailey brothers to get her back up.

"I'll talk to him. Go have fun with your friends."

She walks away.

I only get a little farther when Calista runs up to me. "'Baby Shark'! Deejay no." She shakes her head.

I bend down to her level. She's turning into the spitting image of Rome and Denver. "I'll talk to him."

She hugs me, and I hold her close. "Thank you, Auntie."

"You're welcome."

She twirls away from me, and I follow her until I see Dori stopping her before she can escape the dance floor.

"Sav?" Juno comes up to me, and I raise my hand.

"I'm talking to the deejay. Relax."

"What?" She sips her champagne. My guess is she's had about five glasses already. The woman loves champagne. "I was going to ask about Brent. He called me to say he's tried to reach you several times, but you haven't returned his calls or texts."

"Yeah, I'm not sure about him."

"Why? He said he really enjoyed the date and has been hoping to do it again." She follows me to the deejay.

I really don't want to talk about this right now. Especially with Liam showing up today in a perfectly fitted suit. It only serves as a reminder of us from Austin's wedding a few weeks ago. The way the jacket slipped off his strong shoulders and onto his bedroom floor. How his hands cupped my face when he bent to kiss me.

"Can we talk about it later?" I ask.

"No. I want to talk about it now."

I stop and look at her. Maybe more than five glasses, since she's already ornery. Juno can't handle too much alcohol. "I said later."

I arrive at the deejay's table and realize he's practically a baby. The kid's face is flushed, and his forehead is sweaty while he fumbles with the contents of his table for something.

"Hi. I'm Savannah Bailey."

"Sav?" Juno whines next to me. I put my finger in the air.

"Oh, I need something from you." His eyes light up and

he snaps his fingers, then pushes his hand through his large mane of red, unruly hair. "Mic."

"Okay but first—"

"Do either of you know a Liam Kelly? He has to be mic'd too." His finger is running down a sheet of paper while he reads it. "And Dori Bailey?"

"She's doing a speech?" I ask.

"That'd be why I have to mic her." He might as well have said *duh.*

"Whoa." Juno rears her head back and bites her lip as though she can't wait to see what unfolds from his snarky attitude.

I inhale a deep breath. I will not make a scene and ruin my sister's reception. "My niece wants 'Baby Shark' played."

He's already shaking his head before I finish speaking. "No can do."

"Excuse me?" My forehead wrinkles in confusion.

"I hope you have 'Baby Shark.' Today is not the day to mess with her," Juno pipes in, but I cut her a look. She holds her hands in the air with a whatever attitude, grabbing another glass of champagne from a passing server and setting her empty one on the tray.

"The bride gave an approved list of songs. That's what we're playing," the kid says.

"And you didn't bring anything else?" I ask.

"Listen, guy," Rome interjects, coming up to join us. "I'll pay you fifty dollars to play 'Baby Shark.'" He's already digging out his wallet as baby Dion whines from where he's strapped to Rome's chest in one of those fabric wrap things.

"Oh, give me the baby." Juno puts her champagne glass on the deejay's table and holds out her hands.

Rome shifts his gaze to her. "Sorry, lush, maybe tomorrow."

"What? I'm not a lush." Her words slur a bit, proving that Rome is making the right decision.

"Yeah, okay. Why don't you go find Colton? You can tell him how you really feel."

Juno puts her hands on her hips. "Rome Joseph Bailey!" Her voice rises and the song stops at the exact same time.

I glance behind us to see a bunch of the guests staring at us. Colton's making his way over from across the tent.

"'BABY SHARK'!" Calista screams, running over and wrapping herself around her daddy's leg.

Rome hangs his head, waving the fifty-dollar bill in his hand.

I put my hand over Rome's as I say to the deejay, "We're not going to pay you to play a song. You're already being paid for this gig. If you need the song, one of us has it on our phones."

"But the bride..."

The deejay's words trail off when Liam comes up to my side. The kid takes in his broad shoulders and bulging biceps. If I was a scrawny kid, I'd be scared of Liam too.

"I've got this handled." I put my hand in front of his face.

He lowers my hand from in front of him. "Then why is 'Baby Shark' not playing?"

"Come on, Juno. Calista wants to dance with you once the song comes on." Colton escorts a very pissed off Juno away. Thank goodness, because I wasn't going to be the peacemaker of an argument between her and Rome.

"Liam? As in Liam Kelly? I need to mic you." The deejay reaches under the table and pulls out some portable mics, setting them on the table.

I lean in closer. "Listen."

"Just take my money." Rome sways in an attempt to soothe Dion.

The baby may not be happy, but he looks super cute with his pudgy cheeks and the noise-canceling headphones over his ears to protect him from the loud speakers.

"You're going to play 'Baby Shark,' and while that's playing, you can mic us. After 'Baby Shark,' we'll do all the speeches. Got it?" My hands rest on my hips now. I've had enough of this guy.

The kid looks at Liam for confirmation, so I step in front of him. But now his chest is to my back and my entire body ignites in flames so hot, I fear I'll melt to the floor.

"Don't look at him. I'm the one in charge here."

Because Liam is taller than me, the deejay continues to stare at Liam over my head as though he's the one to make the final call.

"He's not even a Bailey!"

Everyone in the tent goes quiet. There's no more conversation, no silverware or glasses clinking.

Lowering my voice, I lean super close. "Play the damn song for my niece."

The deejay frantically scours his phone and plugs one thing into the other until *doodoodoo* is amplified throughout the tent.

"See, that wasn't that hard." I grab the mic. "Now let's put these on." I push one into Liam's chest and storm off to the side.

"Thanks, Sav. Look how happy you made your niece." Rome dances over to his daughter.

I watch the two interact while Juno's trying some move that looks like she's conducting a rain dance. At least they're all smiling and happy.

"Always putting out fires," Liam says, standing with me to the side of the deejay table.

"I hope your speech is good."

Liam's hands are tucked into his suit pants and he rocks back on his heels. "Wanna make a wager that mine is better?"

"No."

"Scared?"

"Do you always have to be so childish?"

The deejay clips a mic to me and tries to find a spot to attach the battery pack.

"Can't I just use a regular microphone?" I ask.

"These are new. And the other deejay has all the old mics at some other event."

Liam huffs. "Don't mind her, she's a control freak."

"This is my first solo deejay job," he admits with shaking hands as he tries to attach the battery pack to the back of my dress.

Well, don't I feel like slime under a shoe now. "I apologize."

"Well, the little girl looks happy and that's the reason I went into deejaying. I wanted to make people happy. Being a dictator wasn't a goal, but I saw my boss get his ass reamed by a bride once. They can be scary."

I laugh and so does Liam. Our eyes catch for a moment.

"Weddings are stressful. But aren't these microphones a pain?" I ask.

"Of course you have an opinion on it." Liam shakes his head at me.

Just when I thought we could be cordial. Liam is catching me on a shitty day. I had to see my older brother get married weeks ago, and now I'm celebrating Brooklyn's wedding. I'm happy for both of them, but all those worries and insecurities are crashing down on me. I'm going to be my sisters' bridesmaids, but I'll never be the one wearing white.

The deejay looks at me as he clips the mic to my dress.

"You're annoying me," I say to Liam.

Now the deejay looks back at Liam, waiting to see what he'll say. I'm sure we're entertaining when you're not the one who has to suffer from all the unresolved feelings between us.

"But Brent doesn't?" he asks.

Here we go with this Brent shit again. I should lay out what happened that night, but I'm not going to. He doesn't deserve it. "You sure spend a lot of your time thinking about Brent."

He narrows his eyes as the deejay puts the mic on him. "Can you give us a moment?" he asks the deejay.

"Sure thing. You're all hooked up, but I haven't turned you guys on yet. I'll let you know when you're good to go. I think I'll play 'Baby Shark' one more time for the little girl."

I smile at the kid. "Thanks. She'd love it."

He excuses himself, and Liam grabs my arm, pulling me behind the backdrop for the deejay.

I whip my arm out of his grasp. "What?"

"You know exactly why I'm thinking about Brent. Are you going to see him again?"

I rear my head back. "I don't see how that's any of your business."

He steps into me, his hands on my hips, and pulls me to him. "Stop pretending."

"I'm not pretending anything."

"Tell me you don't want to kiss me right now. That if I ran my fingers up and under your dress, you wouldn't shiver from my touch. How wet are you right now, Sav?"

I inhale a deep breath and study him. This infuriating man is not going to let this go. "It doesn't mean it's because of you. I could be remembering my night with Brent."

His fingertips press into my skin a little harder, but he laughs. "Is this all because I don't wear a suit to work every day or have some fancy desk job?"

"What? No. Why would you even say that?"

"Is that the type of man you want? Because a man like that can't take care of your needs. The man who can is standing right in front of you."

My eyes dip to his lips.

A loud crash rings out from the other side of the backdrop, but I can't tear my eyes off Liam. I want to admit my attraction and lose myself in him for a night. Let him make me forget who I need to be for everyone else in my life. Put what I want first for a change and to hell with the consequences.

"Savannah?" Grandma Dori yells.

"Sav?" I hear Brooklyn say right after her.

"I don't know where she is, but the present table is a mess," Holly says with despair in her tone.

Oh fuck it.

I smash my lips to his, allowing his tongue access to my mouth. I grab his shoulders while his hands mold to my ass. Our lips are frantic and needy and hungry for one another.

"Don't stop," I pant when his lips travel to my neck.

"Say the magic word." I feel him grin against my hot skin.

"Please," I beg, and he lowers his body, thrusting his hard length into my center.

God, this feels so good.

"Your wish..."

I grab the back of his head and pull his face up to meet

my lips again. He rests a hand where my neck and collarbone meet. His calloused palms are rough, and I grip him hard, wishing I could strip him down right here. His mouth slides off mine and he casts open-mouthed kisses along my jaw to my ear. A low growl erupts from him and my insides clench.

"Tell me you didn't fuck him," he says in my ear and my body goes cold.

"What?" I whisper, our bodies still entangled. Is this about some pissing contest and marking his territory?

He draws back and our eyes meet under the glow of the lights inside the tent. "I have to know."

"Why?" I step back, my body missing the strong support of his.

"Because I keep imagining his hands on you and I don't like it." His jaw sets in a rigid line.

"Let me ask you a question—do *you* think I did?" I cross my arms, waiting for his answer.

He shoves his hands into his pockets. "Well, all signs point to yes, so..."

"That's what you think of me, huh?" I try to walk away, but he grabs my elbow, circling me back around. "You think I'm someone who would skip from bed to bed? Maybe you think that because that's what you do. We were together and then a few days later you were hitting on Marlene at the bar. Well, I'm not like that. Sex means something to me, and I don't give it up freely like you."

He crosses his arms. "Let's not beat around the bush. That's not you. Tell me what you really think of me."

All of the frustration and anger and outrage that's been building expands to the point where I can no longer cage it in. "You're a whore! You're a man-whore who goes through women like Tic Tacs! But the minute you think I did something even remotely the same, you judge me for it. I'm nothing more than a conquest to you, and once you've conquered me, you'll be on to the next. The only reason you're chasing me is because I won't sleep with you. Tell me, did you make a bet with someone or something?"

He shakes his head and stares at me. "What happened that's made you so jaded?"

I throw my hands in the air. "Screw you. I'm not jaded. It's called being realistic."

"When are you going to start living *your* life instead of living for everyone else? You might as well have died with your parents."

My reaction is automatic. I step forward, slapping him across the face.

Gasps sound from behind the backdrop, and I look down at my mic in horror.

The deejay runs around the corner. "I'm so sorry. I have no idea how the mic turned on, but—"

"You want to know the truth?" I ask, unshed tears in my eyes. "My car wouldn't start, and I spent the night at Brooklyn's. That's it. I'd say you don't know me at all."

"Fuck this. Have a great life." Liam storms into the darkness beyond the tent.

Juno, Brooklyn, and Holly all come around the backdrop and stare at me.

"What? You know we don't get along." I wipe the tears from my eyes with the back of my hand and suck back all the emotions trying to burst forth. "I'll be right back."

I head into the house to compose myself, trying to figure out how it all went so bad.

ELEVEN

Liam

The morning after doomsday, I'm home and working on my bike. I plan on going on a long ride today in order to avoid Savannah, although she didn't come home last night. Not that I blame her. I keep replaying what I said over and over. It was callous and insensitive and if I wanted a cold shower to tamp down my attraction for her, I succeeded.

Austin's Jeep pulls down my driveway, followed by Rome's minivan. Never thought I'd see the day my buddy drove a dadmobil. Denver gets out of the back of Rome's van and helps Calista jump out of the car. "Baby Shark" is playing on his cell phone.

Guess he decided to stay away from this place last night too.

They all make their way over to me.

"Harley has clients. You cool if I put on a movie for her in your family room?" Rome has a bag of food in one hand and Dion's car seat in the other.

"Sure." My guilt stops me from lecturing him about eating in my family room.

He disappears into the house, Calista chattering away with Denver as they follow Rome inside.

Austin slides a stool over, watching me work on the bike. "You going on a ride today?"

"Yeah." I put the tools back and stand to open my fridge in the garage. I grab a water and offer Austin one.

"Sure," he says.

I toss him one. "Looking forward to finally being able to take your honeymoon?" I don't know why I'm making small talk when we both know why he's here.

"I'm counting the days, trust me."

I pick at the label of my water for a minute before I meet his gaze. "I'm sorry, Austin."

My apology comes from a place of respect. I looked up to the guy for being the rock star baseball player in high school, but even more so after his parents died, and he returned home to raise his siblings instead of pursuing a career in baseball. I'm not naïve. I know my words to Savannah last night hurt all of the Baileys, because a little bit of each of them was buried the day their parents died.

"Thanks." He cracks open the bottle of water. "We came here to talk."

I nod. That was clear when the whole brigade showed up. They've talked amongst themselves before coming here to see me.

"She won't give me the phone back," Denver whines as he and Rome rejoin us.

"She will when she's done," Rome says. "I have about ten minutes." He's wearing Dion around his chest again.

"What's Harley doing today?" Denver asks.

"I already said she's working, dumbass."

Denver sits on the counter attached to the one side of the garage wall.

"Listen, guys"—I raise my hand to cut them off at the pass—"I'm sorry. I shouldn't have said what I did, and I regret it. I plan on apologizing to Savannah as soon as she comes home."

Denver cringes. "She's not coming back here. She's moving in with Juno until her place is ready."

My chin falls to my chest. I really blew this one. "Well then, I'll apologize when she picks her stuff up."

"She said she'd be sure to come by when you were working," Rome says.

Fuck me.

"Listen, we know you didn't mean it. That's what we're here to talk about." Rome sways back and forth, patting Dion's back, and it's making me nauseous.

The thing is, I did mean it, I'm just sorry for the cruel way it came out. She was always neurotic and organized, but it's to the extreme now. I rarely see her laugh and let loose and enjoy herself. Telling anyone in her family no is a real problem for her. I think they're all so accustomed to it that they're blind to the person she's become. I never realized how much until Austin was going to leave for California a few years ago and leave the family and business in Savannah's hands. The problem is that it's not my place to tell them this.

"What exactly are you here to talk about then?" I ask.

"You and Savannah are toxic to one another," Austin says before sipping his water. "We thought maybe you guys would work out whatever it is between you. We'd love for you to be our brother-in-law. Especially since we already see you as a brother. But after last night and based on what

Denver's told us... it's probably best for everyone if you put her behind you."

Rome and Denver nod.

"But..." The words die on my lips. My parents left me for Florida and the Baileys are the ones who have treated me like family most of my life. I can't disobey their wishes. If they're here like this, it's because it matters.

"Sorry, man." Denver pats me on the back as though I need consoling. "One of you will end up on *Dateline* for murdering the other if we don't intervene." He laughs.

I nod. "I like your sister."

When I saw the pain on Savannah's face after I lashed out, it was like the quick slice of a blade. Regret poured out of me, and now I'm questioning if it's more than a night I need from her. If it is, I screwed myself royally.

The three of them look at one another as though they didn't expect to hear me voice those words.

"Sometimes people aren't good for one another. You're laid-back and Savannah is high-strung. We thought you'd even her out, but you're both bringing the worst out in each other."

"That's not totally true," I murmur.

"You haven't gone out with me in weeks," Denver says. "Plus, the display at Lucky's with that chick? Then you leave me to take her home so you can take care of Savannah?"

"So?"

"So that's not you. You're fun. Savannah's not."

"She was once." And I keep trying to pull it out of her, but it's hidden so far down that not even Google Maps can help me retrieve it.

But I keep those thoughts to myself. Looking at their

skepticism, I can tell I see Savannah differently than they do.

"Listen, I don't want to get into an argument. We tried to sit back and let this unfold, but now you're both all over Buzz Wheel," Austin says.

"On the upside, you have our thanks for taking the hot seat for a while." Denver claps me on the back.

"We think you guys just need to admit that you're not good for each other. If you both agree that nothing's ever going to come of it, maybe you can be friends," Austin says and downs some more water.

"Is this your polite way of telling me you'll kick my ass if I date your sister?"

They all laugh and share a look between them.

"We'd never start a fight with you," Austin says.

"You're bigger than us," Rome says.

"You'd kick our ass." Denver laughs.

"But?" I wait for them to lay it out. Tell me what they want from me.

"We'd prefer for you and Savannah not to date. Yeah." Austin leans back, crunching his now-empty plastic water bottle.

"Uncle Denver!" Calista yells from the other side of the door that leads into the house. Rome opens the door, and Calista waves Denver's phone. "Uncle Denver, someone was calling your phone."

Rome leans down and reads the screen. "'Wednesday night girl.' You actually put someone in as a contact under that?"

"Stop with the judgment, Daddy." Denver takes the phone out of Calista's hands.

"Who's Wednesday night girl?" Calista asks.

"A friend," he says.

"She likes 'Baby Shark' too."

"You talked to her?" Denver asks.

Calista nods. "She called three times."

We all laugh, though mine is hollow.

I thought I had this in the bag. I'd never been surer of anything in my life. When Savannah had to move in, I thought it was a sign, but I was wrong. The Bailey boys are right. I have to put my desire for Savannah in a box and lock it up tight.

Calista begs for "Baby Shark" again and entertains us with a dance when her uncle concedes. Having her there allows us to ignore the discomfort of them having to come here to politely ask me not to pursue their sister. I never want a visit like this again, so my hands are in the air, surrendering.

Savannah Bailey will never be mine.

TWELVE

Savannah

I sit in Juno's apartment in downtown Lake Starlight, drinking water from the faucet and eating the last of her pizza-flavored Pringles. "He'll be at work tonight, and that's when I'll go over to get my stuff."

"I'll help, but can I just say one thing?" Juno gulps down a large amount of water. The girl is still dehydrated from being wasted off champagne last night.

"You've said enough." And she has. Her pro-Liam speeches need to cease and desist.

"But—"

"He thinks just because we're physically attracted to one another, it means something more than what it is. I can't date Liam Kelly. We're completely unsuited for each other."

Juno's forehead crinkles. "Why?"

She doesn't get it. Juno was only twelve when our parents died. She was so wrapped up in herself, she never bothered to think about how it affected anyone but herself. I don't blame her. We were all wrapped up in our feelings.

That moment changed each of us in different ways. Juno told me once she thought it was romantic that Mom and Dad died together, that they never had to live without one another. I call bullshit.

But Austin and I swore that our siblings' lives wouldn't change any more than they had. I don't regret that, but maybe I'm so mad at Liam because what he said, what he always says, about me is correct. He's not content to let me live in the space I've created for myself. He demands I examine what I really want, who I really want to be.

None of my siblings thought that last night. No one said, "Now that Liam mentions it, Savannah, you *have* changed." That's what scares me the most. Do they think I want to be this way? This OCD person who, instead of drinking champagne and dancing with my niece at my sister's wedding, is arguing with the deejay and making sure the cake cutting cutlery is where it should be and that the present table doesn't topple over? They've accepted that I'm *that* person. I've become my mother without ever giving birth to my own children.

"It's just not a good fit. There are other reasons too."

"Name one." Juno cocks an eyebrow at me.

"He's younger than me."

Juno guffaws as if that's nothing. "Five years."

"Has he even had a girlfriend before?"

"That Rachel girl. Remember?"

I do, but I play dumb. "Maybe."

I straighten her magazines. She always tears out pages that interest her and they end up in a pile on the end table of her living room.

"Sometimes love exists in the place you never thought to look." She shrugs.

I'd tell her to examine her own life, but I'm not going to throw stones.

A knock on the door interrupts us.

"Are you expecting anyone?" I ask. My stomach flips at the thought that it might be Liam.

She shakes her head. "Kingston said he probably wouldn't be back for at least a month. I think last night, with him talking to Celeste about how Stella's doing away from here..."

I nod and take a deep breath. Maybe I'm not the only messed up one in my family.

"Celeste mentioned that Stella might be coming home from school for a little while." I stand and open the door to Grandma Dori with two suitcases in hand. "What are you doing here and why do you have luggage?"

"How about you let me in and, I don't know, take my bags?"

I look over my shoulder at Juno.

"Grandma?" she says.

"Nursing a hangover, I suppose?" She doesn't wait for an answer, plopping the bags down and pushing past me. "I need to stay with you for a while because I have termites at my place."

I bring her bags into the apartment before shutting and locking the door. "Termites?"

"Yep. Can you take my suitcases to Kingston's room and change the sheets? I'm not sleeping on those."

"He rarely brings girls home," Juno offers, not saying anything about how I was supposed to take Kingston's room.

I clear my throat.

Juno looks at me. "Grandma, Savannah was going to sleep in there now." But she bites her lip and shrugs as though to say, 'I doubt this is going to change anything.'

"Why would you leave Liam's? You're already settled there. Plus, this is my excuse to teach Juno how to keep an orderly house." Grandma Dori picks up the stack of torn-out magazine pages and heads toward the kitchen.

Juno flings the blanket off her lap and stands from the couch. "Grandma, what are you doing?" She watches in horror while Grandma Dori throws them in the trash can. "There were instructions on how to build a bookcase in there."

Grandma Dori looks at me with a "yeah right" expression. "That's sweet, Juno, but you were never going to finish it."

"Thanks for the encouragement," Juno mumbles, opening the trash and taking out the magazine pages. She opens a kitchen drawer to shove them in, but it's filled to the max. So is drawer two. After going through three more, she opens her oven and throws them inside.

"Back to me taking Kingston's room." I return the conversation to the topic at hand.

Grandma Dori waves at me. "That's ridiculous. I know you guys had a lovers' quarrel last night, but you'll get over it."

"We're not lovers."

"You know what I mean. Liam is a part of this family, so you two need to make up and stop being so angry at one another."

Just when I think she might understand what I'm going through.

She disappears into Kingston's room. "Savannah, I thought you were going to change the sheets?"

I look at the two suitcases and back at Juno.

"Hey, I don't want her here either," Juno whisper-shouts.

"How did Kingston become a neat freak and not you, Juno?" Grandma Dori calls from down the hall.

Juno's eyes bore into mine. I already straightened his room since I was taking it. The boy is not even close to a neat freak.

"Grandma..." I sigh and take her suitcases into the room. "I really think Liam and I need space. After last night, it's not wise for us to live together. We probably shouldn't have done it in the first place."

She turns to look at me from where she's digging through his drawers. If he only knew. Her shoulders fall and she sits on the bed, patting the spot next to her. I follow her order and sit.

"You two need to be friends. Liam understands you." She lowers her voice. "Maybe better than me, though I don't want to admit it."

My forehead scrunches. "He doesn't know me. He thinks he does, but he doesn't."

"Hmm." Grandma Dori rises and falls on the bed as though she's testing the mattress.

"What are you doing?" Juno asks from where she's leaning against the doorframe.

"I'm testing out the bedsprings."

Juno stares at her. "Why?"

"Get your mind out of the gutter. I have a bad back."

"Can we get back to the termites thing?" I ask, a little exasperated.

Do I want to live with Liam? Hell no, but it's a better option than living with Grandma Dori. Poor Juno.

"How much clearer do I have to make it for you, dear?"

"Um. Is everyone out of the assisted living place or just you?" Juno asks.

"I guess the termites like me because it's only me."

Juno shakes her head and narrows her eyes at me. "Sav, I need a word." Juno leaves the doorway.

"Be right back."

"I'll unpack," Grandma Dori says, so I lift a suitcase onto the bed for her.

By the time I get to the kitchen, Juno's pacing. "She can't live here. This is all because you were going to live here. She's ambushing me so you'll continue to live with Liam."

I nod. "Pretty much."

"This is your problem. Tell her you'll go back to Liam's."

I shake my head.

"Sav?"

"I'm not going back to Liam's. I can take the couch. If I'm miserable, so are you."

Juno huffs. "Why?"

I can't even answer. Other times, I would've crumbled. Admitted defeat to Grandma Dori and said I'll stick it out at Liam's until my contractor fixes my house. But I'm a little pissed that none of my family cares that Liam was right last night. None of them took the time to examine what he said and see if there was any truth to it. No one said, "Oh yeah, Savannah used to want to have a few drinks, skydive, and travel the world. She didn't want to be pseudo mom and run a company at the age of nineteen. I guess I see what Liam's talking about."

Rather than explaining all that, I say, "Misery loves company."

I snag my purse and bag off her chair.

"Savannah?"

I ignore her and dip my head into Kingston's room where Grandma is staring at a strip of condoms as if she's never seen one before. "Bye, Grandma. I'll let you get settled in."

"Bye, dear. I'll see you in the morning. Juno will drive me to the office while I'm staying here since I go in later than you."

I look back at an obviously displeased Juno. "Perfect."

"Savannah..."

There's an extra bit of annoyance to Juno's tone, but I wave goodbye. "See you later."

"Savannah!"

I shut the door and stop on the other side.

For what feels like the first time in years, I really smile.

THIRTEEN

Savannah

Leaving Grandma Dori and Juno behind, my mind slips into fix-it mode. Should I sleep on Juno's couch or find somewhere else to stay? I could stay at Liam's and make myself scarce, I guess. Knowing Grandma Dori, she'll stay at Juno's just to make sure I don't return.

I drive around for a bit and eventually find myself heading down Liam's long driveway. My gut twists at having to see him after last night, but there's a conversation to be had between us. One that's been looming for a long time. The longer we avoid it, the more often incidents like last night will happen.

One single headlight shines toward me, and I slow to a stop, knowing it's him on his motorcycle. I rarely see him ride it. He stops, kills the engine, and straddles the bike next to my driver's side window. The air around us is awkward and uncomfortable and I hate every second of it.

We've never been the best of friends, but before I moved in with him, we coexisted well. We could hold a conversation during the obligatory Bailey functions. Sure, we'd get a few jabs in on each other, but it was all in good fun.

He takes off his helmet. Since it's the middle of summer, dusk won't come until midnight, which means I can see the dark circles under his eyes. He didn't sleep last night either.

"Hey," he says.

I press the radio volume button on my steering wheel, leaving the sound of the crickets chirping as our only distraction. "Hi."

"Can we talk?"

"Are you going on a ride?"

The slight turn of his lips on his right side says he wants to make a smart-ass comment. I admit, I kind of gave him a great opening.

"I was, but I'd rather talk to you."

I gulp and nod. "Is Denver home?"

"Unfortunately, yes." He pats the back of his bike. "How about I take you for a ride?"

"Or I could drive us." I pat my steering wheel.

"That wouldn't be nearly as much fun."

"But it would be safer."

He nods. "Give me a second to put it back in the garage."

After putting his helmet back on, he circles around the back of my SUV and heads back up the driveway to his house. I follow and watch him park the motorcycle and put away his helmet. I'm so busy wondering what's going to happen now with him in my truck that I don't realize he's ready to go until he's knocking on the window.

I fumble to unlock the door, and he slides into my passenger seat. "Thanks."

"Where to?" I do a U-turn in the driveway and head back the way I came.

"I'd rather not be Buzz Wheel's hot news tomorrow."

A sour taste coats my mouth. I never checked the blog last night, but I'm sure it reported our fight. Come tomorrow morning at work, someone will have passed around a screenshot, which means I'll hide in my office until someone else is the center point of everyone's gossip.

"Me neither. What are you thinking?" I stop at the end of his driveway, unsure if I should turn right or left.

"Hungry?"

Since Juno only had a container of pizza-flavored Pringles and some leftover orange chicken from Wok For U, I'm starving. "I could eat."

"Left then."

I turn into the street, and silence encases every molecule in my car.

Liam leans forward, his fingers on the button for the radio. "Do you mind?"

I shake my head. "No." I school my anxious tone. "I turned down the volume and forgot."

He puts on the classic rock station my father listened to when he was doing yard work or out in the garage. It brings a sad smile to my face.

"What made you enjoy this type of music?" I ask, at a loss for what else to say.

His knee bounces to the beat of "Sweet Home Alabama" by Lynyrd Skynyrd. "You really wanna know?"

"I wouldn't have asked otherwise."

He nods with a touché expression. "Your dad. When all you guys told him it sucked, I kind of enjoyed the beat, the lyrics. They wrote about things that affected them back then. Things they lived through. Take this song. It makes me wish I was from Alabama because you can hear their love for their state."

I laugh.

"Take a right here." He points in the direction he wants me to go.

We're leaving Lake Starlight. As we pass the goodbye sign, I release a pent-up breath it feels like I've been holding since last night.

"Funny, since the boys never found a liking for it," I say.

"I think they each kind of like it but are afraid to admit it after giving your dad so much shit. I found Rome listening to Robert Plant once at the restaurant."

"I'm ashamed to admit I never listen to this music anymore. Classic rock tends to depress me."

"Oh, shit. I'm sorry." He moves to hit the button, but I rest my hand on his.

"No. It's okay. It kinda works for me tonight."

I feel his eyes on the side of my head while I drive. "I'm sorry, Savannah. I never should've said what I did."

The sincerity in his tone now hasn't been there for weeks. Somewhere in all this, we've both changed, and not for the better.

"It's okay. There's truth to what you said."

"Well, it was a shitty thing to say either way."

I huff out a laugh because whereas some guys would argue or take back their words entirely, Liam doesn't. Because he doesn't believe them to be untrue. He's just apologizing for vocalizing them the way and where he did.

"Yeah."

"Take another right here. Pull in."

I take in the restaurant on the other side of the parking lot, Carol's Crabby Shack. "You want some crab?"

"Ready to get messy?" He opens the passenger door, one foot hanging out as he waits to see if I'll agree.

"We'll never get in. It's Sunday night." The parking lot is packed with trucks and I can hear the live music from out here.

"I'll get us in. Trust me." He winks, and my stomach somersaults. Stupid involuntary reflexes.

When I still don't move, he turns the keys in the ignition and snatches them.

"Hey!"

"You'll get them back after dinner. Let's go have some fun."

He steps out of my SUV and shuts the door. Waiting in front of my car, he doesn't even turn to look at me.

My stomach growls. "This is one time I'm going to let him think he's getting his way," I mumble to myself before opening my door and meeting him in front of my car.

We walk around to the patio that faces the lake. It's filled with people cracking open crab legs, butter dripping down their hands, laughing and singing and dancing. I haven't been here in years and I forgot how fun it is.

"Liam!" Carol, the owner of Carol's Crabby Shack, kisses Liam's cheek and hugs him. She peers over her shoulder. "Savannah, it's so good to see you."

"Hi, Carol." I wave.

Carol went to school with my mom, but other than a few chance meetings throughout the years, I haven't seen her. I'm not surprised that she recognizes me though. A lot of people see me in the local paper, due to Bailey Timber.

"Come here." She waves me forward then grabs my upper arms and thrusts me into her body. She's taller than me, and her generous chest shakes along my chin. When she pulls back, her hand cradles my cheek. "You're the spittin' image of your mom."

This sentiment has become more common since I turned thirty. Everyone and their mother says how similar I look to my mom now.

"Looks like her mom and business brains like her dad. Perfect combination," Carol says.

I smile politely.

"Carol, do you have a booth?" Liam asks.

She finally draws back and takes in the fact that we're here together. Her smile indents further, and I can almost see her mind spinning with thoughts of us. The one good thing I have going for me is that Carol doesn't gossip. She never has.

The only reason I know that is because we came here as a family when I was five and I had to go to the bathroom so badly. Mom had just had Rome and Denver and between the rest of us, she was too busy to take me. I ended up peeing in my pants. After helping a hysterically crying me get cleaned up and asking Carol for some help, Mom told me, "No one keeps a secret better than Carol."

"We're busy, but for you two, I'll find something. Give me a couple minutes." She smiles one more time and disappears through the crowd.

I stand with my purse clenched in both hands in front of my body, watching couples in front of the band dance to a ballad. A few glances come our way, but no one says anything or stares for too long.

"Want to look out at the water?" Liam gestures toward the lake and I follow his lead to the railing.

"I'm not sure if we should be here. I mean—"

Liam puts his finger over my lips. "I know you owe me nothing. If anything, I should be helping you move out of my house, but please, let me buy you dinner as an apology. We'll listen to music, and I won't hit on you or razz you. We'll just be two people having dinner. I promise." He shoves his hands into his pockets.

Carol comes out and says, "I found you guys a great table." She turns to lead the way but circles back around when she notices us not following.

Liam stands between Carol and me, waiting for me to make my decision.

I could walk out of here and Liam would probably understand. But a large part of me wants to forget for a while. Forget about Bailey Timber. Forget about Buzz Wheel. Forget about my house. Forget about the charity.

I focus on Liam. He's not even smiling because he probably believes I'll reject his invitation. That I'm refusing this olive branch he's holding out between us.

I think it's time I do something people don't expect me to.

"Thanks for fitting us in, Carol." I walk past Liam, whose lips turn up.

"My pleasure." She leads us to a booth tucked into a secluded corner, but we have a great view of the lake. "I'll send Keri over to take your order."

"Thanks."

She disappears, and we both stare out at the water, ignoring the elephant sitting smack-dab in the middle of the table. If I'm going to put it all behind me, we need to clear the air.

"About last night..."

Liam straightens, his eyes focused on me. "I feel terrible. As soon as I—"

This time I put my finger to his lips. "Let me say something."

He leans back in the wooden booth. "Okay."

I tuck my hands under the table, clenching and unclenching them. "You were right. Something in me died when my parents did. I accept your apology, and I need to apologize for the last month. I'm not sure when everything went crazy between us. I am attracted to you, but the girl you seem interested in isn't me anymore. She's just not a part of me."

"She is."

I blow out a breath and my gaze shifts to the water. "She's not, and the sooner you realize that, the better we'll be."

"Sav." He holds out his hand for mine. When I don't place mine in his, he slides it closer.

Knowing he won't stop until I oblige, I put my hand in his.

His calloused thumb runs along my knuckles. "Will you let me help you find her?"

"What?"

"Give me five weeks. One day during each week, I get to choose what we do."

I sigh. "If this is just to get me into your bed—"

"It's not. Believe me, your brothers already squashed any notion that that would ever happen. This is something I want to do *for you*."

His sincerity steals my breath. "Why?" I whisper.

"To prove you wrong?"

I smile because isn't that always the problem between us? We both love to be right. "I'll bet you good money you won't find what you're looking for."

His smirk appears, and my insides zing with awareness. "I'm game, but you're betting against yourself."

"Nah, I know that I'll always be this way. You're betting against yourself."

He shakes his head. "Name your prize. If you are permanently like you are now, what do you want?"

I lean in with a grin. "You show me what's in that barn?"

He lets my hand go. If I had to judge by the speed his smirk vanished from his face, the last thing he ever wants to share with me is the contents of that barn.

FOURTEEN

Liam

She's asking me to share with her something that no one else knows about, and I don't know if I'm ready. But she's putting trust in me with this experiment. If I accept her terms, I'll be putting trust in her too.

A bet might seem stupid. But I'm smart enough to know that if you want Savannah Bailey to do anything she's not on board with, you have to challenge her.

Still, how can I pull out the Savannah Bailey she was before her parents' deaths? We can't time travel or be visited by past, present, and future ghosts. We don't live in a movie or a book. But it's a challenge I want to take on because between last night and this morning, I've figured out that I care for this woman, whether I'm her future or not. I want her to be happy, and I'm convinced this is what she needs to find it.

"So?" she presses.

"Sure, but if I'm right, you go on a real date with me in town at Terra and Mare." This goes against everything

I talked about with her brothers, but the fact is if I'm right, everything they're concerned about is no longer valid.

She inhales deeply and stares out at the water for the thousandth time since we sat down.

"Well?" It's my turn to press.

She turns back my way and holds out her hand for me to shake on it. "Deal."

I take her hand as the waitress comes over, apologizing for taking so long to get to us.

As simple as the bet sounds, I'm going to have to do some research if I want to be eating a steak at Terra and Mare across the table from her.

We end up ordering crab legs, hushpuppies, potatoes, and beer. I'm enjoying the Beatles cover band, but I'm not sure about Savannah. If I can pull just one laugh out of her tonight, I'll call it a success.

"I hear you're moving in with Juno." I spin my beer bottle in my hands.

"I was, but I think I'll stay with you a little longer if that's okay." She picks at the label on her bottle.

Does she really not know how much I love having her in my space? I mean, it's borderline torture, but I'd rather that than go weeks without seeing her.

"It's fine. You're welcome as long as you need."

"Thanks."

I sip my beer. "Kingston back in town?"

A smile creases her lips, but it's a slow creeping smile that pulls out my own because I can tell she's amused by something. "No."

"What then?"

She bites her lip, clearly trying to push back her enjoyment. "Grandma Dori moved in. She says she has termites, which we all know is a lie, but who's going to call her out on it?"

I lean back in the booth. Grandma Dori is a meddler extraordinaire, but I'm not going to argue if it grants me a little more time with Savannah.

"She amazes me." I take a pull from my beer.

"Amazes?" Savannah relaxes, her eyes on me and not the beer bottle or the water anymore. "How so?"

"Just her attitude of 'I do what I want and to hell with you.' She doesn't mean it to be a bad thing. She honestly thinks she's doing a good thing."

She nods. "I know. There's no way I'd be where I am if not for her. You'd never imagine the patience she had with me when I first started at Bailey Timber. I think she's trying the same thing with Phoenix, but Phoenix doesn't want to work in business."

"What do you think you would've done if not for Bailey Timber?" I've wondered that since the announcement of her departure from college to run the family business.

Her mouth twists, and I hate that nothing immediately falls off her tongue. "Honestly, I'm not sure I even knew at the time. I was only in my sophomore year of college. Though my major was business, I hadn't a clue what I was going to do in life. I'm not a creative person at all. Maybe I always knew I'd work for my dad."

"You just got there a little faster then?"

She shrugs. "I suppose, but I would've preferred to finish college without having to schedule it around Bailey Timber. Have fun, do what people do in college."

"Yeah, maybe you needed a few more years before being responsible for hundreds of employees."

Her giggle is low. It's nice, but not the one I want to hear tonight. "Exactly."

"It could be worse. The Baileys could've owned a skeleton cleaning company."

"A what?" Her smile grows, but no laughter sounds from her lips.

Fail.

"I read this article about a company that has to clean skeletons, and not just dust them off. They have to degrease and whiten the bones."

Her face morphs into a disgusted expression. "What on Earth does degrease mean?"

I nod. "They said humans are the worst."

"You're right, I'd rather have to deal with wood." A small, short giggle comes out of her. "Why do they have to clean them?"

"Where do you think all those med schools get their samples?"

Her eyes widen. "I've never even thought about that."

I chuckle and finish my beer. "Me either."

Silence falls over the table, and I try to muster up anything that might entertain her. Luckily, our food comes out and I order another beer. Savannah passes on a second.

"I'll drive you home," I offer.

She shakes her head. "I owe you. I'll be DD tonight."

We crack open our crab legs.

I dip mine in butter while she eats hers without. "No butter?"

She shrugs.

"Do you not like butter?" I ask.

"Who doesn't like butter?" She pops a bite of a hush-puppy into her mouth.

"Exactly. You can't eat crab without butter." I dip a piece of crab in butter and hold it in front of her mouth. She shakes her head. "Why not?"

"Heart attack, artery blockage, calories. How many reasons do you want me to list?"

I put the piece of buttery crab into my mouth and grin. "You're missing out."

"I haven't had it in so long I don't miss it."

I wipe my mouth and hands. "Bullshit."

She peeks up at me through her eyelashes, and yeah, she misses junk food.

"You're the opposite of your brothers," I say.

"I don't know, Rome is beginning to get in shape and eat better."

"He might eat better, but his portion control sucks. He ate my entire container of hummus and pita chips the other day."

She huffs out a laugh. "I swear Calista won't stop with the 'Baby Shark' song. It's imbedded into my brain."

"This morning, she had Denver's phone and was listening to it, and this girl he labeled 'Wednesday night girl' called. Calista answered it and had a five-minute conversation about 'Baby Shark.'"

"No way." Her eyes widen.

"Yep. Imagine that girl's surprise. She probably thinks Calista is his."

She cracks open her second crab leg. "We all thought Calista was his once upon a time."

I remember that. When Harley first came to town, looking for Calista's father, she was asking around for Denver. "Sometimes I'm still surprised Rome has two kids and a soon-to-be-wife."

"How do you think I feel? I'm the second oldest and three of my siblings are settled down. Two married. One with kids. Another trying. I wonder if I should take medication for my cat allergy because I'll never fit in with the rest of the permanently single women."

I gulp my beer, trying not to spit it out because imagining Savannah with cats all around her is funny as shit. "I'll marry you. We can't do Vegas since Brooklyn and Wyatt already did that. Do you have your passport? Maybe we can go to Niagara Falls?"

She shakes her head, but she's smiling at least. "I thought there was no flirting?"

I hold out my hands. "I'm not flirting. This is innocent marriage-of-convenience talk."

"And what would you get if you marry me? There's always an exchange." She wipes her hands and mouth, straightening her back to be poised and ready.

"Maybe that eventually, after twenty years, you'll finally cave and sleep with me."

She laughs. Head tilted back, eyes crinkled with laughter that can be heard two tables over. I relish in the fact that something I said finally made her happy.

"You're laughing at my expense?" She can do it all day long for all I care. This is how I want to see her.

"No." She tries to compose herself but fails once before sobering up. "It's just the way you talk. You'd think you're that nerdy kid in school going after the head cheerleader. I mean, you do look in the mirror every morning, right?"

I shrug. "Yeah."

"And when you walk down Main Street, you catch the women staring at you, right?"

"There's only one woman I want to see staring."

She throws a hushpuppy at me. "You're not abiding by the rules you laid out."

"Sorry. It's harder than I thought." Ain't that the truth.

Her laughter dies off. I kick myself for bringing up my feelings for her again.

"Can I ask you a question?" she says.

"Sure."

"That night with the tattoo... how come you kept that secret from my family?"

"Because you asked me to."

She shakes her head. "No, I didn't."

"You didn't?" I think back to the night she came to me and asked me to tattoo a remembrance of her parents on her skin. I came up with blackbirds flying away together. Later on, her sisters saw it in the book at my shop, and now they have identical ones without knowing Savannah was the original owner. "I guess it felt like a shared moment between us and I wanted to keep it for myself." She watches me silently for a moment, so I add, "I thought it might upset some of your siblings if they knew that."

"Why would they be upset?"

"Because I'm your brothers' best friend. I always felt you were off-limits."

"Until recently?"

I shrug, finishing my second beer. "I guess it finally felt like maybe you saw me as more than just that."

Her eyes lock with mine, and my heart races as I anticipate what she'll say.

"Liam, I've been seeing you for a while."

I slide my tongue over my bottom lip. Damn, that's the last thing she should've admitted.

FIFTEEN

Savannah

Early Monday morning, I place my heels and jacket by my purse at the front door. Liam's in his track pants and sweaty T-shirt in the kitchen.

"I guess I should be thankful your first line of business wasn't asking me to go on a run this morning." I walk by him, pretending not to notice how the wet fabric is glued to his abs.

He unscrews the lid of his water bottle. My guess is it was a giveaway at Smokin' Guns since it has the company logo. He has bottles of water in the fridge for any visitors, but he always uses that water bottle. Maybe he's a closet environmentalist.

"That's step three." His voice is so serious, I turn around with my yogurt in hand and am relieved by his smirk. "Plus, you're already a runner."

"I am, but I like to do it alone."

He nods. "I can respect that, but if you ever want company, let me know." He tips his water down.

I'm not sure I could run with him alongside me. "What is your mile time?"

He laughs, screwing the top of his water back on. "I've never timed myself."

"Really?"

He circles his finger in front of my face from across the room. "I see your confusion, but for me, it's about being outside and getting a workout in because I'm way too lazy to go after work."

"Do you listen to music?"

He opens the drawer and hands me a spoon. I accept it with a nod. Maybe we can stay on solid ground. We're acting like grown-ups.

"Of course. You?"

"Podcasts." I shove a spoonful of yogurt into my mouth to shut myself up. He's going to think I'm a loser.

"Podcasts about what?"

I debate lying, but Liam is so observant, he probably already knows. "How to be a better boss."

His head tilts. A clear sign that he pities me. Great. He's going to go from being infatuated with me to another Lake Starlighter who feels sorry for me. "Admirable, but you should try music. I bet you'll decrease your mile time."

I shake my head, pointing the spoon at him. "That's sly."

"What?" His hands go up and he heads to the coffee pot. "Here or to go?"

"To go."

"So I need to steal a bit of your time every day this week?"

"For?" I finish my yogurt and dump the container in the trash and my spoon in the dishwasher.

He hands me my to-go coffee mug after putting a splash of milk in it. "How soon they forget. The bet?"

Shit. I thought he was talking the charity. We really need to get going on that as well. "Um... how much time do you want?"

His eyes fall over my body, and he inhales a quick breath. "Stop baiting me to say something I'm not supposed to."

"I didn't." But then I run the sentence through my brain again and okay, maybe I did.

"For step one, I'm going to ask you to bend the rules." His teeth latch onto his bottom lip, and I've never wanted to unleash that flesh for someone as much as I do right now.

"Already, Mr. Kelly?"

"I'd like a half hour every night for the week. It adds up to three and a half hours, which is technically less than a day. So you're actually making out on this deal."

I cock my hip out and place my coffee on the counter to cross my arms. "You've done the math, which means you knew you had to make an argument."

"What can I say? I know who I'm dealing with. I'm not going to bring a knife to a gunfight."

I smile. "Okay, a half hour every night. We also have to organize the charity event. Do you have a lunch available to come to the office or maybe I can meet you in town?"

"How about we do that tonight before my step one? You do owe me orange chicken."

I rack my brain. I owe him something?

"Before your date with Brent? At your office?"

"Ah. Yes. Okay, well, Wok For U is closed on Mondays."

He smirks. "I guess that's another time then."

"But..."

He shrugs and sips his coffee. "I understand, really. I mean, it's going to be a pain to be around you for so long anyway, but I can handle it."

I shake my head and turn to the door. "I'm going to work. I'll be home around six. Tomorrow I have a knitting class with Ethel, so I won't be home until seven-thirty."

"How about I get your schedule from Samara and we can figure something out?"

I smile. "Perfect. Thanks. She does my personal and my business."

He raises his eyebrows and I realize again he's withholding making a joke about my personal life. I'm sure with his maturity, it has something to do with sex.

At the door, I slide into my heels and grab my purse, computer bag, and coffee. I need to escape this house before I ask him to take me on the breakfast island. "See you later."

"Have a good day, Savannah."

I turn to find him leaning on the counter with his ankles crossed and a smirk on his face. I hold in my aroused sigh until I'm out of the house with the door shut. This nice version of Liam is going to be harder to resist than the angry Liam who always makes fun of me.

AT NOON, my office door springs open. A pissed-off Juno stands there with her eyes zeroed in on me as though she's been planning my demise for months.

"The polite thing to do is stop by Samara and have her check if I can see you."

The door slams and she throws herself onto my couch, putting her arm over her eyes. "You so owe me."

"Why would I owe you? I had nothing to do with this."

It's clear why she's here having a teenage fit.

She peeks one eye open through her weaved fingers. "You tricked me."

"Me?" I point at myself.

"Don't play dumb. You said you were moving in with me, which put Grandma Dori on the warpath because everyone knows her eyes are set on getting you and Liam together. She's the only seventy-something who pushes her grandkids toward living in sin."

"I'm not having sex with Liam. We're platonic."

She sits up, digs into her purse, pulls out her phone, and presses a few buttons. My gut twists because there's only one thing on her phone that would be worth her pulling it out mid-conversation.

She holds it out toward me. "Really? Because here you are laughing with Liam at Carol's Crabby Shack last night. Where, pray tell, did you sleep?"

I glance at the Buzz Wheel article but don't read it. No need to hear what Lake Starlight thinks about Liam and me. "It was just a dinner. He apologized. I stayed at his house—in my own room."

"Of course he apologized, he wants in your pants."

I sit in the chair adjacent to the couch and remain quiet.

Juno finally looks over and her shoulders fall. "I didn't mean it like that. I mean... I'm just upset. She made me organize the kitchen." She cringes. "She rearranged where my silverware goes."

"Is it by the dishwasher now? I never understood why you had it on the opposite side of the kitchen."

She throws up her arms and blows out a breath so deep, her bangs fly up. "What does it matter? It's my house."

"I'm just saying, it's more convenient—"

"You've turned into her."

"No, I haven't." Grandma Dori has the self-confidence of a lioness fighting a lion. I have the roar of a lioness but the self-confidence of a cub.

"You know what she wants to do tonight?"

"Go to the grocery store?" I guess.

Juno narrows her eyes at me, and I giggle because I razz her non-stop about how pathetic her empty fridge is. I understand Kingston and his bachelor ways, but I was surprised at Juno.

"It's sexist that you think just because I'm a woman, I should have a stocked fridge."

"Sorry for being sexist. In all honesty, Liam has a full fridge."

"Because you're there."

"That's not true. But he is different than I thought."

A low spark lights up her bored eyes. I'm giving the happily-ever-after queen reasons to believe in true love again. "How so?"

"He's just being a good friend. That's all."

She holds up her phone. "A funny friend, huh?"

I throw my pen at her and she catches it effortlessly. "Don't tell anyone?"

Usually I'd go to Rome to discuss something I don't want the other Baileys to know, but Liam is his best friend. That puts an awkward spin on the whole scenario.

"I won't."

She probably will.

I sigh. "I'm not saying I like him or anything. But we called a truce on the whole thing."

"And what exactly is the whole thing?"

She shouldn't know about Austin's wedding night. We didn't sleep together, but we were physical. "The whole him always coming after me thing. Making fun of me."

Her eyebrows fly up on her wrinkled forehead. "You mean like in the fifth grade when boys make fun of the girls they like? Is that what Liam was doing?"

"Maybe? I guess."

"My philosophy with you two is sleep together and get it over with. Then the world will return to order again." Juno picks up her phone, thumbing through either her emails or Snapchat. She's obsessed with both.

I attempt to make sense of what she's saying, but I'm not sure I can. "Meaning?"

Her eyes shoot up as though she doesn't understand what I'm asking.

"Sleep together and get it over with?" I prod her.

"Well, I mean, you and Liam aren't riding into the sunset. You're riding him into the bedroom."

She must sense my distaste, or my body language is telling, because she rushes to correct herself. "I mean you and Liam as a couple." She cringes.

Strike that. She isn't rushing to correct herself—she means it.

"Does that upset you?" she asks.

It does. Why does it?

"Wasn't it just a few days ago that you were Team Liam?"

She inspects the ceiling as if her answer awaits there. "I don't remember. Was I?"

"Yes, you were. Tell me, Juno, what—or should I phrase it as *who*—changed your mind?"

She smiles. She always smiles when she gets caught. When she was fifteen, the sheriff caught her and her friends out past curfew. When I say past curfew, I mean it was three in the morning. She'd snuck out. Austin and I arrived at the police station to find her pearly whites on display through the cell bars.

"Grandma Dori?" I fill in for her. "The same woman who suggested I become friends with the man?" This reverse psychology stuff feels amateur for Dori. Maybe she's losing her touch.

"Sorry, the sooner she gets her way with you and Liam, the sooner she's out of my apartment." Her head falls into her hands. "She wants to do pedicures tonight."

I laugh, imagining Juno painting Grandma Dori's toes. "Bonding time with your grandma is good."

She throws the pen at me that I'd thrown at her. "I think I'm gonna call Kingston's commander and tell him there's a family emergency."

I shake my head but don't say anything. She won't do that to him. Standing, I figure I'll grab my salad from the fridge to eat lunch, but Juno stands and hesitates in front of me.

"So things with you and Liam are..."

"Civil. He apologized, and I accepted."

Juno doesn't need to know about the little bet we made because she wouldn't understand. Sometimes I wonder when my family stopped seeing me as a sibling and more as a fictional superwoman character.

"Denver said it was quiet this morning."

"We don't fight every morning." I roll my eyes.

She smiles at me. "I thought maybe it was what you guys did. Got all heated because make-up sex was so good." She laughs and dashes out of the office as the pen I throw at her hits the glass door.

Payback is a bitch though, because Juno runs right into Grandma Dori—who's holding up a bottle of bright orange nail polish with a wide smile.

SIXTEEN

Liam

I arrive home to find Denver's truck in the driveway. Looking at the bags of candles and incense in my passenger seat, I wonder how I'll get those into the house without his curious eyes catching me. Then again, for all he knows, they're groceries. It's a foreign concept to him since I'm pretty sure he thinks food magically appears in the fridge. I don't mind feeding my friend, but how we're the same age and he has no drive to have his own space, I'll never understand.

I get out of the car and pull out the bags. He said he was leaving today. I hope that's still the case, because the things I have planned for my exorcism of Savannah Bailey, her brother would either try to join or call bullshit. All depends on his mood.

His music is loud and banging when I walk through the door, which means he's in the shower or getting ready. This annoying ritual of his drives me to the barn most afternoons. Since he has the power to make his own hours as a bush pilot, he tends to only take later flights so he can sleep in. Lucky me. It should give me time to stash the bags somewhere though.

"Liam!" Denver yells, and his feet are barreling down the stairs like an elephant. No cat burglar future for him.

I open the pantry and toss in the bags. The crash of glass tells me I'm less one candle. Great.

"What's up?" I slam the door as Denver stops, staring at me quizzically.

He points at the pantry door. "Do you have a chick there?"

"No." I step away from the door, but not far enough away that I can't block him if he goes to take a look.

"You look guilty."

His hair is damp from a shower, and he's shirtless, the various tattoos I've given him are on display.

"I'm not guilty. Is that completely healed?"

He looks down at his shoulder and runs his hand over the ink. "It's still peeling a bit, but it's close."

I nod, happy to see there's no redness around the ink. "You heading out?"

Now that he's sufficiently distracted from the pantry, I fill up my water bottle from the fridge.

Denver slides up on the counter. "Let's get back to your guilty look."

I smile with my back to him. He's quicker this time, which means he's not wrapped up in his own life. How can he be? He doesn't do shit except party. The guy could be making bank with his outdoor skills, but he sits on his ass most days.

"I'm not guilty."

"Blonde, brunette, or redhead?" His eyes light up at the word redhead.

"There isn't a girl in the pantry." I lean against the counter, sipping my water.

"Here I thought you got your shit together and were finally gonna get some ass."

"I'm not sure I understand your line of thinking."

He jumps off the counter. "Because we're out of sync. Before, you'd have known exactly what I meant, but I'm a lone wolf now. You and Rome have deserted me. At least he's getting laid on the regular. You..." He points at me, walking toward the stairs, thank goodness. "I don't get your new vow of celibacy."

"When do you leave?"

He circles around at the bottom of the stairs. "In about five minutes. I just have to grab a shirt. We're setting up camp tonight. Then I get to watch dumbass executives try to get themselves out of the wilderness with a piece of flint and a machete." He twirls his finger in the air.

I laugh, relieved that I distracted him from talking about me.

"A hundred dollars says the 'boss' tries to slip me some cash to get them out sooner."

"I thought you liked doing the excursions?"

"I like doing them for people who love the outdoors. People who look at a moose with awe. People who want to hike to the highest mountain just for the view and the satisfaction of making it. Not these self-entitled shitheads who give up trying to start a fire with two sticks because it hurts their hands."

"Maybe you need to start your own company. No shitheads allowed."

He points at me, stepping on the first stair. "You have a point, but no way would I run a company. That's a sure-fire way to screw up my life."

"How so?" My forehead wrinkles.

"Everyone knows the boss has no fun." He snaps his fingers. "That reminds me. Do you know if Savannah called the exterminator for Grandma Dori's place?"

"Why would I know?"

"Juno's going crazy having the old bat at her place. I heard you and Savannah kissed and made up."

I shrug. "I apologized and we agreed to be civil until her house is done."

He steps back down and heads halfway back to me. "Thanks, Liam. We all feel shitty about the talk because we want you to be happy, but you two are so opposite. It could never work."

"Opposites attract?"

"Not when neither of them wants to change." He raises his eyebrows.

"Go get ready, Denver."

He nods, fully aware it's a topic I'm not up for discussing. I'll honor the Bailey brother wishes. Until I can prove them wrong.

"Miss me." He winks.

"Counting the days until you return," I holler up the stairs after him. "Not," I whisper.

Five minutes later, Denver leaves with a duffle bag swung over his shoulder, three bottles of water, two apples, and my battery pack for his phone. I grab the bags out of the pantry and set up my night with Savannah.

SEVENTEEN

Savannah

The house is dark when I return home from work. Liam must've had somewhere to go. He told he was going to start his "find the old Savannah Bailey" experiment tonight, and I assumed he meant immediately after work.

Ever since we made that bet last night, I've contemplated how a man like Liam whole-heartedly believes he can pull out my old self. I'm not even sure I'd recognize her if he did. He'd tried the strong-arming me with digs and passive-aggressive comments until we ended up causing a scene at Brooklyn's reception. I can't imagine what he has in store for me now.

I open the front door and realize I was wrong. The house isn't dark. Candles are glowing on every surface, which I couldn't see because the blinds were shut. Some big, some small, but there are enough that I think Liam's taking his mission in a different direction. Does he think romancing me is going to drive out my type-A personality?

Putting my purse on the table by the door and dropping

my keys next to his, I slip off my heels. Damn, that feels so good. I stretch my toes and circle my ankles, and that's when a smorgasbord of smells hits my nose, leaving it begging for mercy. Cinnamon, sage, vanilla all mix to form an overpowering scent. Walking by a candle, I spot Orange Blossom embossed on a pretty label. What the hell is he doing?

Liam walks downstairs in a loose-fitting pair of lounge pants and a snug T-shirt. "You're home," he says as though he's been waiting all day.

I take inventory. No flowers. No smell of dinner in the oven—but I'm not sure I could smell it over the array of candles burning. He's not dressed up, and his hair isn't gelled like he does before going out for the night.

"Are we having a seance or are we masking the smell of burned popcorn?"

He laughs. "Look at the magic of scent. Your funny self is already returning." I admire the way the lounge pants hug his ass as he walks over to the kitchen counter, picks up a bag, and hands it to me. "Go upstairs and put these on."

"Please?"

"Please." He smiles warmly.

I peek inside the bag, thinking there will be some sort of skimpy lingerie inside, but all I see is gray. "So this is step one?"

He grins. "It is."

"If you're going to put me in the middle of a circle of people and chant, hoping to pull my soul out of my body, I have to say now, I'm not cool with it."

He laughs again. I'm glad he finds this funny.

"Liam, what is going on?"

"You'll see."

My nose tickles, and I bend over in a sneeze.

"Bless you," he whispers, leaning forward. "Now go."

I jolt for a moment, because having him so close is doing crazy things to my heartbeat.

After I walk up the stairs, I hear the flick of a lighter before I shut my bedroom door. There's no possible way he has anything else down there with a wick to light.

I unzip my pencil skirt and slide it down my legs, unbutton my blouse and look down at my bra. Oh, how I'd love to take the damn thing off, but no way can I be around Liam without a bra on. When I open the bag, I take out the items and place them on the bed. There lay pants and a shirt like Liam's except they're four sizes smaller.

"Holy moly," I say as I pull the lounge pants over my legs. Damn, they're so comfy. The shirt would be so much better sans bra, but it still feels like a T-shirt I've cherished for years. Looking at the bag, I realize that he must have driven to Anchorage to shop at a yoga store.

Then everything clicks. We're going to do yoga. Fear freezes me in place for a moment. Yoga? I'm the least flexible person on the planet. I didn't even know Liam was into yoga.

Paranoia runs through my body and I pick up my phone to google yoga poses. Downward dog—which I know of but have never tried. Cat pose—looks easy enough. I scroll past the woman who looks like a pretzel. I try to move my leg up and hold it straight, standing on one leg, but I teeter to the side. Shit. I can't hold this position for more than one millisecond. I'm going to look like a complete idiot.

"Savannah?" Liam knocks on my door.

"Just a second." The sudden awareness that he's right on the other side of the door causes me to lose what little balance I had and my arm twists around my leg. Before I can recover, I lose my footing and fall.

"Sav? You okay?" He knocks again, more frantically this time.

"Yep, sure am."

He's silent for a moment. Probably ready to call me on my bullshit, but we're playing nice now. "Hurry up. I don't want us both to be homeless if a fire breaks out."

I chuckle. "Yep. I'll be right out."

I wait to hear his footsteps head back toward the stairs. I put my clothes from today in the dry cleaner bag and head downstairs.

Standing at the top of the stairs, I realize Liam has lit incense, and now there's a new mix of scents in the air. I inhale and stop breathing for a moment.

Liam's pushed back the couch and coffee table and placed pillows and blankets in a circle. I might as well tell him where my insurance card is, because if he expects me to do yoga on blankets, I'm going to break my neck.

"Come into the circle." He waves me in as if he's the knowledgeable instructor granting me permission.

"What's going on?"

"Are you ready?"

"For what?"

"Just stay with me." He grabs my phone out of my hand, puts it on silent, and places it on the kitchen table.

"Whoa. You never said I couldn't have my phone."

"You can't have your phone." He winks.

"Not sure I would've signed up then."

He ignores my comment, coming back into the pillow circle. "Sit down."

I sit.

He sits across from me. "Cross your legs."

I do as he says.

"Put your hands on top of your thighs like this." He displays a classic meditation pose people use in movies.

I release a breath. Thank goodness, no yoga. "We're meditating?"

He picks up his phone, scrolling through. "What did you think we were doing?"

"Um... meditating. Yeah."

He smiles brightly as though he's trying to show me this plan isn't bad. "This app has great reviews, so we're going to go with it. Usually I'd say screw reviews, but I'm a novice here."

I hide the smile that wants to break out. He did all this work for me? I can't remember the last time someone put so much thought into something for me.

"So you've never meditated before?" I ask politely, because the influx of every scent imaginable says he's new and bought anything and everything that said it would be good to clear your mind. But I'm not going to complain. It's a nice gesture.

"Nope. We're newbies together. Okay. Are you ready?"

I nod.

He presses his screen, and a woman's sweet voice instructs us to breathe. I peek my eye open to see Liam's eyes are closed and his back is straight. She talks about anxiety as if we need a definition of it—telling us the repercussions, how it manifests, what causes it. Hello? If you want me to forget about my anxiety, shouldn't we not talk about it the entire time we're meditating? It's more like she's selling a product than helping me.

"Okay, maybe that's not the right one for us." He clicks off, and silence echoes throughout the house. I laugh and he looks at me, smiling as though he enjoys it. "Let's try this one."

A new woman's soothing voice instructs us to breathe once again. She talks about the pressures of life and how people rarely take the time for themselves. Giving us the Cliff's Notes version of how great meditation is for people.

I bust out laughing, and Liam opens his eyes.

"Shit. I should've tested these."

"Fast forward and see if it starts after the sales pitch."

He nods, and his thumb slides across the screen. The woman is giving instructions on how to meditate, telling us how to still our body and be aware of our breath.

"Okay, now we start," he says.

I bite my lip to stop my laugh and close my eyes, trying to take this seriously. He put a lot of time and effort into this.

The sounds of birds behind her, along with a wave slowly cresting on the shoreline every few seconds, fill the room. My mind is still on Liam's ass in those lounge pants, then it travels to how I'm here for a week alone while Denver is away. Then I think about the charity event we need to nail down some specifics for. How the workers' union wants more money and better benefits. Grandma Dori telling me she wants to lower her hours. The contractor saying he has to wait two weeks for the matching tile to arrive.

Liam hasn't made a sound or moved a muscle. Of course he can sit quietly with his own thoughts and push away his worries. If anything, the quietness of the room is making me *less* relaxed and *more* anxious.

"Relax," Liam says as though he can feel my nervous energy.

"I'm trying," I bite back.

"Try harder," he whispers.

"I can't erase my calendar from my mind."

He chuckles but stops, and I peek an eye open. He's staring back at me.

"Your eyes aren't closed," I whisper.

"We're doing this for you. I'm being nice by doing it too," he whispers back.

Oh yeah. I forgot about that. "I'm not sure I'm a meditation kind of person."

"Well, we're going to do it for seven days. So you need to just sit there for fifteen minutes each time. It's not going to come with immediate results, Sav."

I shut my eyes tightly and listen to the woman.

Silence falls around us as she stops talking. All the worries and fears and to-dos pop up in my mind like file folders stacking on top of one another. I keep my back straight. If anyone walked in right now and they didn't throw up from the smell, they'd think I was a master of meditation. But I'm far from relaxed as our session draws to a close and the woman tells us it's like exercise and we must do this on a daily basis to reap the results. Great.

My eyes open before Liam's, and I use the moment to soak him in. The calmness over his body compared to the chaos inked on his skin. His lap looks so inviting, I wish I could crawl into it and have him kiss my forehead and tell me all will be well one day. How I'm navigating my path the best I can, given the circumstances. That one day in the future, I'll have a man who loves me for me, even though I might make more money than him and my hours are crazy, and I like things just so and I put capitals T and A in Type-A personality. There's a man out there who thinks I'm worth the sacrifice.

His eyes open and I stand, picking up the pillows to put the room back to normal.

"Getting right to it, huh?" He follows suit, helping me tidy up. "We could have done another one."

"No need to do squats and bicep curls all in one day."

He laughs, grabbing the pillows from me.

"Mind if I blow out some candles?" I ask.

His smile vanishes. "Go ahead."

He helps me. It seems like a waste for only a half hour of our time. Though technically we only meditated for fifteen minutes. I notice Liam's shoulders are hunched and he's quiet.

"Hey, Liam?" I say before heading toward the stairs to go back up to my room and work.

He peers up from sliding the couch back into place. His smile has dimmed slightly, like a disappointed kid who showed his parents a drawing and they asked what it is.

"Thank you."

He nods, his lips tipping back up into his amazing smile. "Any time."

EIGHTEEN

Liam

We're in the middle of week one of this experiment, and we've meditated every night. Three nights of hearing her light breathing across from me. Three nights of watching her breasts squeeze into that tight T-shirt. Three nights of having her help me put everything away before she heads back upstairs. I have no idea if she's enjoying it or is just in it to see what's in the barn. It'll be a let-down if it comes to that because I'm really hoping she gets something out of all this and isn't using it as a means to an end.

I approach the security desk at Bailey Timber, and Carrie eyes me and slides over my name tag. "They're expecting you in the conference room. Fourth floor."

"Thanks."

I pin on my badge and head to the elevator. The doors ding open on the fourth floor, and Phoenix stands there with a half-eaten burrito in her hand. A microwave burrito I'm thinking she got down at the 7-Eleven.

"Hey, Liam," she says, turning on her heels to head toward the conference room. It's the giant room in the middle of all the offices on the north side of the building. I would've found it without Phoenix's stellar handholding.

"What kind of burrito you got there?"

"Red hot beef." She holds it out, offering me a bite.

I put my hand in the air. "I'm good, thanks. Where's it from?"

She takes a bite and swallows. "7-Eleven. Don't knock it. It was my splurge in LA."

I give Phoenix props for trying so hard to make her dream come true. But I think she and Denver might be cut from the same cloth.

"They had Wok For U catered in. I think Savannah purposely told me after my burrito finished in the microwave, which I'm supposed to think is a privilege to use. The other day I accidentally put the popcorn in for twelve minutes instead of a minute and twenty."

I cringe.

"Yeah. There was talk about banning me from the microwave, but come on. It was an honest mistake."

I sniff. "I think I can still smell it."

She laughs and punches me in the upper arm. "Funny."

I'm not joking. That scent lingers for eternity.

I hear Savannah talking to someone, and Phoenix detours us another way.

"I know you work here, but I think we're supposed to go that way." I point in the opposite direction.

She crunches up the burrito wrapper as her eyes follow my finger. "Oh, Savannah is in a meeting that way, and if I take you past the office, you're sure to distract her."

Distract her in a good way, I hope.

"Phoenix Bailey having consideration for others? Has hell frozen over?"

She punches me in the arm again, and we arrive in the conference room a moment later. I can still overhear Savannah. She's telling the other person that Bailey Timber can't afford to pay more, but she'll see what she can do on the benefits.

Grandma Dori's sounds out next. "We just upped their benefits last year. I understand the tough spot they're in, but we're not in a better one."

What? Is Bailey Timber having problems? They're a staple of this community.

Phoenix shuts the door of the conference room. "Orange chicken and fried rice. Li said he made special fortunes."

"I don't even wanna know."

She snags a cookie and sits at the head of the conference table, pointing toward an empty chair. "So tell me, Liam Kelly, what are your intentions with my sister?"

I quirk my eyebrow, and she laughs. We both know I'm not answering, and she probably doesn't really care unless I hurt Savannah. Then I'd see the wrath of Phoenix Bailey. She might seem like she doesn't care about her family, but she does. She's just a self-absorbed twenty-year-old like all twenty-year-olds.

"How's Sedona?" I lean back in my chair.

"Fine, I guess." She rolls her eyes.

The twins might be opposites, but they're entwined in each other's lives regardless of whether they share the same bedroom or are thousands of miles apart. With Sedona in New York for school and only returning for family functions, I imagine Phoenix feels like Denver did when Rome went to Europe to study under the famous chefs. The difference is, Denver had me. Phoenix is living with her older brother and his wife while they try for a baby. Her dream has died—at least for the time being.

"What does fine mean?" I ask.

"That douche Jamison is back in the picture, I guess."

"The foreign exchange student she was dating your senior year?"

"Jeez, no one could call you a dumb jock."

I shake my head. "Watch it with the stones. I can hurl boulders back if I choose to."

She smiles, a bring-it-on one, but the last thing I would do is razz Phoenix when she's healing a bruised ego after returning from LA. "Anyway, she's talking about bringing him home after she graduates."

"I thought he was some hot-shot soccer player in Europe now?"

A hollow laugh escapes her. "He was, but he's playing for the North American Soccer League now."

I act as if that's impressive, but I don't follow soccer, so I really wouldn't know.

"It's like the minors for baseball," Phoenix clarifies. She's obviously searched out answers. "He's all Sedona can talk about. It's nauseating. And she wants to be a travel writer, but how is that going to happen?"

"Your mom did it and she was based here in Alaska."

Phoenix's gaze shifts to the table. The mention of her mom is a sore spot. I wish I hadn't asked about Sedona.

Lucky for us, Grandma Dori comes in to join us. "Liam," she coos.

What can I say? The woman loves me.

"Dori." I stand and kiss her cheek.

"Savannah will be right in. She's finishing up a meeting." Dori looks at Phoenix, and she nods. What are these two planning? "Phoenix would be happy to get you a drink."

Dori and I look at Phoenix, but she's inspecting her nails now.

"Phoenix? Drinks?" Dori nudges.

Phoenix looks up. "Sure. I'll have an iced tea." She returns to examining her nails.

Dori sighs next to me. "No, dear, you get the drinks."

"Oh. Okay. I'll be back." She slides her chair out and leaves the room.

"I'm not sure her heart is in it," I say and sit back down.

Dori takes the seat Phoenix vacated. "I know, but until she figures out her next step, she needs to learn what the real world is like."

I love Grandma Dori. She's a great mentor to not only me but all her grandchildren. I'm not sure I agree with Phoenix working at Bailey Timber though. If anything, this will turn her off becoming a responsible adult with a nine-to-five job.

The light bulb goes off in my head. I get it now. Dori's showing her what her life might be like if she gives up on her dream. Sly Dori.

"Hungry? Eat, Liam." My stomach growls as she speaks and Dori laughs.

I stand from my chair. "Can I fix you a plate?"

Phoenix opens the conference room door, and I catch Savannah's rising voice in the background. She looks at Dori, sighs, and at the other end of the table, cracks open her iced tea bottle. Dori waits silently for Phoenix to look at her.

Finally Phoenix notices. "What?"

"Liam might like a drink," Dori says.

"I'm good, Phoenix." I wave her off.

"You're not going to eat without a drink. Phoenix." Dori's tone is the one she gave us when she babysat the Baileys and I happened to be over. It has a bite to it, suggesting Phoenix not test her. A few of the Baileys are immune to that tone, Phoenix being one of them.

"Tell me where to get them and I'm happy to do it," I offer.

"No, Liam, Phoenix will get you a drink." Her eyes shoot invisible lasers at Phoenix.

"*Ugh*!" Phoenix sighs dramatically, sliding her chair out from the table and standing. "What do you want, Liam?"

"I'd love a water."

"And I'll have a Diet Coke, dear." Dori smiles at her.

Phoenix pushes the door open and Savannah can still be heard. Where are they and why has no one shut the door wherever she is?

"She really should try her hand at acting instead of singing." Dori puts her fingers on her temples and massages.

I put a plate of orange chicken and rice in front of Dori. I'm about to sit down myself when the door opens, and Savannah appears.

I missed her this morning because I'm trying to be a gentleman and give her space. It's clear now that I missed out on some beat-off material, because her dress is enough to turn my mouth into a water fountain. All I can do is commit her to memory. I haven't seen her this dressed down for work the entire time she's lived with me. Maybe it's because we're in record heat, or maybe the meditation is having an effect on her. Either way, she looks good enough to eat—for hours.

"Sorry I'm late. I'm glad you started without me." She glances at Dori.

They share a look of worry, and I realize maybe Savannah is under more pressure than just being the mother hen of her family. Could she be trying to keep a failing company from sinking?

NINETEEN

Savannah

Liam stares at me as though I'm naked. His tongue skates over his full bottom lip as his gaze slides down my body. He takes in the patterned, clingy wrap dress I'm wearing and his hands clench on the table. Forgetting the fight I just got into with the union leader would be divine right now. Liam's hands could make me forget that the workers' demands are more than we can give them.

"I'm going to help Phoenix. She probably forgot she was getting us drinks." Grandma Dori stands. I'm vaguely aware of what she said until she touches my shoulder. "What would you like to drink?"

I blink and peel my gaze off Liam. "I'll just grab my water from my desk."

"I can get it. You two eat. I'll be right back." Grandma Dori leaves.

Liam clears his throat. "I love your dress." He leans back, not shy about his appraisal.

"Thanks for mentally stripping me just now." I head to the buffet table because I'm starving.

"You're welcome. Thanks for enjoying it so much."

I whip my head around, and that smirk I love is on his face. "Is this the way it's going to be now? We openly say what we're thinking?"

I take my plate and sit across from him. His eyes dip to my chest as my wrap dress falls open a little bit. I tighten and tuck it, my cheeks heating.

"Are you okay with that?" he asks. "I never said my attraction to you had waned."

"You said you weren't going to openly flirt with me." I fork a piece of chicken.

"For that dinner. But if you expect me to go through the next five weeks without noticing all your... assets when you're wearing a dress that could be pulled open with one tug on a piece of fabric, you're fooling yourself." He scoops up his fried rice.

"It's a tug and button," I clarify with a wink.

He laughs. "I could still undress you in under two seconds."

"Are you hoping I take the bait and make you prove it?"

His face reddens. Liam Kelly embarrassed? That's not something you see every day.

"I wouldn't be opposed to it, but I always find the harder I work for something, the sweeter the reward."

My lady parts go into a flurry of activity—clenching while nerve endings fire to life. I shove the biggest piece of chicken into my mouth in order to shut myself up from provoking flirtatious comments from him. Liam smiles over his fork, and I bury my head in my dish.

The door opens, and Dori and Phoenix rejoin us, arguing about time spent on the computer. Dori's telling her that the IT department checks all activity. They don't actually, but they could if we asked. This Phoenix-in-the-office experiment needs to come to an end.

Grandma Dori looks in horror at the bulge in my cheek. "Savannah dear, a lady should never eat that much food at one time."

For being a feminist and pro-woman, Grandma Dori still holds on to some of those stupid beliefs about how a woman should act. Funny how she shacked me up with Liam in the first place but is flabbergasted that I have too much food in my mouth.

Ignoring her, Phoenix sits at the opposite end of the table.

We chat about all the siblings as we eat. Austin and Holly are topic number one since Phoenix is the only one who sees them now that they're actively trying to have a baby.

"I worry it's taking too long," Grandma Dori admits.

Compared to Rome and Harley, it does feel that way. But Harley gets pregnant if Rome just looks at her.

"It's only really been, like, a month. She could already be pregnant for all we know," I say.

"True. Why did they tell us anyway? Now I feel like I'm waiting for Christmas to come," Grandma Dori says.

Phoenix raises her hand. "I told everyone."

Of course she did.

"All right, let's talk about the charity event now that Brooklyn and Wyatt's reception is over." Grandma Dori gets down to business.

"I was gonna go around town tomorrow and inquire about what everyone is willing to donate," Liam pipes up.

"I haven't had time yet, but I have a list of venues to call. That said, I was thinking about doing something a little different." I bite my lower lip. Liam clocks the movement, and I let it go.

"I still don't understand why I can't plan this thing." Phoenix practically pouts.

"What are you thinking?" Grandma Dori asks me.

"I thought about having it open to the entire town. I know we usually sell tickets and have tables and make it really fancy, but maybe we have a silent auction. Do it in the square with the gazebo and get food catered in—"

"That's a big endeavor, Savannah."

I was certain Grandma Dori wouldn't agree, but I had to try. "We could do art in the park. We'll need pictures and art pieces for the new extension. Maybe we make it a contest or something."

Liam buries his head in the plate. I guess he's not going to help me win this fight. Either that, or he thinks it's the worst idea ever.

"I think the people who donate money like the exclusivity of the event. You have all the people outbidding each other just to beat the other one."

Grandma Dori has a point. People with big checkbooks generally have the egos to match.

"I just think that we're doing this for the library, which will be for everyone to enjoy. Why not make everyone involved in the donation process and make them feel like they're contributing?"

Dori sighs.

Liam peeks up at me but says nothing.

"I don't think it will work," Grandma Dori says. "The silent auction is okay but we don't have a ton of time to arrange something in the square that the entire town could participate in. Let's just stick with the gala and we'll revisit your idea of opening it up to everyone for the next event."

I slouch back in my chair and push my plate away, sipping the water Phoenix brought to me.

"I'd like a big cake, maybe decorated like a stack of books or something. We should pick a theme. What's a popular children's book? Did either of you have a favorite?" Grandma Dori asks.

"*Charlotte's Web*," I answer.

"*Cat in the Hat*," Liam says.

"*Tikki Tikki Tembo*," Phoenix says.

I've never even heard of it. All three of us turn our heads her way.

"What?" She sips her iced tea.

"There's a ton we could do, and everyone has their favorite," I say.

"We could do different stations with the themes," Liam says. "Maybe we pick, like, six books and the desserts could be themed that way. Maybe we could figure out a way to do a fun poll and let the guests decide either when they purchase the table or when they arrive."

"I don't understand," Grandma Dori says.

Liam looks at me and I nod that I do understand, which makes him smile. I shouldn't like that something I did gave him enjoyment.

"Let's say Smokin' Guns bought a table," he says. "I'm asked at the time of purchase, 'Out of these six books, what's your favorite?' Then my table is decorated like that book. Or you could tell me I'll get to pick them when I get there. We have the tables set up with the themes ahead of time, and sponsors pick when they arrive."

Grandma Dori seems to think it over. "I love it. I'd love to get a poll going to pick the books." Her eyes light up. "Phoenix, you can handle that. Email Buzz Wheel and ask them if they can include a link to the poll for the next couple of weeks. We'll get it up on the library web page and make handouts. And see, Savannah, this way the town is involved."

I give her a tight smile.

"This is perfect. But I think I like the way they pick a table when they arrive." She scribbles on the pad of paper she brought. "Savannah, you'll talk to Greta down at Sweet Suga Things?"

"Once we figure out the books."

"Yes, that's right." Grandma Dori points at me. "I'm so excited I got ahead of myself." She giggles.

I don't, and Liam chuckles. Phoenix is lost in her head somewhere, so she doesn't even seem to know what's going on.

"Savannah, you secure the venue. Liam, start going around to businesses. Phoenix—Phoenix?" Grandma Dori inhales a deep breath.

"Phoenix!" I yell.

She startles in her chair. It tips back and she loses her center of gravity but recovers quickly, grabbing the edge of the table, her face ghost-white. "Jesus."

"Get the poll going. Let's come up with a list for them to vote on."

We decide on the books to include in the poll, and even Phoenix's pick gets on the list. After it's done, Grandma Dori and Phoenix excuse themselves, leaving me alone with Liam. We're both done eating, and I'm highly aware that we're surrounded by windows. I can probably expect to find myself in Buzz Wheel again.

"Why don't you push your ideas more?" he asks.

"It's no use. Grandma Dori always gets her way. She's technically the owner." I'd like to point out that it's not as though he came to my defense. He could've sided with me and maybe she would've folded, although I highly doubt it. Two years into taking over the company, I tried to get more ideas of my own into play, but Grandma Dori likes things her way. How can I refute her advice on what's right and wrong to do for Bailey Timber? She's been a part of it for the majority of her life.

"You never know until you try."

I nod. "Is that lesson number two? I have to tell off Grandma Dori?"

He laughs. "No. I'm not going to be that forceful with you, but I was thinking that maybe you could come along on a couple visits to the local businesses, asking for donations?"

My forehead wrinkles. "I'm not sure that's a good idea."

"Why?" He leans back, crossing his arms.

"Because everyone in this town loves you. Me, not so much. We don't have to pretend you didn't overhear my heated discussion with the union rep. Those people live in this town. They think I want to keep all the Bailey money to myself. Now I'm going to ask their sister, brother, cousins, and whoever else to donate something to give away during an exclusive dinner only accessible to the wealthiest people in the area?"

He stares at me for a moment, soaking in my words. When he opens his mouth, I'm already turned off to anything he's going to say.

"I think you've not only lost sight of yourself, you've lost sight of the people of this town." He stands and tucks in his chair. "I'll leave it in your hands."

Unsure of what to say, I stare at him while he walks around the conference table.

He rests his hand on my shoulder and leans down to my ear. "I'll see you at home, honey."

With the click of the door shutting behind him, I search

for meaning in his earlier words. I've never imagined living anywhere other than Lake Starlight. I love it, but Liam's right. Lately I dodge downtown as though it's flush with flesh-eating zombies. Who is Liam Kelly? Lake Starlight's Buddha?

TWENTY

Liam

On Sunday, I'm sitting at the breakfast island, reading the paper and drinking my coffee, when Savannah returns from a run. She doesn't notice me right away because as soon as she comes in, she's logging something in a small book in her purse, staring at her watch.

"How fast were you today?" I ask.

She startles, dropping her pen on the floor.

My gaze soaks her in like a dry towel. Sweat has left a sheen on her skin, and her running shorts stop right at her ass, making her long legs appear even longer. Her tight sports bra and tank top don't hide her figure in the slightest, and I have to shift in my seat to find a comfortable position for my growing hard-on.

"Too slow."

"Listening to a podcast?" I arch my eyebrow. I knew she wouldn't take my suggestion about switching to music.

"Yes." She drops the booklet and pen back into her

purse, toeing out of her running shoes. She pads across the room and opens the fridge.

"Denver returns today," I say with my eyes on the paper as though I'm not pissed about it.

I love my buddy, but having the place to ourselves has been nice. Had we meditated in front of Denver, he would've razzed me forever or joined in—you never really know with that guy. Friday night, we ordered pizza and watched *When Harry Met Sally*. I never pegged Savannah as liking romantic comedies. Maybe because it's so rare that she laughs.

"I know." Am I imagining that her words sound deflated like mine?

"How do you think the meditating thing went?" I ask.

She turns around, yogurt in hand, and grabs a spoon, then she slides out the breakfast stool next to me. She props up one foot, and I can't help but notice the way her shorts are wide enough that they hang down a bit. If she was mine, I'd have free access to slide them down, pick her up, and position her on my lap. But sadly, she isn't.

She says, "I liked it. I'm going to keep it up. You're probably going to make fun of me for this, but... I see it like a challenge to clear my mind. To be able to eventually sit there for twenty minutes with a clear mind."

I laugh and put the paper down, sipping my coffee. She's adorably predictable. I'd love to be able to kiss her and say, "Yeah, I get it." She's not going to turn into that naïve nineteen-year-old who looked at the world with hope and an unsullied view. She went through a hurricane in a dingy, stranded in the middle of the ocean. It changed her in ways there's no reversing. But it doesn't mean she can't enjoy her life a lot more than she does at present.

"I'm not going to make fun of you as long as you don't

tell anyone that I might continue doing it too." I get up to refill my cup. "Coffee?"

"Sure."

I fill her cup, add a splash of milk, and return to the island. After I set the cup in front of her though, I keep my distance because I'm having a really hard time being so close to her when she has so few clothes on. "I got you something."

"What? Why?" Her face wrinkles in confusion, or irritation maybe.

I head to my den where my desk is and grab the box with the nice ribbon the sales lady added for me. Placing the box in front of her, I step back to take in her reaction. She stares at me with awe and a small smile. It looks as if she's trying not to let it shine too brightly.

"Open it," I urge and return to my coffee, slightly embarrassed. I've only ever bought a woman a gift once in my lifetime, and that was in high school.

She unties the ribbon slowly as though she's savoring the anticipation. With her hands resting on the sides of the box, she peeks at me again. I wish I could snap a picture without her knowing because I want nothing more than to savor her expression. It's one of true happiness, and I'd buy her a million more presents for the rest of our lives if I could see that same look every time.

"I'm so excited." She's practically giddy, and I'm eating up every moment. After opening the box, she carefully moves the tissue paper away and looks at the contents for a breath-halting moment before picking up the leather journal.

"It's red because I think it's one of your favorite colors?"

The sales lady had asked me, and after running through

Savannah's outfits in my head, I realized that she wears red more than any other color.

"It is." She smiles.

"There's a pen in there too."

A small sigh leaks out of her throat and she shifts in the chair. "Liam—"

"It's for you to write down thoughts. Anything you want, but I read an article that said you should write down at least one thing you're grateful for every day."

She thumbs through the empty pages that are ready for her deep thoughts, or what her day was like, or just to doodle flowers and stars on. "I love it."

"I'm glad."

Our eyes lock over the breakfast bar, and she slides off the stool. Our gazes don't waver the entire time she rounds the counter. Instinctively, I place my coffee mug on the counter and open my arms.

She rises on her tiptoes, wraps her arms around my neck, and hugs me. "Thank you."

I wrap my arms around her waist. We stand with mere inches between our bodies, and I breathe her in. Even after her run, this must be what heaven is like.

"You're welcome," I whisper, and she shivers before falling down to her heels. I let her go and step back.

"You could've just told me I should buy one."

I shake my head. "Keep it locked up if you don't want anyone to read it."

"What?" She heads back to her stool, looking over the journal again as though she can't wait to put a pen to paper and jot down everything that runs through that pretty head of hers.

"You used to leave your diary in easy-to-find places."

The journal drops out of her hands onto the granite counter and her mouth hangs open. "You read my diary?"

"I was a twelve-year-old boy." I shrug. "I was only a reader, not the seeker."

"Denver?" she asks.

I nod.

"And what did you find out about me?"

I dump my coffee in the sink and put my cup in the dishwasher. "Just that you hoped Ian Troppel would ask you to prom and you were going to make a voodoo doll of Mr. Japlin because he gave you a B on a paper."

She laughs. I love the way the sound bounces off the walls and fills the room. Even more, I love that I caused it. "I wonder what happened to my old diary?"

I shrug.

"You guys didn't take it or anything?"

"I can't speak for your brothers, but I didn't."

She hugs the journal. "Thanks again. I'd gladly pay you—"

I put up my hand. "Stop. You're welcome." Her small smile says how grateful she is I got her a gift. I shouldn't push my luck, but I'm going to. "Want to go on a ride with me today?"

"As in?" She puts the tissue paper and journal back in the box and secures it with the lid, bunching the ribbon in her hand.

"A ride on my Harley. I'm doing it for a charity, and I thought you'd like to join me."

She raises her chin slightly. I can see I'm going to be shot down. "And I'd have to ride?"

I try to fight back a smile, but it breaks through. "On the back of my bike."

Her body sinks down on her stool, but not in a way that

indicates she thinks that's the worst option available. "Um..."

"Well, you can think about it. I have to go shower. I'm leaving in about an hour." I head to the staircase.

"Liam?"

I circle back around, raising my eyebrows in question.

"What is the charity for?"

My lips desperately want to turn up. "It's for this bar I go to. The waitresses need new tube tops."

Her nostrils flare until she catches on that I'm joking.

"Remember the trooper who died a few months back? A car hit him while he had a vehicle stopped?"

She nods.

"For his family."

Her phone dings. We both glance at her purse on the opposite counter.

"That's a nice thing to do," she says.

"Like I said, you can think it over and let me know." I shrug as though it doesn't affect me either way. It does though.

Her phone dings again.

I point at her purse. "You better get that. Family members to tend to. Fires to put out."

I run up the stairs before she can give me a quick comeback. After shutting my bedroom door, I turn on my shower, hoping she takes the bait. Not only because having her arms wrapped around me would be the best thing to happen all week, but it'd be good for her. She doesn't understand how freeing and peaceful it is to take a ride on a motorcycle.

Ten minutes later, I'm wrapping a towel around my waist when there's a knock on my bedroom door. I could ask her to wait a minute while I get dressed. That would be the right thing to do after we agreed to leave whatever sexual tension was building between us in the past. But I feel as though if I don't help her along a little bit, she'll stall out at some point.

I open the door, and Savannah's eyes zero in on my abs before dipping lower. I guess I was wrong about that. Who knew?

"Get that Cheshire Cat grin off your face. You're trying to tempt me." She points at me and I laugh.

"Sorry." I bite my lower lip, which I know drives her crazy.

"Oh. My. God. I was just about to agree to go with you, but now." Her hands wave at my body.

I snatch her hand and she tries to pull away. "I'm sorry. It was convenient for me to answer, but you're right, I knew what I was doing. Just to be fair though, you walking in a sweaty mess in less than a yard of fabric isn't exactly fair either."

The apples of her cheeks pinken.

"Come. I promise a good time." I squeeze her hand.

She slides her palm out of mine and pokes my chest. "No monkey business."

"Okay." I hold up my hand. "I promise not to swing from limb to limb and throw poop."

There go her nostrils again, but she turns on her heels and locks herself in the guest bathroom.

It feels like a small victory, but a victory, nonetheless. I won't tell her yet that she has to make sure to hold on tight today. I mean, we don't want to crash.

TWENTY-ONE

Savannah

We arrive at a bar on the side of a highway way out of town and park in the long line of bikes already there. From the huge building hangs a banner with a picture of the deceased trooper and his family. Liam fist-bumps a few people on our way to the registration table, but he doesn't introduce me. I catch lingering gazes with silent questions in them. Spotting me in this crowd is as easy as finding a burned piece of white rice in a bowl. Maybe coming here was a mistake.

At the table, he says, "Liam Kelly," and the woman places a checkmark next to his name and hands him two tickets. "Thanks."

He leads me away, only millimeters of space between us, and we end up in a circle of guys who look super familiar, but I can't place them.

The big one with a black leather vest that doesn't cover his stretched stomach raises his water in greeting. "Kelly!"

"Hey, Slim," Liam says. "I had no idea you guys were doing this one."

Slim eyes me up and down with a slow creeping grin. "This your girl?"

"Me? Oh—"

"Yeah." Liam places his arm around my waist, pulling me into his side.

I draw back and look for some silent non-verbal reason why he's lying. But with the way Slim's vision has zeroed in on my chest, I think I'll go with it.

"Didn't know you'd put the handcuffs on," another guy to my right says. He isn't as scary as Slim. At least he smiles at me and looks me in the eye.

"News to me too." A brunette two people over from Slim, standing next to another brunette, examines me as though I'm less than nothing.

Liam's hand grows tighter on my hip. "Nina." Her name comes off his tongue like vinegar.

She's wearing a leather vest, but it's shorter than Slim's. All she has underneath is a halter top that barely contains her boobs and shows off her flat stomach. I glance down at my jeans and plain white T-shirt. I was going to wear a black T-shirt, but Liam said that it would be too hot. Now I just feel out of place.

"Liam," Nina seethes.

My gaze shifts between them. I'm uncomfortable with whatever subtext is going on that I'm unaware of. I realize in this moment that Liam has or had a whole other set of friends I knew nothing about.

"I told Kathy we'd find her before the ride starts. I'm sure we'll see you at a stop or something." Without waiting for a goodbye, Liam walks us away.

"Who is Kathy?"

"An old friend," he mumbles, his hand still not leaving my hip.

"An old friend like Nina?" I snipe.

He stops me by the end of a table where they're serving fresh fruit, pastry items, and drinks. Turning me so my back is to the table and he's in front of me, his hands land on my hips. "Nina was a long time ago, so you don't have to worry about her. I lied because Slim likes the new girls. He wouldn't have left you alone the entire ride even if Nina's riding on the back of his bike. This way he knows you belong to me, and he's not one to try to take what isn't his."

I lean back to look in his eyes, and there's sincerity there. "I wouldn't have allowed him to *take* me anyway."

He shakes his head. "I know that, but it doesn't mean he wouldn't try. Is it so horrible to act like my girlfriend all day?"

No. Not at all.

Shit.

Yes, it is.

"All those people, aren't they your friends?" I ask.

"Not much anymore. I run into them sometimes at a bar or something, but I cut ties years ago."

"Why?"

His hand slides into mine. "I'll tell you later. Come on. We only have about fifteen minutes before everyone has to ride."

I allow him a pass on telling me about his relationship with Slim and his groupies, and we weave through the crowd. He nods hello to various people who refer to him solely by his last name. I feel as though I'm in a different world. Denver and Rome never mentioned anything about this part of Liam's life. Then again, why would they? I never showed interest.

After what feels like a mile, he stops me in front of a woman with dyed red hair and nails so long, she could literally scratch out someone's eyes.

"Kathy," Liam says.

She turns from her conversation with a man and smiles brightly. "Liam." She's the first person other than Nina to use his first name.

He hugs her and picks her up off her feet. Over his shoulder, she zeroes in on me. A smile indents dimples into her cheeks until he sets her back down.

"Who do we have here?"

Liam doesn't take my hand or put his arm around me this time. "This is Savannah."

"Hi, Savannah." She puts out her hand, and I shake her boney hand with rings on almost every finger. "I'm Kathy."

"Hello."

"And are you guys...?" She wags her finger between us.

"No." Liam does something behind me that makes Kathy laugh, but when I turn around, he pretends to just be standing there.

"What did he do?" I ask.

"Mother-son confidentiality." Kathy beams at Liam like she loves him like a son. "Slim and his roadies are here."

I feel the tension wafting off Liam. "We saw. As far as he's concerned—"

"She's yours?"

My head volleys between them as they finish each other's sentences.

"Nina?" she asks.

"Green with envy."

"I figured."

Liam doesn't once look at me during the conversation. Kathy turns around, and that's when I see the patch stitched onto the back of her black leather jacket. Chicks Brigade. I point, and Liam, finally paying me attention, laughs.

He bends down to my ear as Kathy answers a question someone else asked her. "She runs the Chicks Brigade. If you want a membership, I can get you in."

I look around and see mostly all women in this area, next to bikes that have some sort of girly flair to them.

Just then, someone gets on the microphone and tells the crowd to line up.

Liam leans over and kisses Kathy's cheek. "We'll see you after."

"Nice to meet you," I say, putting out my hand.

"You as well. Watch out for that one. He heals hearts, doesn't break 'em." She points at Liam.

But he snags my hand and says goodbye to Kathy before weaving us back through the mass of black leather. When we reach his bike, he puts the helmet back on my head, secures it, then puts on his own.

"I thought bikers always wanted to feel the cool air breeze through their hair?"

"Believe me, you'd rather have helmet hair and be alive than have perfect hair and end up a pancake on the road." He checks the strap of my helmet one more time then climbs on the bike, waiting for me to join him.

I put my feet where he instructed on the way here, climb on, and circle my arms around his stomach.

"Ready?" When he feels me nod on his back, he turns on the engine and we line up with everyone else.

I'd never admit it but having Liam in my arms makes me feel a lot like my old self. And I don't hate it.

LIAM WAS RIGHT—HELMET hair sucks. Luckily, out of the three stops, our last is at a gas station, so I run in and buy some ponytail holders. I found out at the last stop, from some more of Liam's secret friends, that a band is playing after the ride tonight and that's when the party really starts.

The people on the ride are super friendly and outgoing. None of them look at me as if I'm some stuck-up bitch who's trying to date a bad boy, which is what I worried in coming here. Liam hasn't been too handsy except on the two run-ins we had with Slim and Nina's kept her distance, so all in all, I'm having a great time.

Let's be honest, having my arms around Liam's waist for the majority of the day doesn't suck.

"Ready?" Liam leans on his bike, his dark sunglasses shielding his eyes.

"Yeah." I touch my hair. "You're right about the hair thing."

He stands up straight and puts his hand behind his ear. "What was that?"

"Ponytails." I hold up the package I bought.

"No, I mean about me being right?" His smirk grows.

With that smirk, the dark sunglasses, and the bike behind him, I think my ovaries just made a ruling that only Liam's sperm can meet my eggs, otherwise pregnancy is off the table. I can't even argue with them. "You were right, but I've never—"

His finger comes to my lips. "Let's just leave it at that."

All the bikes line up again, so I drop the ponytail holders in the saddlebag of his bike and pull out the sanitizer. Liam, knowing the drill after the first two stops, puts out his hands.

"You'll thank me later," I say.

He rolls his eyes and massages the sanitizer into his palms. "Yeah, you said that already."

"Maybe it will be you saying I was right next week when all your friends have a cold."

"It's summer."

"There's such a thing as summer colds. Germs don't just live in the winter. And believe me, summer colds are the worst." I rub sanitizer into my hands while Liam tries not to laugh at me.

"Let's go, Kelly."

We both turn to find Slim, Nina on the back of his bike. Liam's body stiffens.

"You really need to tell me why we hate him," I say low enough so only he can hear me.

Liam waves Slim off, who pulls ahead a bit, then narrows his eyes on me. "You don't even know him. Why would you hate him?"

I let him put my helmet on again because somehow he thinks I can't secure it myself. But like he's dealing with my sanitizer, I'll deal with his manly macho act. "If you hate him, I hate him. That's how it works. You're my friend, he's not, and I trust you have valid reasons."

He stares at me for longer than necessary as though I'm a Rubik's Cube.

"Kelly! Let's go!" Slim yells, and Liam purposely ignores him.

"Sorry about him." Liam straddles his bike.

I hop on, feeling much more confident now. "Don't apologize. Just ignore him."

He starts the bike. I'm pretty sure my panties are going to soak through from watching his forearms flex each time he revs the engine. I pass him his jacket that was lying on the back of the bike, and he thanks me as he leans to the side to slip it on.

My head is on his back, my arms around his waist when he pulls back onto the highway. We've gotten used to one another today. I'm not so anxious, and I've learned how to shift my weight to go along with him on turns as if we're one person. He was right again about being on a motorcycle, though I wouldn't tell him—it's peaceful and relaxing and I haven't thought once about all the troubles at Bailey Timber.

As I'm thinking about telling him he should take his motorcycle out more often and that I might join him, we take the curve around the bend. There's a large puddle of standing water on the other side of the road where the road seems to dip. It must've rained out here overnight. Without warning a huge wave of water hits us and the bike jerks. I can't hear what Liam says, but his body straightens, and the bike slows and fishtails, straightens, fishtails, straightens, fishtails, and straightens. Once we're through the worst of it, Liam runs his large hand up and down my leg as if he's telling me it's okay. He's got me and I'm safe.

If I'd known the wave was coming, I would've probably had a panic attack, but it happened so fast that I didn't have time to prepare myself. Adrenaline rushes through my system. Though I'm soaked and shaken, I've never felt more alive.

TWENTY-TWO

Liam

Fuck. Someone was watching over us through that wave a semi on the other side of the road threw onto us. I didn't even see the water until we rounded the bend. I'm not sure what caused the puddle in the first place, since it's not raining, but all I care about right now is that we're on dry land again.

We reach Poppy's bar, and I hurry to get off the bike after Savannah. My hands reach for Savannah, and I tear off her helmet and stare at her as if I'm a doctor. "Shit, I'm so sorry. Are you okay? It came out of nowhere."

"Kelly? You okay?"

I wave to Riley as he parks a few spots down.

"Savannah?" I ask.

Her hands cover mine on her cheeks. "I'm good. I was just surprised, and now I'm wet."

I look down at her white T-shirt that's now soaked, revealing her lacy bra that does jack shit to hide her nipples. I shrug off my jacket and put it over her shoulders.

"So it wasn't a grand master plan to get a peek at my boobs?"

She can't be serious. We were this close to dying. I let her get on the back of my bike with no jacket. Not even a sweatshirt. God, I'm so fucking stupid.

"No."

She laughs and takes my hands off her cheeks. "I know that. I'm joking."

"Let's just go home. Forget this. We'll grab food and go shower."

When she nudges me, I step back. "Okay."

She pulls her hair back into a ponytail, and I spot some dirt on her neck. I slide my thumb down the curve and wipe my thumb on my drenched shirt. She looks skeptically at me.

"Dirt." I hold up my now-clean thumb.

The band—which must be out on the back patio since we can hear them—announces that they're starting and that they're a Guns N' Roses cover band. Savannah's eyes light up. What am I missing?

"We can't leave. Guns N' Roses! Remember how much my mom loved them? How my dad would groan every time she'd dance around the kitchen to 'Sweet Child O' Mine'?"

"Vaguely, but—"

She glances behind her and back at me. "Do they sell T-shirts in there?"

"Yeah, but—"

She nods and starts walking. I think I may have created a monster.

"Whoa, Sav."

She stops and looks at me like I should have no problem with her going into the bar and buying clothes. Which is true. But Poppy's isn't exactly known for their array of sweatshirts, but Savannah wouldn't know that because she hasn't been inside yet. Something I was hoping wouldn't happen. It's not really her scene. She's doing so well, and I don't want to send her scurrying back into her shell.

"I don't think they'll have what you're looking for," I say. "We can go, and I'll find out when these guys are playing again and where and I promise we'll go."

She studies me for so long, I shift my stance. Then her hand lands on my hand that's currently gripping her arm. "Relax. There's no harm in checking."

And she's gone, up the front steps of the bar.

Shit.

"Hey, Kelly!" someone behind me calls, but I put up my hand.

I weave through the people, catching her right before she opens the door of the bar. Where did the shy woman who was practically velcroed to me earlier go? Her face was pasty white, and she looked so uncomfortable, but now I think she'd knee Slim in the balls if he tried anything on her. Is this what a near-death experience has done for her?

She pulls from my grasp and steps inside the bar. "Excuse me," she says to a waitress passing by. "Do you guys sell T-shirts with the Poppy's logo on it?"

I bite my lip and shake my head. Does she not see the Hooters-type clothes the woman is wearing? There are three rips across her shirt's tit area, and it stops mid stomach.

"Are you looking for a job?" the girl asks, looking over Savannah's shoulder at me. "Hello," she says, her gaze roaming my body.

I'm not naive enough to think she's shooting me a pair of bedroom eyes for any reason other than she wants what's in my wallet. But Savannah looks from her to me, giving me the scowl I haven't seen once this week.

"No, I just need to change," Savannah says.

"Well, sweetheart, head over there." The waitress points toward the corner where I already knew she could find their merchandise.

"Savannah," I say.

She raises her hand when we have to stop to let a line of people through. "It's fine. I knew you were kind of a man-whore, so I shouldn't be so surprised by all this." She waves at the sea of people in black leather and chains.

"What does that mean?"

A woman stops in her tracks, her eyes zooming right between my legs. I roll my eyes and keep walking, but when I catch the maddening Bailey woman, she's standing in front of the clothing booth with wide eyes as though we're at a BDSM store.

"Wow," she says, her gaze wandering over every item.

"Hey, sweetie, can I help you?" the woman behind the counter asks. She's wearing a replica of what the waitress was wearing. It might be the most conservative thing they have.

"Let's go home," I whisper in her ear, putting my hand on her hip.

Savannah glances up and there's some fear in those baby blues, but she shakes her head. "No. I think I can pull one of these off." She taps her wallet on the counter.

"Oh, sweetie, you can definitely pull these off," the woman behind the counter says.

"Get her the Poppy T-shirt. Men's extra-large." I pull out my credit card, and the woman stares at me but never moves. "Hello?"

She eyes Savannah. "I think I'll let the lady decide."

Savannah giggles but continues to peruse the T-shirts. They're all ripped across the breast area, all short and all tight. The only bottoms they have are skin-tight booty shorts and mini-skirts. If she puts those on, I won't be able to control myself. Neither will any other male in her vicinity.

"The men's long sleeve shirt looks nice and comfy. You must be cold."

Savannah thumbs in my direction. "He's trying to cover me up."

The woman leans across the counter. "Men. Always trying to keep us down."

She couldn't have said anything more to Savannah's liking. And after that, Savannah's fingers are a fury of activity, pointing to different items and choosing sizes. Before I can do anything, she's running Savannah's card through the machine.

"Can you tell me where the restroom is?" Savannah asks her.

"Right down the hall."

"Thank you."

"Stop on by, I gotta see how hot you look in those." The clerk nods at the array of black fabric in Savannah's hands.

"Sure thing." She waves and heads down the hall, not caring whether I'm behind her or not. She stops right before going through the door labeled with a picture of a cat. "Oh. Here's a shirt for you." She tosses it to me then grazes her fingers over the cat on the door. "How cute, they used a cat to label the restroom."

After she goes into the bathroom, I shake my head and glare at the rooster on the men's room. I should probably change in there, but I'm not taking any chances of losing her in this crowd, so I pull off my shirt, tuck it into my back pocket, and pull on the fresh shirt with a woman's open legs printed on it and the words, "Poppy's – Home of the Horny Biker."

Crossing my arms, I wait outside the women's restroom for Savannah. And I keep waiting, shaking hands with a few people who pass me. Just when I think she might've snuck out a window—because I'm acting like a protective father and she's the belligerent teenager in this scenario—the door opens, and Savannah emerges.

I'm not sure how long I've been standing there gawking when she tugs on the T-shirt, stretching the three slits over her cleavage and drawing me from my reverie.

"Say something," she begs, her voice a lot less confident than when she went in.

"Um..."

"Ugh. I have to put these on your bike." She holds up her wet jeans and T-shirt.

Please tell me she's still wearing her panties. Especially with the red-and-black plaid skirt that barely covers her ass. I already know she's wearing her bra because I can see it clearly through the gaps in her T-shirt.

Before I have a chance to ask, she's off again, stomping out of the hallway and through the crowd to the door. We reach the fresh air. There will be next to no darkness tonight. The most we'll get is twilight for six or so hours.

"I really think we should go home."

She ignores me and throws her clothes in the saddlebag on my bike then tugs at her skirt.

"You don't have to prove something to me. Is this your way of saying you're not the OCD Savannah or something? Because I'm not comfortable with you in there"—I point toward the run-down building behind us—"in that." I motion to her outfit, barely able to look at her without getting hard.

Who am I kidding? I'm already halfway there.

"I'm trying to go with the flow. This is your event. We shouldn't leave just because my clothes got wet. Not when they have some available. Is it ideal? Hell no. But I'll survive." She turns, but I lightly touch her elbow and she circles back around. "What?"

"I'm not sure *I'll* survive." I let my meaning sink in as she blinks a few times. "I haven't been shy about my attraction to you, and right now you're dressed like some... I don't even know what. A wet dream? There's just so much skin."

She giggles, steps forward, and puts her hand on my chest but retracts it right away. "Try not to stare."

She's kidding, right? She has to be. How can I not stare?

But I might as well admit defeat. How can I say "live your life" then try to shelter her in the next breath? If she's willing to go along with it, I shouldn't try to change her mind. A month ago, she would've thrown a hissy fit and reamed me out for what happened, so this is progress.

Three guys walk by and whistle, each of them envisioning her naked. I know because I've already done it four times.

"Fine." I come up alongside her. "But to everyone in there, you're my girlfriend, got it?"

She smiles at me. "I kind of like this protective side of you, Liam Kelly." She touches the shirt I'm wearing. "Sorry. It's all they had in extra-large."

I look down at the woman with her legs open and shrug. "Going with the flow, right?"

"Right." She smiles.

This is the first time in so long that I've glimpsed the old Savannah who loved life more than spreadsheets. The

Savannah who lived in every moment while it was happening. Not the one afraid to step out of her comfort zone. It might be brief, but later that night, as I stand at her side and watch her twirling around to "Knockin' on Heaven's Door" with not a care in the world, I wish we could stay in this moment forever.

TWENTY-THREE

Savannah

Two weeks into Liam's experiment and I've meditated every morning. Liam's been joining me because Denver is usually asleep. I've also written in my journal every day since I received it, and I give Liam props—I enjoy these quiet moments to myself late at night with only my thoughts. Somehow, writing down my worries about the things I can't control frees my mind.

I'm interrupted by a knock on my door, and I roll over on my bed. "Come in."

The door creaks open and Liam fills the space, holding a jar filled with multi-colored papers. He must be getting ready to go to bed, because he's in the track shorts and T-shirt I've seen him wear the mornings he doesn't go for a run.

"Hey," I say.

"Week three, are you ready?" He waggles his eyebrows.

I sit up on the bed, crossing my legs, as eager as a child

staring at all the presents Christmas morning but being told they have to take pictures first.

"May I?" He nods toward the bed.

I slide up toward the pillows and pat the space. "Of course. Technically, it's yours."

"Which reminds me, I'm going over to your house tomorrow. I'm gonna talk to the contractor."

"You don't have to do that."

"I want to."

I grimace a bit. "I'm sorry, I'm overstaying my welcome, aren't I?"

He's shaking his head before I can finish my sentence. "You're welcome to be here as long as you need, but I want you to be here because you want to be here, not because you have to be here."

I sit back, the giddiness of getting another present from Liam fading. "We should talk."

He holds up his hand. "I didn't come here for a talk. I understand the reasons why you think we wouldn't work out, but if I'm honest, I'm finding it hard to keep them forefront in my mind."

I nod because a large part of me feels the same way. Especially after the charity motorcycle ride. But then I'll remember Nina and the way other women look at him as though they've had him. As though they know how he makes love—or as is more likely in his case, how he fucks.

"Regardless, I do want you here, and I don't want to talk about us. We said we wouldn't do that. This process is about you. I'm going to see the contractor tomorrow because it's ludicrous that it's taking so long. He's screwing you around."

"I'll go with you."

"No. Let me scare him a little." He grins and flexes a

bicep.

I laugh. "You like playing bodyguard, huh?"

"More than I care to admit." He runs a hand through his hair, and the sudden urge to kiss him makes my lips tingle. He peers at me from the side.

"Liam," I scold, but he's quick to recover.

"This is step three. You take a piece of paper out of this jar every day and you have to do the task."

"And if I don't do it?"

"I'll spank you." He waits for my reaction. Truth is, my body is red hot at the prospect and I'm sure my face gives away that I find the notion a little exciting. "Jesus, don't look like that."

"Like what?"

He blows out a breath. "Like you're about to turn over and ask me to get started."

"I was not."

He shoots me an expression as if to say, "Yeah, yeah, you were."

"This is exciting. Do I start now?" I try to push our flirty banter behind us before I really do ask him to smack my ass.

He runs a hand through his hair again. "Sure."

I wiggle my ass and get comfy on the bed, dipping my fingers into the jar. I pluck out a pink piece of paper. He watches me unfold it, and there in his scratchy handwriting is my task.

Have dinner by yourself out in public.

I DROP IT, and sourness rumbles in my stomach.

"What did you get?" I hold it out to him, and he nods. "Ah, FYI, that's probably the one you'll find the hardest."

"I'm not sure I can do it."

A meal alone probably wouldn't be a big deal to most people. I know that lots of people eat on their own at restaurants. I've just never been the kind of person who's comfortable doing it. I'd feel as though everyone was judging me and wondering why I didn't have a companion.

"Sure, you can." He stands and stares at me for a moment. "You got this. You've been doing great."

I slide my legs off the bed, and I'm about to approach him. Hug him and maybe linger there so I can smell him. Anything that doesn't cross the line but quenches some of my thirst for him.

But the door flies open and a big body jumps on my bed.

I grab the jar at the last second and place it on the floor by my bed.

Denver misses it entirely because he's self-centered. "I thought I'd find you guys bumping uglies!" He laughs, sitting up to chomp on his piece of pizza.

"Where did you get that pizza?" Liam asks with a scowl.

"It just got delivered. Get it while it's hot."

Liam inhales a deep breath and his eyes find mine for a moment. I guess he wasn't planning on going to bed.

"Jesus, can't you buy your own fucking pizza?" Liam stomps out of the room.

Denver looks at me. "What's his problem?"

"You need to grow up and, I don't know, contribute around here a little bit."

"Where's all this coming from?"

I shake my head. "I'm not going to live forever, Denver. One day you'll have to take care of yourself."

He stares at me with wide eyes and a shocked expression.

I rerun the words through my head. "I didn't mean, I just meant—"

Denver sits up on the bed. "Do you want to talk about something?"

For whatever reason, the genuine concern in my brother's gaze brings a surge of emotions to the surface. A tear almost slips from my eye and I wipe it away, but Denver sees it.

He inches closer. "Talk to me. What's going on? Did something happen while I was gone? I mean, he's my best friend and all, but blood first. I'll kick his ass if I need to."

But it's not that. It's so much more than that.

My head falls into my hands and the tears pile on top of one another. I'm not even sure where it's all coming from, but I can't hold in all my worries and fears anymore. They're overflowing and I want them purged out of me. "No. I'm just so messed up."

"No, you're not. I mean, you can be a little crazy about germs and neatness, but there're people much worse than you." Denver puts his arm around my shoulders. "Look at me. I'm not perfect."

I wipe my eyes. "You enjoy your life, right?" I peek through my eyelashes to see his reaction.

"I fucking love my life. Yeah."

"I hate mine," I admit.

Every muscle in his face droops at the same time. "No, you don't. It's just stress that has you saying this. It does crazy things to people."

I shake my head. "I hate my life. I hate who I've become."

Denver looks around. "I'm not equipped to handle this,

Sav. I'm not the fix-it one of the Baileys. I'm the make-you-laugh-at-your-problems guy, not the serious one. Want me to get Liam? You guys have some weird connection. He'll probably know what to say."

"No. I don't want anyone to know. I shouldn't even be telling you this. I'm just having a bad day. Tired after a long weekend. I'm sure that's it." I know I shouldn't have admitted that anything is wrong. No one can handle it if I lose my shit. I have to squash this before he calls someone else in the family and says something to them. "Plus, it's my time of the month. Probably hormones."

Denver leans back. "Well shit. That's it. Women murder men on their period. Thank God, you scared the shit out of me."

I nod, wiping the tears away. "I'm just going to go to bed."

"That's a good idea. Do you need me to go to the store or anything?"

I smile at my sweet brother. He's lazy and a freeloader, but he'd do anything for any one of us when it comes down to it. "No, I'm good. Thanks."

He heads to the door but turns my way. "Hey, Sav?"

"Yeah?"

"You know that it's okay to want more, right? That if you really want to change yourself or your life, you can? You just have to give it a go."

I nod. "Thanks. Goodnight, Denver."

He shuts the door, and I sit on my bed, staring at the jar of notes Liam made for me. Standing, I look out my window and spot Liam heading into the barn with the pizza box. I inhale deeply. Am I strong enough to take what I want without caring whether or not things will work out perfectly?

TWENTY-FOUR

Savannah

On Friday night, I sit down at Lard Have Mercy to have dinner by myself. Yes, I've put it off all week, but between work and organizing the charity event, I've been swamped, so Liam gave me a pass. As long as I did it before the end of the week, it was okay.

The place is pretty empty for a Friday night. There's just me, two families, and a few people on the stools. I take a picture of the empty bench seat across from me and pull up a text message thread I have going with Liam.

Me: *Care to join me?*

Three dots appear right away, and I wonder how he can be so fast when he's at work.

Liam: *You got this. Enjoy your own company.*

I put my phone on the table, happy that Holly's mom,

Karen, isn't working today because then I'd be having dinner with her.

Splurging—on calories at least—I order a burger and fries along with a strawberry milkshake, then I pull out the magazine I brought. I purposely didn't bring something business-related. I flip the pages, reading articles about how to make your eyes pop, all about the fall trends to get excited about, celebrity news, and what used to be my favorite—astrology. I used to love reading my horoscope back in high school.

Scrolling my finger down the page, I find Virgo.

Venus enters your sign on Wednesday, making all your wishes come true—and perhaps a romantic one in particular? The weekend boosts your love life in a major way.

Love. Romantic partner. I'm not sure about a partner, but I'm growing tired of not having Liam, that's for sure.

I start an article about sex positions that'll give you mind-blowing orgasms. If only I needed the advice. Lately, all roads lead to sleeping with Liam. Pretty soon, I suspect, we're not going to be able to hold back, so I better make sure I can compare to all the women who came before me.

"Excuse me?" A small voice interrupts my thoughts.

I glance at the end of the booth, shut the magazine, and slide it off the table into my lap because there's a little girl standing there, and she doesn't need to be traumatized.

"Hello," I say with a guilty voice.

"Are you Savannah Bailey?"

I look around and locate the girl's parents two booths over, smiling at our exchange. "I am."

Is she going to slap me? Is she going to tell me I stole money from her family and now she has to sell all her toys and wear hand-me-downs?

"Can you please sign this?" She slides over one of the

paper placemats and places a pen on it.

I glance at her parents with confusion. "Why do you want me to sign it?"

"Because my mommy told me that you're an amazing businessperson. I'm going to run a company one day." She leans forward. "I'm sorry about your parents." She draws back again and puts her hands behind her back. She can't be more than seven, maybe eight. "Mommy says everyone thought you were going to fail, but you didn't. That if I was looking for a real-life hero to look up to, you should be her."

My eyes well with tears and I look at the mother and mouth, "Thank you."

She nods, but she really has no idea how much I needed to hear this as our company sits in limbo, barely profiting for the last couple of months. Not that anyone knows that but Grandma Dori, a couple guys in finance, and me.

"What's your name?" I ask.

"Paisley."

"Well, Paisley, you just made my night." I scribble her name and "The future is female," then I sign my name.

She reads it when I hand it over. Her eyes widen. "Thank you, Mrs. Bailey."

I smile. "It's Miss Bailey, and you're very welcome."

She runs over to her parents, and I give them a little wave. I feel embarrassed yet still honored. I look around to see if someone set me up. This feels like something Liam might do to make me feel better about myself, but there's no one in sight.

A few minutes later, I'm still waiting for my meal and sitting in awe over my encounter with Paisley. Her parents stop at the table to say their thanks, and I slide out of the booth to shake both their hands, but my magazine falls to the floor and opens up on the sex position page.

You've got to be kidding me.

The mom looks down and cracks a smile. I scoop it up before Paisley sees it, since she's begging her dad to buy something from the small machines in the front of the diner. Thank goodness.

"Have a great evening, Miss Bailey." The mom touches my shoulder, eyeing the magazine.

"Thank you."

She stops and silently tells her husband to move along with Paisley. "I wanted to thank you myself. My husband worked for North Forest Lumber Company, and when it closed so abruptly, we suddenly didn't have a paycheck coming in. Bailey Timber taking on so many of those workers saved a lot of families." She tears up. "You saved us before we ever had a chance to drown, so I wanted to thank you."

I grab her arms and pull her into me. "You've made my night. You and Paisley and your husband. Thank you so much. Thank you so very much."

She giggles into my shoulder and I catch Paisley staring at us with questions in her eyes.

"I'm sorry. I'm such a mess." I let loose an awkward chuckle.

"It's okay. Please enjoy your night." The woman pats my shoulder and joins her husband and daughter walking out of Lard Have Mercy.

"Very nice people," the waitress says, and I slide back into the booth, tucking the magazine into my purse. "They paid for your dinner."

"No. I can't—"

"It's done, honey. They wanted to do it." She slides my burger, fries, and milkshake on the table.

I'm chomping on my first fry when my phone dings in

my purse.

Liam: *How's it going? I'm between clients.*
Me: *Better than I could have imagined.*
Liam: *Please tell me you're not getting an orgasm from the blueberry pie?*

I laugh, and the waitress glances over.

Me: *Well, it HAS been awhile.*
Liam: *We could solve that problem tonight. ;)*
Me: *I thought you weren't supposed to flirt with me.*
Liam: *I may have to take that back and call myself a liar. It's too hard not to.*
Me: *LIAM.*
Liam: *SAVANNAH.*
Me: *Thanks for making me do this.*
Liam: *You're welcome.* <3

I tuck my phone into my purse and eat my burger and my fries, thinking about how taking on the workers from the North Forest Lumber Company is what's put a dent in our profits. We didn't take over as many contracts as I thought we would after Clint Edison was arrested for embezzlement and his company shut down. But seeing the result of that decision—a family that isn't out on the street—seals for me that it was the right decision. I'm confident the contracts will come. We just have to stay afloat until they do.

I'm finishing my milkshake when the bell above the door rings.

"Hey, stranger." Juno slides into the booth across from me, the ever-present Colton at her side.

"Hey."

"I would've joined you if I knew you were coming." She looks at my plate.

There are things I would never keep from my siblings, but this one is between Liam and me. "I wanted to eat by myself. What are you guys doing here?"

Juno rolls her eyes. "Denver's dragging us out to Sunrise Bay. Some new bar opened up. He said he needs a wingman."

"And you are the two for the job?"

Juno shrugs and looks at Colton.

He answers, "Guess so."

"Wanna come?" Juno asks, sitting straight up as if she just had the most brilliant idea.

I shake my head. "No."

"Come on. It'll be so much fun. Colton is supposed to be Denver's wingman, and we can be each other's."

"Why are you going if Colton is Denver's wingman?"

She shrugs. "Colton asked me to go."

"I'm not sure you guys understand the meaning of the word." I want to scream at them to just date one another, but they both swear they only have platonic feelings for each other.

I said that once about Liam. Lies. All lies.

"Come on," Juno whines. "I haven't seen you in, like, two weeks. What've you and Liam being doing? There have been no reports on Buzz Wheel or anything."

"I've been swamped at work."

Her face lights up as if she just remembered something. "Grandma Dori is finally moving out!"

I'm surprised. I would've thought she'd be there until my place was fixed and she lost her leverage to keep me at Liam's. "What made that happen?"

"She started the oven and the magazine articles I'd tossed in there filled my place with smoke. She said she can't fix me and she's out."

Colton and I laugh. Few could live with Juno. Kingston can, but he's barely in town for half of the year because of his job.

"That's good news for you."

She smiles and nods. "One hundred percent. Bad news for you though—rumor has it that Ethel's on the hunt for you. You've missed two knitting classes."

Shit. I completely forgot to ask Samara to cancel those lessons.

"I have no idea how I forgot." I lean back in the booth and cross my arms.

"Well, you know Ethel. She'll figure out a way to punish you," Colton says.

"Are you guys nailing each other?"

Juno's question throws me for a moment. "What?"

"You and Liam. Come on, Sav. Your behavior has all the 'I just started screwing someone' signs. I haven't seen you in weeks. You're skipping out on your commitments."

"Knitting class is hardly a commitment. I'm not even paying her."

"Still. This is like high school, when the girl gets a boyfriend and stops talking to her friends because she spends all her time with said boyfriend."

Colton stands. "This sounds like a sibling thing. I'll be over there." He sits at the counter and pulls out his phone.

I lean in across the table. "Well, I'm not doing anything with Liam."

"Why not?"

"Juno, can we all just stick to our own business?"

She rolls her eyes and slides out of the booth. "Not sure

why you're here alone when you have a hot guy down the street who clearly wants you. I always thought you were the smartest Bailey. Have a fun night with your vibrator."

She collects Colton and leaves. Too bad she missed me flipping her the bird. She's so snarky when it comes to Liam and me.

It takes me a minute, but I realize that Juno is kind of right. Why am I fighting this? Liam and I are obviously attracted to one another. We can take it slow and see where it goes. Maybe it will fizzle out as quickly as it ignited.

With Liam's help, I'm getting better at taking things as they come, without any guarantees. I think back to the motorcycle ride, the different tasks scribbled on colorful paper that he's had me do all week, and the journal and meditation. Mostly I think about that little girl, Paisley, and what she said about everyone doubting that I could successfully run the company. It wasn't like I didn't know that at the time, but did I care? No. I wasn't scared stiff by failure back then, so why am I now? Maybe things with Liam will be amazing, and maybe they won't. But either way, I've already been through one of the most painful, life-altering crises a person can go through and survived.

The waitress comes over to take my empty milkshake glass.

I turn in her direction. "Can I please get a piece of blueberry pie?"

"A la mode?"

"No. Just plain. To-go."

She smiles and disappears behind the counter.

Should I think this over some more? Weigh the pros and cons?

My phone dings in my purse, and I pull it out.

Liam: *Why do I feel oddly competitive with pie tonight?*

I laugh.

Me: *Not sure how to respond to that.*
Liam: *Are you dodging my question? I'm not going to be able to concentrate. Tell me you didn't orgasm from pie.*
Me: *I didn't orgasm from pie.*
Liam: *Phew. That's good to hear. My last client canceled so I'll be home a little earlier. You know in case you wanted to greet me naked on my bed. No complaints here.*

The waitress brings the pie over, and my phone vibrates in my hand.

Liam: *That was a joke. Kind of. I mean I'll fully support you naked on my bed if you feel strongly about it, but I know we're supposed to have this line drawn in the sand so you can wear lingerie in my bed, too. Your choice. ;)*

I laugh again.

The waitress catches my eye. "The ones who make you laugh are always the keepers."

I tuck my phone into my purse, slide out of the booth, and grab the pie. "You're right about that. Thank you so much." I hand her some money. "Keep the change."

"Don't try too many of those positions. You want to be able to walk in the morning."

My face heats up as I turn back to see her grinning.

Okay, Liam, be careful what you wish for, because your wish is about to be granted.

TWENTY-FIVE

Savannah

One bell announces my departure while another announces my arrival. Smokin' Guns Tattoo shop is jam-packed tonight and I'm wondering how Liam can leave when this many people are waiting.

"Savannah?" Rhys is sitting at the front desk. "Did Liam know you were coming?"

I approach the desk with a million drawings scribbled on top. Everything here seems to be fair game for the artists.

"No. I brought him pie," I say like an idiot. Maybe if I brought him a beer or something, it would've made more sense.

Rhys's perfect eyebrows shoot up to his hairline, and I realize what he's thinking.

"Oh crap, not like that pie." I hold up the clear to-go container that contains the actual pie. "This pie. Blueberry pie. A real pie. Not." I glance down between my legs.

Rhys laughs but sucks in his lips to stop himself when he sees my complete mortification. My face hasn't felt this hot in years. I look behind me and thankfully don't recognize anyone.

"Gotcha. Let me check in with him. He's in the private room, working on a client," he says.

"Oh. Well, I don't want to interrupt."

He shakes his head. "It's for the customer's privacy. Sometimes tattoos are in... well, you know."

"Yep." The P pops out of my mouth as I rock back on my flats. "Tell him no rush."

Rhys winks and walks behind the counter and past the other tattoo artist, who looks my way. Some I recognize, but it's not as though I hang around in here.

Rhys returns a minute later. "He's almost done. Asked if you'd feel more comfortable waiting in his office?"

"I'm good here, but thank you."

"Want anything to drink?"

Some kid who's definitely not twenty-one raises his hand. "I'd like something to drink. Alcohol preferably."

Rhys ignores him.

"I'll just wait out here."

"He was very intrigued when I told you came bearing pie." Rhys winks again. I'm pretty sure this guy is trouble. But the good kind.

I wink back. "Now I'll just look like a tease."

He laughs, snapping his fingers and pointing at me. "I don't remember you having such a funny side."

I take a seat in the rows of chairs. Two girls across from me eye me curiously.

One leans forward and whispers, "You're waiting for Liam Kelly?"

"Yeah." I nod.

"He's with our friend right now. Getting a heart tattoo

right by her area." She points a little lower than her hip bone.

I understand the need for privacy now. They're probably in their twenties. "Nice. He gave me one years ago and I love it. He does great work."

They look at me with wide eyes. "You have a tattoo?"

"Yeah."

"Oh." They lean back and cross their legs, snickering to one another.

Ignoring their juvenile behavior, my mind drifts to that night I came in here, lost in my grief.

Liam had opened Smokin' Guns a year prior, but his reputation was such that people were coming down from Anchorage to have him do their tattoos. When a friend of mine showed me a tattoo she'd gotten, it planted the seed in my head, but I rolled it around for a few months because I wanted something unique.

When I walked into Smokin' Guns, Liam and Rhys were at the front desk. Rhys's Vans-clad feet were up on the edge of the desk, and Liam had a sketchpad in his hands. He wasn't as muscular as he is now, but he still made my heart race. Maybe because he's always looked at me like he was thirsty, and I was his favorite thirst-quenching beer.

Walking in was risky, because of my brothers—Denver was known to spend the majority of his time at Smokin' Guns. Not to mention anyone could walk in and see me and I'd be fodder for gossip. The president of Bailey Timber shouldn't be getting a tattoo.

But that night, after Liam dropped the sketchbook on the table and rounded the desk, I didn't care. I wanted to do something for me. Something I wasn't supposed to. Something I could look at in years to come.

"Savannah?"

Liam came so close, I backed up. He shoved his hands into his pockets and my nerves surfaced, doubts leaking in past the strong pep talk I'd given myself in the car. What was I doing? I should be anywhere but there. I should be at Bailey Timber or at the house, helping Austin with the twins.

"Hi," I said.

"I'm going to head to the back for a second." Rhys's feet fell to the floor and he disappeared into the back.

"Hold on a sec." Liam rushed past me, flipped over the 'Open' sign, and locked the door.

I held my purse tighter by my side. "Oh, I'm sorry. Are you closing?"

"Are you here for a tattoo?" He lowered his head to look straight into my eyes.

I swallowed and nodded, unable to say the words. Seriously, what had happened between the car and the shop? I had been all strong and confident before walking in. Who the hell cared if I got a tattoo? To hell with everyone's expectations of me.

"And you want me to do it?" He pointed at himself as if he'd be the last person I would trust.

"Yeah, but if you're closing, I can come back." I turned.

He lightly grasped my elbow—similar to how he does now. Not a lot of pressure, but the surge of electricity I felt that night still happens today. "No. We're open... for you. I just figured you'd feel better if no one came in while we were doing it."

I smiled and my shoulders relaxed. "Thank you."

"No problem." He waved me forward. "Come on over to my station. Do you know what you want, or do you want to look through some books?"

"I don't want something from the book. I want something original, I think."

His smile widened, and he grabbed his sketchpad on the way to his station. He didn't have nearly the amount of stations set up that he has now, and there was no privacy room back then. Although he did put up a partition for me after he got started.

He patted his bench and I slid onto it, putting my purse next to me. Sitting in his rolling chair, he propped his ankle on his knee and grabbed the pencil from behind his ear. "What do you want it to represent?"

"My parents. Something to remember them by."

"Names?"

I shake my head.

"Date?"

"Date?" I ask.

He clears his throat. "Death date? Some people want it."

"No."

He nods. "Anything personal about them?"

I inhaled deeply, and he tossed his sketchpad on the bench, rolled up between my legs and placed his large hands on my thighs. My blonde hair had fallen like a veil on either side of my face and tears threatened to fall.

"Sorry, I just wanted to get a feel for what you were looking for," he said. "I promise I'll never ink anything unless it's perfect. You can trust me."

I stared into his blue eyes that nearly matched my own. They held sincerity and empathy and kindness. I believed him, and the scared little girl crawled back inside. "Thanks."

"Give me five minutes. I have something in mind."

"Okay, I'll just come back?"

He laughed. "No. You can just sit there and wait."

He grabbed his sketchpad again and propped his ankle on his knee. Five minutes later, he hopped up alongside me. Thigh to thigh, upper arm to upper arm, and handed me his sketchbook.

I looked at the drawing of two blackbirds flying away. One larger than the other but practically side by side. My mom and dad used to play The Beatles song "Blackbird" all the time. It was one of their favorites. It wasn't their wedding song but over the years it kind of became their song and my dad would always try to buy my mom things with blackbirds on it—greeting cards, tea towels, paintings. Liam must've remembered. A tear slipped off my cheek, blotting the perfect picture.

"I'm so sorry." I wiped at it, but that only made it worse.

"It's okay." He took it from me, but I couldn't take my eyes off it. "So is this good?"

"Yeah. I love it."

He hopped down. "If you have any hesitancy, I can keep working. It doesn't have to be done tonight."

"No, I really want it."

He smiled again. A perfect mouth full of straight white teeth. "Perfect. Where do you want it?"

I cringed, and he tilted his head. Hopping off the bench as well, I pointed at my hipbone but inside, closer to my private area. He nodded, but I saw his Adam's apple bob.

"If you'd rather someone else do it, I understand," I rushed to say. "You're my brothers' best friend and all."

"No." The word croaked out of him. "I'll do it."

"Great. I hoped it wouldn't be a problem."

"I'll be right back. Let me get the stencil done."

Just as he said that, Rhys came back into the big room. "Getting ink, huh?"

"You can call it a night. I'm going to close up," Liam said to him.

"Oh." Rhys looked at me. "*Oh*. Gotcha." He went to the front desk and returned a second later with his coat and backpack. "Have a great night, you two." He winked just like he still does.

I laugh now, remembering how uncomfortable I felt in that moment. As though Rhys would spread gossip that I was sleeping with Liam. I wondered how that would look. What my family would say.

I remember how Liam came over with a partition and laid out everything. "Now's the time for you to strip down. We can do this two ways. You can take off pants off completely, or you can lower them to your knees. Your choice." He looked nervous. The tips of his ears were pink, and he kept dodging my gaze.

I lowered my pants to my knees and laid on the table as he directed. Liam did all the prep work, put on gloves, and applied the stencil. After I approved the placement, he slid forward and one hand reached out to touch my hipbone. I retracted slightly.

"Last chance?" he said.

I shook my head. "I'm good."

The music over the speakers changed and Counting Crows, "Colorblind" came on. Between the buzz of the needle, Liam's hands on my body, and the lyrics to the song, tears leaked from me like drops from a faucet. Slow and steady and consistent.

Liam said nothing, allowing me to have my moment. His hands were steady on my bare skin, and he didn't feel the need to fill the silence with words. He didn't assure me that things would get better. He was just there, and it was the first time since my parents died that I felt some sort of acceptance creep in.

He finished, and I missed his presence as soon as he rolled away. He wiped the tattoo one last time and held up a mirror for me to look at it. I could have stared all day.

"Liam, it's beautiful."

"I'm glad you like it. Do you mind if I snap a picture? It's just for original tattoos I do myself." I nodded, and he pulled out his phone and took a shot. He showed me the picture. "Just the tat. None of you."

"Thanks."

"Let me put some ointment on it and bandage it up." He went back to work, and after he took off his gloves, he disappeared before returning with a box of tissues.

I wiped my eyes, and he still didn't say anything about my meltdown.

"What do I owe you?"

He put his hand on mine as I reached for my wallet. "It's on the house. Do you need a ride home?"

I shook my head. He unlocked the front door, and I stepped out into the cold winter weather.

When I turned around, he was still in the open doorway. "Thank you, Liam."

"I'm here whenever you need me."

I waved, and he watched me slide into my car and drive away. If I had to pinpoint when things shifted between us, I'd have to say it was that moment.

"Savannah?"

My name being called pulls me back from the memory and into the present.

Rhys waves. "He said two minutes."

I nod and notice the two girls who were across from me are now standing with a third girl. Her shirt is all tangled, the buttons not aligned, and my stomach clenches. I quickly remind myself that it's his job to tattoo people and I myself was pant-less on his table once.

"So?" one girl asks.

"He said he's kind of with someone. That he wasn't interested," the girl who got the tattoo says.

The other girl glances my way and murmurs to the other two. The third nods.

I'm so busy watching their interaction that I don't notice Liam coming out from the back.

"I heard someone has pie?" he says, hopping over the small partition.

I stand and hand it to him. "Here you go."

"Oh. Okay." He rocks forward. "I have to be honest, I was hoping for a different kind of pie." He gives me that sexy grin that makes it impossible not to smile back.

Rhys finishes running the girl's credit card and she signs, her two friends ushering her out.

"Do you get a lot of offers like that?" I ask him.

He looks at the girl who just left. "No, but I'm rarely asked point-blank. It sucks, but I'm just a tattoo artist, and I'm not giving any mixed signals."

Perfect. Now that that's out of the way, I gather my courage so I can say what I came here to say. I nod and step closer to him. "Take me home, Liam."

He turns but he must hear something in my voice because he does a double-take, asking me with his eyes my definition of "take me home." When we lock eyes, he shouts, "Rhys, close up!"

Someone groans behind me as Liam puts his hand on the small of my back, escorting me out of the shop.

"I think someone else wanted your services."

He grabs my hand and we walk by the three girls, which I kinda feel shitty about.

"I'm only servicing you tonight." He picks me up over his shoulder and I squeal.

Why have I held out this long? It's been Liam since he branded me with ink. How was I so blind?

TWENTY-SIX

Liam

I shouldn't press my luck, but when Savannah slides into the front seat of my car, agreeing to leave her SUV behind and get it tomorrow, a question rattles around in my head. And I'm probably the world's biggest dumbass for asking, because it could derail this entire thing, but I have to know.

"Hey, Sav?"

She's grabbing the seatbelt, so she can't see that I'm not moving to start the car yet. "Yeah?" After she fastens her seatbelt, she finally notices.

"Why the change of mind?" I insert the key into the ignition to get the air conditioning going but turn down the music.

She swivels in the leather seat, the pie sitting between us. Her heated gaze in my direction diminishes, and I grab her hand before she can run in the opposite direction. She doesn't pull away and my heart catapults at the idea that she finally might feel what I do. What I have for so long. That there's something here we need to explore.

"I want to be here. With you. These past few weeks, things have shifted. Don't get me wrong, I've been attracted to you for years, but I've used every available excuse as to why we wouldn't work. You're younger. You're my brothers' best friend. You're easygoing and I'm uptight. But I've figured out that I never knew the real you. I thought I did, but I didn't."

"And?" I can't keep the hope from my voice.

She smiles a bit. "I don't have all the answers, if that's what you're looking for. All I know is I'm exhausted from fighting whatever is happening between us. My arm is weak from holding you back."

I tighten my grip on her hand, bringing it up to my lips to kiss the inside of her wrist. "Okay."

"Okay?"

I nod. If I've learned anything about Savannah, it's that she can't be pushed. It's taken me months to get her here. I tried to strong-arm her into seeing it and that didn't work. Who knew standing back and being her friend would change her opinion of us? Asking her to define what we are right now isn't the way to win her long term.

"Yep, okay. There's just one promise I need from you."

Her back presses to the window, and she examines me. "What?"

"You can't run out of my bed this time."

Her lips tip up and she slides closer, her free hand reaching for my face. Her fingernails thread through my hair and a shiver runs along my spine. "You'll have to kick me out."

I'm dying to kiss her, but there's no way in hell I'll be able to control myself if I do, and I'm not screwing her in my car for our first time. Maybe the second time, but definitely not the first. "Hold on, because this is going to be the fastest ride home."

She giggles and slides over, holding the pie in her lap.

"I don't give a shit about that pie now." I eye it, pulling out onto Main Street.

"It'll make for a good post-orgasm snack." I can hear the smile in her voice.

"Babe, you're gonna need an entire pie after I'm done with you."

She laughs, and her fingers slide along my hard thigh. I capture her hand and entwine our fingers.

This is what I've wanted for so long. Savannah in my bed, sure. But the two of us like this, comfortable and happy in each other's presence. That's what makes me feel like a fucking king right now.

We pull up behind a Cadillac and Savannah and I glance at one another, seeing a familiar blue-haired woman behind the wheel. Dori brakes hard, forcing me to brake hard. Savannah barely grabs the pie before it smashes into my console.

"Thank you for that."

She smiles at me then looks back at Dori's land yacht. "She's not supposed to be driving."

"I know."

After stopping for a full minute at the stop sign, Dori accelerates as though the white flag just got waved and there's only one lap left. We hit the next stop sign, and again she waits a full minute. I check the clock. Turns out it's only thirty seconds, but still.

"My guess is she doesn't check her rearview mirror," I grumble.

"There's a reason the sheriff told her he better not find her on the road."

Savannah crosses her legs and my mouth waters, eager to have them spread open for me. I love Dori, but in this moment I'm not thrilled with her interfering with Savannah and me. "I'm gonna go around her."

Savannah throws her hand over mine on the steering wheel. "You'll scare her and then who knows what will happen?"

I blow out a breath. "She's making what should be a ten-minute trip a twenty-minute one. Where is she going? Northern Lights is the other way."

We turn toward one another at the next stop. Yep, we both realized it at the same time.

"Why would she go to my house?" I ask.

Savannah bites her lip. "I don't know, but should I call her and tell her we're not there?"

"If she'd look in her rearview mirror once in a while, she'd know that."

"Clearly she doesn't use her mirrors." Savannah points at her rear bumper, which has matching dents on each side.

"Clearly. But I'm really doubting whether I can keep it together for one of her lectures, knowing what—or who—is coming after." I grin.

Savannah rolls her eyes then shrugs. "We have no choice at this point. We'll have to wait until she leaves."

We finally get out of downtown Lake Starlight and onto the rural roads where the speed limit is fifty-five, but we're tailgating Dori at a whopping thirty-three miles per hour. My hands grip the steering wheel with my arms straight out in front of me, my back pushed against the leather seat.

I'm so annoyed. Savannah's uncontrollable laughter at my sexual frustration isn't helping. How many times did I want to pull that laugh out of her? But right now, it feels like fishing for hours and only catching seaweed.

She catches me side-glancing her and pokes my upper arm. "Come on. It's funny."

"You never find anything funny, but you finally give me the green light and your grandma ends up cockblocking me. I don't see the humor."

"That's the funny part. And yeah, I'm laughing. I've laughed more these past three weeks than the entirety of last year."

I smile at her, grab her hand, and once more kiss the inside of her wrist. I could easily become addicted to the small moan that escapes her every time I do it. "I'm glad I make you laugh."

"I never said you made me laugh. I just said I've laughed. I could be laughing *at* you."

I cock my head to the side when we stop at the last stop sign before my house.

"I'm kidding." Her smile is like the first glimpse of the sun after a thunderstorm—refreshing and warm. To think I played a small role in pulling this woman out of her shell is humbling.

Dori speeds through the intersection. All we see are her taillights until she turns into my driveway, her back end fishtailing when her front tires hit the gravel.

"My only hope is that Denver's here and can drive her home," I say, driving past her car.

She's stopped in the middle of the driveway, leaving me to pull across the grass to get to the garage. No way will I be wasting more time when she leaves by needing to move my car out of her way.

"He went out with Juno and Colton."

I blow out an annoyed breath and turn off the engine.

Savannah shifts to get out of the car, but I grab her thigh to stop her. "We're in agreement, right?"

"What?" she says through a laugh.

"We get her out of here as soon as possible, and the minute she walks out the door, we flick the lock and get naked, right?"

She presses her lips to my cheek. "Deal. But the faster we talk to her, the faster we're naked."

"That's why I like you so much. You're smart." I tap her temple, and she laughs again.

She opens the door, and we walk out of the garage. I'm a little concerned that Dori isn't standing at the garage opening, waiting for us. She's at the front door, her finger on the doorbell.

"Grandma?" Savannah says and looks at me with the same unsure look I'm wearing.

"There you are."

I glance at my watch. Eight o'clock. I thought elderly people went to bed early?

"We've been following you since downtown," Savannah says.

Dori eyeballs me behind her granddaughter. "I knew that."

She didn't.

"The sheriff said you're not to drive."

She waves off Savannah, and I have a bad feeling we're going to be the ones to drive her home. I could call her an Uber. The half hour it'd take to get her to Northern Lights and back does not sound as appealing as finally getting Sav naked in my bed.

"The polite thing to do is to ask me in," Dori whispers to Savannah.

"This isn't my house," Savannah whispers back.

"Kind of is," Dori says.

"Dori, would you like to come in for a coffee?" I ask loudly enough for them both to hear.

Her face lights up as she peers around her granddaughter. "How sweet of you, Liam. That would be nice."

I groan. Savannah shoots me a look to say, "be nice," but all I can think of is the many ways I'm going to make her scream my name tonight. Now I'm stuck having to make her grandma coffee. Weaving between them, I use my key and unlock the front door, heading directly into the kitchen.

"Am I interrupting something?" Dori asks Savannah, but not softly enough that I don't hear her.

"No. It's fine."

I sigh, deciding to use my Keurig because it brews faster.

They sit at my kitchen table. No one ever sits at my kitchen table. Everyone sits at my breakfast bar. I don't care except for the fact that choosing the kitchen table somehow makes it feel as though this won't be a brief visit.

"Decaf please," Dori says.

I switch the K-pod to decaf and start the brewing. "Sav?"

She shakes her head. "I'm good."

She crosses her legs, and my eyes track every movement. I wish I'd have taken a little longer on the tattoo for my last client. Then maybe Dori would've come and left before we returned home and I'd already have Savannah naked, my mouth between her thighs.

"Do you guys want some privacy?" I ask, setting Dori's coffee in front of her.

"No. You can join us." She signals to the empty chair across from her, which I find humorous since we're in my home. Classic Dori.

"Why are you risking jail time to drive over here? Wouldn't a text have done the trick?" Savannah asks.

I slide my hand under the table to her thigh. She moves her hand over mine, digging her nails into the top of my hand.

"I wanted to check in on the library gala. The votes are tallied, but I wanted to know how many tables we've sold so far."

Savannah glances at me. All our previous conversations about the gala have been at Bailey Timber. It's Friday night.

"I thought we were going to talk about that on Tuesday when Liam comes to the office?" Savannah asks.

"Well, I thought it might be worth checking in early," Dori says, sipping her coffee with an innocent bat of her eyes.

"Grandma, what's going on?" Savannah squeezes Dori's hand, and I use the excuse to slyly run my hand down her back. She shifts away from my touch.

"Ethel went to see her friend Mildred, so..."

Savannah laughs and glances at me. I don't like the look on her face. She better be fucking kidding me. Inside my head, I'm screaming *hell no*.

"Do you want to play cards or something?" Savannah asks.

Dori smiles and digs into her purse, producing a deck of cards. "I'd love to."

I inwardly groan and slide out the chair.

"Is Liam okay, honey? He seems crabby tonight." Dori must think she's whispering when I open my fridge and pull out a beer.

I get that Savannah can't say no to family, but I sure as hell can. Maybe. Okay, not Dori, but the other Bailey family members.

"He's good," Savannah reassures her.

I sit back down, twist the cap off my beer, and guzzle down half the bottle. I pull out my phone.

Me: *You owe me for this.*

Her phone dings. I have no idea why she never puts it on silent. Dori's so busy shuffling that she doesn't pay any attention to Savannah pulling her phone out of her purse.

Savannah: *Don't worry, I pay my debts in full.*

My dick twitches and I shift in my seat.

Who knew Savannah's grandma was such a cockblocker?

TWENTY-SEVEN

Savannah

"Bye, Grandma. Text me when you get home." I hug Grandma Dori with Liam at my back. His hands have secretly landed on me the entire evening.

"Behave, you two. I don't want the sheriff calling me and saying one of you got arrested for assault."

"I don't know, I think Sav can pull off a pair of handcuffs." His hand slides down my side to my backside and gives it a squeeze.

I school my features so that nothing seems amiss to my grandma.

Dori laughs. "Thanks for keeping an old lady busy." After directing him to bend down, she kisses Liam's cheeks.

We shut the door and Liam leans over me to flick the lock, his hot breath on my neck.

"Time to strip," he whispers.

Goose bumps rise on my skin. "I feel bad sending her in an Uber. What if the driver takes advantage of her?"

He slides my long hair off my neck, one hand splayed

across my stomach. "It's Duke Thompson. He does it as a side job from his airport security job. She's fine."

Using his strong hand, he turns me, one hand landing above my head and one steady on my hip. He's caging me in. I remember the morning when he referred to me as his prey. The way he's staring at me now makes me feel like a caged animal, but instead of feeling intent on escape, I'm more like a stray dog that's starving and skittish from years of never being pampered. One who welcomes the cage—Liam's cage anyway.

He brushes my hair off my forehead and tucks it behind my ear while his thumb makes lazy circles along my hipbone. "Do you know how long I've waited to kiss your tattoo?"

My palms are plastered to the door as shyness swells inside me. I haven't been with anyone for a while, which Liam probably knows. Even though I'm five years older, his experience outweighs mine by a ton. His chest remains inches from mine, but all I can think about is having the weight of his body on top of me. How nice it will feel.

"I've been waiting since I gave it to you," he says. "That night sealed my fate—I'll never get you out of my system. I thought it was a typical crush on my friends' older sister. But that night, the trust you had in me... a trust I know doesn't come easy to you. I knew then that no other woman would ever satisfy me the way you would."

Is he serious? My hand slowly leaves the safety of the door, and I run my fingers down his stomach. He inhales a deep breath, watching as my hand slides under the hem of his T-shirt.

He takes another step and leans in. My self-confidence locks in my throat. Almost sensing my hesitation, he runs his cheek along mine, his hot breath at my ear. "We don't have to. We can take this slow."

But his thumb hasn't stopped running along my hipbone and my fingers have found their way inside the waistband of his jeans. I want this. I just have to take it. Pushing aside my demented belief that I'll prove unworthy while Liam holds the *Guinness Book of World Records'* title for best and most thorough deliverer of orgasms, I meet him toe to toe and strain my breasts toward his chest.

He inhales deeply and our eyes lock. "I'm gonna sound like a loser, but I'm kind of nervous."

My lips tip into a grin. Maybe I'm not the only one unsure what to expect after we cross this line. "Me too."

He bends and I raise up on my tiptoes. His eyes are open while my hand slides from under his shirt, up his strong biceps, and into his hair. We're millimeters apart and my eyes drift shut as I wait to experience Liam again. Our first couple of kisses were nice, but we were frantic, and I'm not sure either of us was processing anything other than getting to a bed. This time is different. We've dished out our problems. We've laid our cards on the table. We might not have classified what this is, but we're invested in seeing what can happen.

His lips are almost pressed to mine when a key sounds in the lock behind me. We can't react fast enough before the door whips open, hitting me in the back and catapulting me into Liam. He stumbles, grabbing my upper arms but unable to stop us before we crash to the floor. As I lay on him on his hardwood, he glances over my shoulder with a gaze colder than ice.

I look over my shoulder to find Denver looking at us, shaking his head. "Ever heard of a bedroom? I thought you two were going to stay away from each other?" Denver laughs, stepping over us.

I look at Liam and he sighs, his eyes squeezing shut and his head falling to the wood floor, defeated. Even his arms have fallen off me and are now limp at his sides.

No. No. No. I wiggle off of him as gracefully as I can in a sundress and stand up with a hop.

Denver's head is buried in the fridge when I reach the kitchen. "What happened to the salsa that was in here?"

"Never. Happening," Liam whispers and sits up, propping his elbows on his knees and leaning against the wall.

He's wrong. This is going to happen.

I march over to Denver, grab the back of his T-shirt, and drag him out of the fridge.

"Whoa. What's going on?" He barely manages to set the open container of orange juice he just drank down on the counter as I push him forward. "What's with this?"

He tries to look over his shoulder as we pass a laughing Liam still sitting on the floor. Finally, Denver uses his considerable strength to screech to a stop. When he does, my bare feet slide on the hardwood and I end up on my ass.

Liam shifts to get up, but I give him my palm. I stand, then open the front door and use all my muscle to turn Denver around and push him out the door.

"What the hell?" he says, whipping around once he's on the porch.

"The Kelly house has no vacancies tonight. Go couch surf." I slam the door.

Liam barely hides his laughter as he points at the side window.

Denver is peering in with a confused expression.

I open the door. "What didn't you understand?"

"Are you two, like, really... doing it? I was kidding. Thought maybe I'd walked in on you strangling him."

I glance over my shoulder at Liam and he shrugs, leaving the ball in my court. At this point, if I don't sleep with him, my lady parts are going to revolt and close up shop.

"We were about to until you barged in." I grab Denver by his T-shirt—which I'm fully aware is overkill, but Denver has to be threatened within an inch of his life to keep any kind of secret. "If you tell anyone what you saw or anything that has Liam's and my names in the same sentence, I promise you, Denver, I will put you on every dating app with a sappy post about how you're looking for monogamy and leave your cell phone number in your profile."

He rears back, eyes wide. "You would not."

"Try me."

I release his T-shirt and he stumbles back a step. "Fine. Jeez." He smooths the front of his T-shirt. "I'm going."

"Don't come back until one of us texts you, and remember." I act as though I'm zipping my lips shut.

He nods and rolls his eyes. "You didn't have to be so mean about it. I would've understood."

He wouldn't have.

"Have a good night, Denver." I shut the door, flick the lock, and turn off the porch light.

"Nice, Savannah!" Denver yells as I hear him stumble.

A laugh bubbles up inside me.

Liam doesn't waste any time and picks me up. I wrap my legs around his waist, my arms around his neck.

"Impressive," he says, carrying me up the stairs.

"Thanks. I feel like I could take on King Kong right now."

He laughs and deposits me on his bed. I grab his T-shirt

and he falls on top of me, his arms firm on either side of my head. "We're finally alone."

"That we are." I widen my legs a bit, and his thigh nudges them farther apart. My sundress rises up to my waist, and even through his jeans, his hard length causes a rise in my body temperature.

"No more distractions." His words sound like a warning.

"No more."

Our eyes lock and he lowers his body down on mine. A satisfied exhale leaves my lungs. He circles his hips while his hand cups my cheek. I'm ready. Ready to have him.

He presses his lips to mine. I sink into the mattress as his solid frame loses all its rigidity, as though he felt the same monumental change I did the moment his soft lips touched mine. My hands run along the back of his head and I wrap my legs around his waist.

Our lips shift and he slides his tongue into my mouth. It's like sinking into a hot bath—soothing, exhilarating, and perfect. It's not the rushed messes we were the other two times, and his hands haven't ventured from my cheeks.

Too quickly, an ache builds inside me. I need more. More of him touching me, me touching him. More skin, because although my dress is thin, the jeans and T-shirt on Liam have got to go. He must read my mind because he ends the kiss. His eyes light with a promise that we'll be doing that again as his hand hovers over the front buttons of my dress.

"I'm not going to lie, I would've preferred to test out my two-second theory on the other dress." He flicks open three buttons with ease, and he stares at the fullness of my breasts.

"I'll wear it next time."

"I'd rather have you naked twenty-four seven. Is that too much to ask?" His million-watt smile sears me, and I scold myself for waiting so long to experience this with him. Three more buttons and my dress falls to the sides, giving him a clear view of my lace-covered breasts.

"Hard to explain that at work," I say.

"Who needs work?"

The cool breeze from his ceiling fan makes my nipples pebble even more. Another three buttons are open.

"To earn money," I say.

He finishes unbuttoning my dress and shifts to one side of me, running his large hand over my skin and pushing the fabric off my body. His hand stays on my hipbone, one finger gliding under the elastic seam of my panties. "This dress takes way too long."

"You managed pretty fast."

"Had this not been our first time, I might have ripped it open." His devilish grin says he's wondering what I would think of that.

"Even with this being our first time, I might not have minded."

He kisses me again, his tongue seeking entrance to my mouth. Shifting over me, he holds his weight off me, but I press my hand to his chest.

"You need to strip." I run my hands under the hem of his shirt.

He grabs the shirt from the back of the neckline and tears it off himself. I stare at the muscular planes of his body, the images tattooed on his body. He's busy unbuttoning his pants and I miss the weight of him. But I know it's worth it when I see him slide off the bed and push his jeans down his legs before stepping out of them.

With my arms open for him to return to me, he stands

above me, almost gawking but in a good way. "I never thought I'd have you."

"You make me sound like an unattainable jewel or something." I'd never admit that I like it.

"You are. To me, you are. Can't you see that?" His hands grip my ankles and he pulls me to the edge of his bed, falling to his knees.

I sit up and rest my weight on my elbows to see what he's doing. With that glint in his eyes, he slides my panties aside on the left, exposing my tattoo. Leaning forward, he watches me as he kisses the blackbirds.

"I wish you could see yourself through my eyes." He shimmies my panties down my legs, groaning when he has to close my legs to get them all the way off.

I wish I could see myself through his eyes too. More than he'll ever know.

TWENTY-EIGHT

Liam

She's so beautiful and sexy and stunning, lying on my navy sheets and waiting to see what I'll do to her. All the women I've had before should've prepared me for this moment. I know what women like in bed, but I want to know what *Savannah* likes.

My hands slide up her torso and pull down the cups of her bra. Her head falls to the mattress. I kiss my way up her flat stomach and reach around to unhook her bra.

Capturing her lips with mine, I roll onto my back and bring her on top of me. I sit up and give her tits a squeeze, pinching her nipples until she lets out a breathy exhale. She arches her back, pushing them into my hands.

I lean back and she falls forward, her blonde hair forming a veil around us. She kisses me, and I'm lost in the taste of her and the softness of her skin. My hands explore every inch of her that's been forbidden for years. Her body slides along mine, her fingers hooking under my boxers, pushing them down. But my hands now cup her face. I'm not done kissing her yet.

Somehow, between her hands and my movements, my boxers join the rest of our clothes. She lies back down on me, her tits pressed against my chest and my dick poking up between her ass cheeks. The soft plea of my name coming off her tongue drives me crazy. Makes me want to flip her over and take her here and now like an animal staking his claim, but I don't want that between us. Not tonight anyway.

I slide up to the headboard and rest my back against it. She follows, crawling toward me. I motion for her to turn her back to me, which she does and leans her back against my chest. I turn her chin so that her lips are accessible as I reach between her legs, feeling the slickness of her wet pussy, while my other hand lands on her breast, squeezing and pinching.

Her head falls back to my shoulder. Our tongues explore one another, deeper and deeper with every swipe. I circle her clit with my thumb and slide my finger up and down her slit, teasing her entrance. She bucks once, but I bite her bottom lip and she sinks back down to me.

Her hands clench the tops of my thighs, and my dick grows harder with every moan that falls from her mouth. A strangled whimper crawls up her throat, and I smile, knowing she's close. I increase my speed and she bucks into my hand again, but I bite her lip one more time, sucking it as she comes apart on my hand. I watch in fascination as she cries out then draws in a breath, her hips riding out her orgasm in jerky, uncoordinated movements.

"Shit, I'll never tire of watching you come," I whisper then kiss her temple.

She relaxes back into me, like a woman who's been thoroughly satisfied, but as she slides back, she must feel my straining dick poking into her. She turns all the way around.

"Then make me come again," she says, straddling me.

"Condom?" I ask, and she widens her eyes as though she forgot. "Top drawer."

She grabs one from the box then tears it open. I watch her shaking hands and figure if we don't want to end up having a kid before we're ready, I better help. I pinch the tip, and she rolls the rubber down my length. She shifts off me with the foil condom packet in her hand and eyes the trash can in the corner of the room.

Not happening.

I swing my arm over her hips and hold my hard dick to guide it into her. "We'll clean up after."

"Okay."

I run my hands over her soft hair. Fuck, I love her. I mean not love love, but really, really like. Shit, I need to get this crap out of my head right now. I can't afford to scare her off.

Every frantic thought in my head evaporates when she sinks down on me. All I can think now is please don't let this be the first and only time she's wrapped around my dick.

I pull her to me, our lips joining, and her hard nipples run along my chest as I push up and she gains a steady rhythm to ride me. Her hands go above my head, gripping the headboard, and her speed increases.

My hands run along her back and down, spreading her ass cheeks and pulling her up my dick and back down. Her knees widen and she clenches around my length.

Unable to stop, we stay in that position and I bring her tit to my mouth. I suck on her nipple, and the whimper I heard right before she came last time escapes her throat. I lightly nibble then suck as much as I can into my mouth. She pants and clenches around my dick before moving faster. I use my hands to spread her ass cheeks again and push them back together, pulling her up and driving her down hard.

This time the whimper is repeated over and over, growing in volume and length until she bites her lip, staring at me as if I'm some orgasm angel brought down to earth only for her.

Damn, I could get used to that look.

She falls apart in my arms. Her tit falls out of my mouth, but I don't stop driving in and out of her because I'm almost there too. How couldn't I be when I'm finally inside the woman I've wanted for so long?

I hit the breaking point when she arches her back, placing her hands behind her on my thighs, and my only view is her naked form on top of me. Her tits jiggle as she takes me over and over until I come with a groan and empty myself.

We both breathe deeply, trying to gather ourselves while our gazes are locked. After a bit, she gets up and wraps her arms around my neck. I roll us over on the bed, kissing her until her lips are swollen and red.

For the first time, the actual sex was better than the imaginary beat-off wheel in my head. I should've known. Savannah Bailey has excelled at everything she's ever put her mind to.

TWENTY-NINE

Savannah

I've woken up in Liam's bed before, but waking up with his arms around me, nestled into his strong chest, hearing his breath in my ear makes me regret that I didn't do this earlier.

Liam fell asleep before me, which surprised me because the man has endurance. But he earned his sleep. We dozed for an hour before I was awoken by his hands exploring my body and his lips on my skin, and my favorite—his dick pressing into me. I'm not complaining at all. It's a night I'll remember forever. After the last time, my mind began running through all the possible scenarios as we move forward. But I can't dwell on that. I need to relish the moment now.

I wiggle out from under his arm, but before I can stand, the mattress shifts and my back hits his strong chest.

"I said no running." His voice is groggy but still delicious.

"I was gonna make you breakfast."

He laughs. "On that note." He releases me.

I turn around and give him a quick kiss on his lips. I climb out of the bed and he sits up, resting his feet on the floor.

"Go back to bed," I say, putting on his T-shirt and my panties.

"Nah, I'm going to eat up all the time I have with you."

Cue the swooning. "You act like I'm going somewhere."

He stands and places his hands on my shoulders. I forgot how he towers over me when I don't have heels on. "I have to work tonight."

My shoulders slump and I wrap my arms around his waist. "That sucks, but I'll be here when you get home."

"Week four starts tomorrow," he reminds me.

I roll my eyes and walk out of his bedroom.

"You're running."

"I'm cured. I slept with you and my former self would never do that. Hallelujah." I race down the stairs with him half-heartedly chasing me.

When I open the fridge and his arms wrap around me, I yelp until I feel him kiss behind my ear. His hands sneak under my T-shirt, his pinkie gliding under the waistband of my panties.

"I'd say you've done an awesome job, but we have to finish out the five weeks."

I grab the egg carton and turn in his arms. "Fine."

"Or we call it quits and I make the reservation at Terra and Mare." He lifts a brow.

The last few weeks have been, for lack of a better term, awesome. Soul-crushing swooning over a hot guy. But I'm not ready to go hand-holding down Main Street just yet. I'm not ready for the pressure of questions and being the main topic of the rumor mill. I witnessed what happened when Austin and Holly started out. I can't handle that right now, not when Bailey Timber is floundering.

"Can we talk?" I ask.

Liam's smile fades and he steps away from me as if I just said last night was a mistake.

"No, it's not that."

He doesn't look convinced, so I rush to put the eggs on the counter and take his hand, leading him to the couch.

"Just say it, Savannah." There's that familiar bite to his tone, the one he had with me after Austin and Holly's wedding.

"Do you promise not to be mad?" I ask.

"No," he deadpans.

"Promise."

He rolls his eyes and blows out a breath. Everything about his body language says he's pissed right now. "Fine. I promise."

"What if we keep this thing between us a secret for a while?"

He stands from the couch so fast, my hand flies off his thigh, almost smacking me in the eye. Okay, wrong thing to say.

"I should've realized it would come to this. I'm curious, what is it you're so ashamed of about me? Because Smokin' Guns is a successful business. I own my house outright. I'm a standup guy."

"It's none of that. I'm not ashamed. Why would you think that?" I shake my head because we'll address that later. "I just can't do it yet. I'm not ready to be in the public eye, and if you sit back down, I'll explain the reason."

He stays standing with his hands on the back of the couch, not looking at me.

"Please, Liam. Just... can we have a conversation about this?"

He releases another long breath through his nose, but he rounds the couch and sits back down. I slide closer and take his hand, but it's as limp as a dead fish. We're going to have to address his thoughts about not being good enough for me at some point, but I'm about to tell him something only Dori and I and our accountant are aware of.

"You know how North Forest Lumber closed its doors a bit ago?"

He nods.

"Well, Bailey Timber hired a lot of the workers at the plant and a few of their admins. They weren't going to get severance and we figured—well, *I* figured we'd get the contracts that Clint had stolen off us, plus some of their other customers. But that hasn't been as successful as I hoped. Another competitor has popped up in Anchorage and wooed some away. I put the company in a bad position. If we don't secure at least five new contracts by the end of next month, I'm going to have to lay people off for the first time since I took over the business."

His hand grips mine. I knew he'd feel for me. That's Liam. He's always empathetic to others, which is probably why so many people in town love him.

"I'm sorry you're having to deal with that, Sav, but that's business. And you and I are definitely not business. I understand that people will be upset, but you tried to help when they had nowhere else to go. They'll get it."

I shake my head. "I failed them. I failed the town. I took a risk when Grandma Dori told me not to. She said to let them go on unemployment and we'll hire them once we got the contracts. But I was so sure that the only reason our clients left was because Clint Edison bad-mouthed us that I fought her on it. I wanted to have them hired and trained in our way of doing something before the contracts moved over."

"I understand the pressure you're under and I get that you feel bad for what's going on with the company, but I'm not sure what that has to do with us right now."

I press my lips together. "If I go out there and say I started this new relationship and Buzz Wheel reports their bullshit stories, next month when I have to announce lay-offs, people are going to say it's because I was too busy dating you and I wasn't paying enough attention to the company."

He sinks back into the couch. Either he agrees or thinks I'm crazy, I can't tell. But he has no idea what it's like to be picked apart for every decision, to be under the microscope for every little thing. "Just because you run a company doesn't mean you don't get to have a life."

I nod. "I know, and I agree. But give me some time. I have some more conference calls this week. We're close to getting some commitments. But I promise you..." I slide one leg over his lap and straddle him, placing my hands on either side of his face. "This has nothing to do with me being embarrassed or thinking you're not the type of man I'm supposed to be with." I press a kiss to his lips but draw back when he doesn't reciprocate. "Last night was amazing and I'm all in for this thing between us. Just give me some time. I'll email Buzz Wheel myself."

"What would you say?" He looks intrigued now.

"I'd say I saw Savannah Bailey and Liam Kelly making out in the gazebo and she was all over him. When they tore apart for a minute, her smile radiated, and I'd say she's met her Prince Charming."

He laughs and I smile at him, still not letting his face go. "Will you refer to my dick size?"

I laugh and swat his chest.

He uses my moment of weakness to flip me onto my back on the couch. "All in?"

"All in."

"You have one month."

"Deal. Seal it with a kiss?"

"Tempting, but I'll pass." He pretends to get off me, but I grab at his shoulders.

"Hey!"

"You know, I should hold out on you until we go public."

"Well. You have to do what you have to do." I slide out from under him, but I'm halfway off the couch, my head hanging over the edge, when he locks his hips to mine.

He pushes my T-shirt up over my head and his mouth descends on my breast, twirling my nipple with his tongue.

"Hey!" I kick my feet, but he doesn't stop except to push the T-shirt completely off of me—which doesn't take much since it's so huge on me.

"Shit!" We both slide and end up on the floor. But that's okay, rug burn never put anyone in the hospital.

We spend the entire day in bed in our own secret paradise, ignoring Denver's desperate messages asking if he can come home.

Best. Day. Ever.

THIRTY

Liam

I finally convinced Savannah to accompany me to some of the local businesses to solicit donations for the library gala auction. I've already gone to most of them, but I have a few more to hit. First she made me go to Sweet Suga Things, but I'm not complaining about getting to taste-test cake and icing.

Now, we're at Lifetime Adventures, which is way out of her element.

"Ready?" I ask, almost taking her hand before we walk in, but catching myself and sliding my hand into my pocket instead.

"I guess."

"Relax. This is Denver's mentor, remember? No pressure. Plus, he always donates. I gave you an easy one."

She laughs, but there's a nervous hitch to it. I wish I could put my arms around her and kiss her forehead, but her rules dictate that I can't. As much as I understand that Savannah has always worried about her reputation in Lake

Starlight, I hate that she's put us on the down-low. It makes me feel like I always do with her—that I'm not good enough.

The bell chimes as we push through the door of the log-cabin-style building. The office is small with a ton of brochures on display, along with a TV mounted up high, rotating video clips of various excursions. Denver's mug is front and center in a few. There's a small table set to the side to discuss the different offerings.

"Look." Savannah points at an article about Denver and that music producer, Griffin Thorne, he saved after his small plane went down a couple of years back. I read it when it first came out, and in it, Denver praises Chip for everything he learned that got him out of the bush. "I should've come here ages ago. My family owes Chip for working with Denver so much."

"Stop worrying."

Right before I ring the bell for service, the door to the back office opens. Out steps a blonde who's close to my age and dressed like Savannah in heels and executive wear. Her hair is pulled into a low ponytail, and she stops in her tracks when she sees us. "Oh, hi."

"Hi," Savannah says.

"Is Chip around?" I ask. She clearly has something to do with this place if she's behind the closed office door, though I wonder where Nancy, Chip's long-time office administrator, is.

"No."

Savannah looks at me. "Okay, what about Nancy?"

"No."

This woman sure makes it easy to hold a conversation. "I'm Liam Kelly, and this is Savanah Bailey."

"Bailey? As in related to Denver Bailey?" she asks as if that wouldn't be a good thing.

Savannah looks at me again. "Um... he's my brother."

Her hands go up in the air and her eyes roll back. Oh shit. I wonder whether Denver screwed her or screwed her over. "Well, Chip and Nancy aren't here. If you want to book a tour, do it online. Someone will get back to you."

"Do you know when they'll return? We have to talk to Chip about donating to the charity auction for the new extension on the library. It's going to be a children's wing." I pull out the info sheet we put together—but this girl clearly isn't interested in hearing any of it.

"Nancy should be here, but I think she's out at lunch. Priorities, right?"

I inhale and lean forward as if I'm asking her a secret. "And you are?"

She laughs. "Of course you have no idea who I am. I'm sure my father never talks about me." She sticks out her hand. "Cleo Dawson. Daughter of Chip Dawson."

I knew Chip had a daughter, but I've never met her. I run into Chip a few times a year, and most of those times are when I'm with Denver and he drags me here. Chip's a cool guy, but I never pried into his personal life.

"It's nice to meet you," I say.

Savannah and I shake her hand.

"Now if you'll excuse me, it's time for me to get the hell out of this frozen tundra."

It's summer now, not winter, but I don't bother correcting her. Cleo breezes by us and we're left alone, staring at one another in confusion.

"Thanks for giving me the easy one, babe." Savannah punches me lightly in the upper arm.

I should be questioning what's going on, but Savannah Bailey just used a pet name for me and everything else that happened blows out the door with Cleo. I take Sav in my arms and smash my lips against hers. Surprisingly, she doesn't pull away until light from outside falls on us when the door springs open again.

"Jesus, no. I do not need this. First I get the wrath of Cleo Dawson, then I have to see you two sucking face." Denver steps fully into the small room.

Savannah pulls away from me. "And you'll keep this a secret too."

Denver rolls his eyes. "Fine, but I hope you realize the truth *will* come out. You guys have been holing yourselves up at Liam's so much the family is already talking. Even Rome and Harley have caught on and they have a new baby. If they've noticed, you can bet everyone has. Besides, if you keep sucking face in public, it's not going to me that walks in on you next time."

Ignoring Denver's little rant, I change topics. "What the hell is going on here? We just met Chip's daughter."

Denver runs his hand through his hair. "She's a peach, right? I bet her vagina has little spikes around it to keep guys away, like a Venus flytrap or something."

"That's a shitty thing to say. You have no idea what she might be going through." No surprise that Savannah sticks up for her—I'm sure someone said something similar about her at some point.

"She's horrible. It's like she enjoys living in her little unhappy bubble."

"I don't think I've heard of her being up here for a long time, right?" Savannah asks.

"Not since she was a teenager." He shrugs like 'who the hell cares, the woman is the devil.' "Anyway... Chip is kind of sick."

"Kind of? And what do you mean sick?" Savannah asks, lowering her voice.

"I'm not exactly sure, but he's in the hospital right now." Denver's shoulders slump and he looks away.

"Sounds serious," I say.

His gaze meets mine. I see his silent plea to let this go for now, that he can't really talk about it because no one is supposed to know. The good thing about being best friends your entire life is that words don't need to be exchanged sometimes. "Anyway, as of today, I'm running this place for the time being until he's back on his feet."

"You?" Savannah couldn't sound more surprised or confused.

Sometimes I think Denver got the shit end of the stick. Everyone has their place in his big family, and he took on the role of immature kid for life. But at some point, I hope he fights back and grows up.

"Yes, me. Thanks for the encouragement, sis."

She tries to backtrack. "I'm just surprised..."

I wrap my arm around her, and although she steps away, I bring her to my side because it's just Denver.

"Yeah, well, I'm surprised each time I run into the two of you on the cusp of doing 'that which shall not be named.' I'm still not a hundred percent comfortable with this yet." He waves his finger between us.

"Sorry not sorry." I kiss the top of his sister's head then slide my hand down to her ass and slap it.

"Fuck, Liam." Denver shuts his eyes and turns around. "Go do that somewhere else."

He disappears through the door to the office.

Savannah shakes her head and stomps out of the small log cabin. I follow her to the gazebo area set up for when groups are waiting to depart, and we sit on a bench that overlooks the opposite side of Lake Starlight.

"Mind enlightening me on what I did wrong in there?"

She blows out a breath. "Can I ask you a question?"

"Always."

She takes a moment, I assume to pick her words carefully, before glancing around to make sure no one is lurking. We're basically in the middle of nowhere. "Why do you like me? Or are you just attracted to me physically and that's it?"

I stare at her long and hard. She truly is lost inside herself and has no clue how amazing she is. Life has beaten her so far down that she just doesn't get it.

"I'm attracted to you, clearly. But the best way I can describe why I like you is to say that I see you. You've captured my attention since I was fourteen. True, back then it was probably teenage lust, but somewhere, that lust turned into more. And then when you moved in, all these emotions and feelings made me feel like I was drowning. I didn't know how to handle them. They came out as me challenging you and maybe picking on you at times. So when you ask me why I like you, it's a hard question for me to answer. It's like asking why the sun rises in the morning. It just does. It's how it was meant to be."

She twists on the bench to face me.

I can't stop myself from brushing her hair behind her ear. "That's the best answer I have. But I have to say that you underestimate the woman you are. You're so much more than you give yourself credit for. I think somewhere, you lost sight of what you love. Once you find that and fight for it, you're going to be happier."

"When did you get so smart?" she asks in a soft voice, and I chuckle. "Can I ask you another question?"

"Yeah." I'm wondering if she'll ever not have one to ask.

"What's the story with Slim? And Nina? All the other girls? How many women have you slept with?"

I knew this was one of her hang-ups about ever dating me. I don't want to lie to her, but my past is my past and bears no weight on the future I'd have with her. "Let's start with Slim."

She nods, waiting expectantly as if I'm telling her a fairy tale. There's no happily ever after with this one though.

"When Rome went to Europe and Denver was busy getting his pilot's license, I found myself alone a lot. Smokin' Guns was already off the ground. That summer was when I bought my bike and started riding regularly. Slim was the first person I met. I hung out with that crew and met Nina through them, but things went south fast. They were into some shitty things, the least of which was intimidation and picking fights. It wasn't my scene. Nina loved it, so we broke up. Though I'd bet money she was already sleeping with Slim before we were over."

"Why didn't you hang out with Austin or some of the other guys from school?"

I sigh. "You and Austin had your hands full, and a lot of our friends were finding their way, just like Rome and Denver. Getting involved with that crew was a mistake. Kathy is the one who showed me they couldn't be trusted and that they weren't the kind of people I wanted in my circle. I jokingly called her Mom once, and she kept the joke going."

She slides closer and looks around before putting her hand on my leg. "Thanks for your honesty."

"Don't thank me yet." She retracts her hand, but I reach for it. "I've had women. Probably not as many as you suspect, but I've had periods of my life when I wasn't looking for a relationship and took what I could get—which was quite a lot. I'm not proud of it, but I never told a lie to get a woman to sleep with me. If you're with me, you have to be okay with my past."

I hold my breath as she looks away. I could've skated around the topic, and months ago I would've done just that, but I want to be the best version of myself for this woman. A man she's proud to stand next to.

"Okay, that's sort of the answer I was expecting. I don't like it, but it's in the past. I'm not going to let it affect the present."

I squeeze her hand, feeling as if the weight of a glacier has been lifted off of me.

"I want you to know something too." She puts her other hand over mine. "I see you. I'm scared shitless, but I see you. These past few weeks, everything you've done for me, the time you've taken, I see it all and I appreciate it more than I can say. But I'm a bit of a hot mess and nearly broke in front of Denver a few weeks ago."

Ah, that makes sense now. "He told me you were emotional because you had your period. I wondered."

She rolls her eyes. "He freaked. I thought he was going to start screaming your name because he didn't know how to handle me. I want to find the pieces of myself that I lost. I want to see myself how you do. And I'm getting there, I think. But right now, public affection makes me uncomfortable."

Of course it does, and I'm a PDA junkie. I'm not going to go screwing her in broad daylight in the middle of the town square, but I want the hand-holding, the kissing whenever I want. I want the luxury of displaying affection toward the woman I'm falling for. But if I give her time, I know she'll turn around. Look how far she's already come.

"You want me to keep my hands in my pockets at all times?"

"Maybe until I feel more comfortable?" Her voice is small and reserved, as though she thinks I'm going to be mad at her.

"I really hate this. At some point, you have to stop worrying what people think and live your life for yourself." I stand, stuffing my hands into my pockets. "But I'll go along with it for now. Ready?"

She stands and sighs, but I'm not sure how she expects me to react. I want everyone in this damn town to know she's mine, but she keeps finding reasons to keep us hidden.

THIRTY-ONE

Savannah

It isn't until Friday that I realize Liam never gave me a task for the week—when he told me this morning that he took off tomorrow and kicked Denver out for the night. He said tomorrow I'd get my fifth and final task. Since I'll use any excuse I can to contact him these days, I pull out my phone at lunch and type him a text.

Me: *You never gave me something to do for my week four.*

The three dots appear so fast, I wonder if he was about to send me a text. It shouldn't make me happy, but it does nonetheless.

Liam: *You went with me to get donations for the auction, plus you were supposed to be pulling things out of the jar every day since last week. Did you not follow my directions, Miss Bailey?*

Me: *I did. Most days. But I probably have a few more to do.*

I pulled one the other day that said to say hi to a stranger, and another today that said I was to have a meaningful conversation with an employee. I spent twenty minutes in the break room, talking with one of our employees about her adverse reaction to food smells. In the end, she told me she wanted to file a complaint about Phoenix. Not all of Liam's ideas are stellar.

Over the last week, I've slept in Liam's bed, eaten dinner with Liam, meditated with Liam. I even allowed him to run with me last night. He beat me though, so that's never happening again.

Liam: *Maybe I should replace them all with sex favors?*

Even I know my smile is cheesy as my stomach quivers instead of flutters now. I've fallen for Liam Kelly—hard. Now it all has to come into place. I have two meetings next week, and if they sign to make us their lumber supplier, I'll be ready to scream my feelings from the rooftops.

My mom always told me to imagine what you want, work hard, and it will come true. So I close my eyes and imagine that in less than a week, I'll have turned Bailey Timber around and have a steady boyfriend.

My phone dings and interrupts the images in my head. Probably a good thing since they might have been going too far into the future anyway—what kind of ceremony we'd have, Liam carrying me over the threshold, and what our baby might look like. My eyes pop open. I'm almost horrified by how easily that came to mind.

Liam: *Is that a no?*

Liam: *Can't handle it? ;)*
Me: *Sorry, I was lost in thought for a second.*
Liam: *I hope it was about me.*
Me: *I can't lie, you are what the majority of my thoughts consist of nowadays.*
Liam: *I'm smiling so wide I look like a goon.*
Me: *Good.*
Liam: *Tell me you'll be in my bed when I get home...*
Me: *I guess you'll find out. :P*

There's a long pause. I assume he got pulled away by a customer, so I place my phone down, but it dings before I can continue eating my lunch.

Liam: *Here's your task:*
Liam: *Be naked in bed when I arrive home.*
Liam: *Have whipped cream and chocolate sauce next to the bed.*
Liam: *Don't forget the cherries. I LOVE cherries.*

I put the phone face-down on my desk and laugh so loudly, my assistant, Samara, peeks through my glass office door. I wave her off, and one last giggle escapes as I pick up my phone.

Me: *Why don't I just pick up a maid's outfit? All of this is very cliché. I would've assumed you had more original ideas.*
Liam: *We have to start with cliché. Don't worry your sweet lil ass, babe, there are things I'm gonna do to you that will make your toes curl.*
Me: *I think my toes already curled last night.*

Liam: *You're hard to please Miss Bailey. How about this then...*
Liam: *I'm gonna do things to you that'll have you coming at your desk as you relive them in your mind.*

My face heats and job complete, because all his message did was make me remember what he did to me last night. The way he bent me over his bed with his hands on my breasts, his mouth trailing down my spine while he thrust in and out of me.

Knock.

The phone fumbles out of my hand and bounces off my desk to my chair, landing with a thud on the floor.

Austin peeks in. "Do you have some time to chat?"

My older brother looks happy and tanned. But I guess most people would if they just got back from their honeymoon where they pretty much screwed every second of the day trying to make a baby. I imagine it's like Christmas morning every day for those two.

"Yeah, come on in." I bend down to pick up my phone and walk over to the couch he's already sitting on. "How was the honeymoon?"

He nods. "Good. Relaxing. Had a great time."

"That's wonderful. Is Holly as tanned as you?" I smile.

"Not quite." He chuckles. "She spent most of her time under the umbrella and took great pleasure in lecturing me about the risks of sun damage. She considers herself the expert since she grew up in Florida."

"Well, she's right."

He rolls his eyes at me.

Never one to beat around the bush, especially with Austin, I get right to it. "I heard you're trying for a baby."

His head falls into his hands. "Seriously, the gossip in

this town." He looks at me a second later with obvious questions of his own. "I ran into Denver in town. We took Calista and Dion their souvenirs."

I cross my legs and keep my phone tucked into my lap just in case Liam messages me. How can one twin be a vault and the other the exact opposite? "I told him if he told anyone that I'd put him on every dating site, saying he's desperate for monogamy."

He leans back and spreads his arms across the backs of the cushions. "Then I'd start downloading dating apps to your phone."

I shake my head.

"Listen, I'm not here to tell you what to do. Before we left for the honeymoon, things were a little intense between you and Liam. I honestly worried one of you would be going to jail for assault. But Denver says when he's allowed in the house, you guys seem cool with one another."

If anyone understands taking the responsibility for your family at such a young age and how that can mess with your head, it's Austin. We each did our part after our parents died. "I think I like him."

He cocks his eyebrow. "You think?"

"Fine, I know I do." My phone dings in my lap, and I grin.

"Is that him?" he asks.

I turn it over, see Liam's name, and turn it back around, not reading the text yet. "Yeah."

"From the smile on your face, I'd say things are better than cool between you two."

Ever since Holly came into Austin's life, we haven't had many heart-to-hearts. Then again, she came as soon as the twins turned eighteen. Once he was no longer responsible for the day-to-day responsibilities of any of our siblings, his job was done. I'm the one who signed up for the forever job —being responsible for Bailey Timber Corp.

"Yeah. Though I'm sure it doesn't make much sense to you."

He smiles. "It makes sense."

"He's so easygoing."

"Opposites attract."

"He's a recovering playboy... I hope."

Austin sits on the edge of the couch. "Liam isn't a playboy. I'm not sure he ever really was. I know he might've gone through a phase, and sure, he had his share of fun, but the guys used to hang at the house a lot. As bad as this sounds, our brothers were the bad influence on *him*. He helped them when they got in over their head more than once."

"Really?"

He laughs and shakes his head. "Do you know your brothers at all?"

"Of course, but I always figured Liam was right there with them."

"He was, but not with the same dumbass ideas. I mean, he had that house and the barn long before Denver or Rome got their shit together. He owns Smokin' Guns, and he's at all the fundraisers and town events."

I don't need reasons to think highly of Liam. In my mind, I put his past where it belongs—BS, Before Savannah. Which also happens to stand for bullshit, which is what I think of him sleeping with other women, but I can be mature about it. Regardless, hearing Austin go to bat for him is nice.

"All right, well, I wanted to see your face when I confronted you about it. But just so you know, if I was only in town for eight hours before Denver told me, I'm pretty sure all of us Baileys know. But I'm the only one who will bring it up."

He stands to leave, and I do too, then hug him. When he hears me sniffle from the tears that are building, he not only puts his arms around me but tightens them.

"Are you okay, Sav?"

I draw back, wiping my eyes. "I'm going to tell you this, and if you tell a soul, I will kill you."

"How well do you know me?"

Austin's right. We were each other's confidants for so long, but since he's been married, I've felt that he was only Holly's.

"I let Liam do this whole experiment thing with me."

"Yeah, let me call Holly. I'm not sure this is something I wanna know about." He turns toward the door, but I grab his arm.

"Not anything sexual."

He stops and waits.

"It was about finding the person I was before Mom and Dad died."

He nods and rocks back on his heels. "And?"

"And I think it's working and now I'm constantly crying. I'm a hot mess!"

He laughs and squeezes my shoulder. "Then I'd say you're almost there. You're finally getting back in touch with your emotions. That's huge for you."

My forehead wrinkles. "What does that mean? I've always cared for everyone."

"I'm not saying you're heartless, but right after Mom and Dad died, you and I were thrust into new lives. We had to worry about getting our younger siblings through the grief of losing our parents and set our own aside. Through the years, I've noticed you shut down your feelings."

"That's not true. I cried at your wedding." I teared up, but close enough.

He sighs. "I don't think you ever properly dealt with your feelings about losing Mom and Dad. After a while, any time you felt something—good or bad—you kind of... pushed it away. Other than anger, I'd say your emotions are pretty locked down."

"I'm starting to take offense." My jaw clenches.

He laughs, running his hands through his hair. Him and his casual shorts and T-shirt because he's a teacher. And his baseball team just won state. And he just got married. Mr. I Have Everything I Ever Dreamed Of is calling me out for not showing my emotions?

"Tears are awesome. If Liam is responsible for you finding yourself or whatever you want to call it, I couldn't be happier. I love Liam. He's like a younger brother to me." He runs his hand down my upper arm.

"That's another reason I questioned this thing between us. We're five years apart. When I was nineteen, he was only fourteen. Isn't that creepy?"

Austin laughs again. "Now you're thirty-one and he's twenty-six. You're both adults. And seriously, I mean, if Liam was my friend, would it have been a problem? If he was the one who was nineteen when you were fourteen?"

I chew on my lip. What he's saying is true and I want to be all female power about it and pretend I don't care, but I'm hung up on it for some reason. "I guess you have a point."

My phone dings again and I try to bite down my smile, but Austin points. "That's the emotion you want to focus on right now." He glances behind him. "Now, I need to get out of here before Grandma Dori finds me. She wants to come over for dinner, and I really don't want to answer all her questions about us trying to have a baby. I'm going to kill Phoenix." He snaps his fingers. "Actually, if you move in with Liam, can Phoenix stay at your house? Maybe she and Denver can live there."

"I'm not moving."

Shit. I haven't even thought about moving back into my house. I mean, it's been so long since I lived there. The thought of going back kind of depresses me now that I think of it. Liam has a better couch and all the kitchen gadgets you could want. His bed is pretty great too.

"I'll let you contemplate that."

Austin looks down the hallway before sliding out of my office as if rumor hasn't already spread that he's here. Just as he's slipping down the hallway, Grandma Dori comes into view. He stops, his shoulders sagging a bit, but he opens his arms to hug her.

I laugh when he glances over her shoulder at me, then I return to my desk to read Liam's texts. It's going to be a long night of waiting for him to finish work. Somehow, it just doesn't feel like home unless he's there.

THIRTY-TWO

Liam

The family room light is on when I return home at ten o'clock. I half expect to find Denver and Savannah in a screaming match, because Denver's big-ass mouth sent three of the Bailey siblings to visit me at Smokin' Guns today. Austin and Brooklyn had the courtesy to wait until I was between customers to talk to me, but Rome busted in, stole Rhys's chair, and rolled over next to me while I was finishing Gerald, a client who was there on his fourth visit to finish a large family emblem on his back. Thankfully, all of the Baileys gave me their blessing and said they'd keep it quiet, per Savannah's wishes. However, thanks to Rome, I have to make sure Gerald, an accountant from two towns over, keeps our secret too.

By the time I reach the door, I hear music coming from inside—"Dancing in the Streets" by David Bowie and Mick Jagger. When I step inside, I spot Savannah dancing in the kitchen with a spoon to her mouth, lip syncing.

I drop my bag, cross my arms, and watch her. Her hair is

pulled back in a high ponytail, and she's in yoga pants and my old Lake Starlight High School T-shirt, which is tied in a knot at her waist. I want to kidnap her and hold her hostage in my room until she's had at least three orgasms. But it's rare to see her like this, so I don't dare. She continues dancing while she puts the wooden spoon in a bowl and stirs, her hips swaying to the beat.

Denver slides into the room in his socks as though he's Tom Cruise in *Risky Business*, then he grabs her and they dance. He has one hand on her hip and his other hand in hers. Every step is exaggerated and they're both laughing so hard by the time the song comes to an end, Denver falls onto a breakfast stool and Savannah bends over the counter, giving me a perfect view of her ass.

Denver spots me at the door and nudges Savannah, pointing at me. "Daddy's home."

Savannah glances over her shoulder and smiles.

Damn. I know with certainty that I could come home to that smile every night for the rest of my life and be a happy man.

She swivels around and leans her elbows on the counter. "You're just in time. We're about to frost."

"Frost?" I push off the wall, happy to see she didn't give Denver a black eye but wishing he'd disappear so I could place her on the counter, spread her legs, and make her scream my name.

"The cake," she says when I fist-bump Denver.

I wrap my arm around her waist to bring her flush against my chest. "My entire eight-hour shift, all I could think of was doing this."

I bend her down and capture her lips. At first, she pushes me away but relents for a half a second before pushing at me again.

"I guess I have to get used to this now, huh?" Denver heads to the other side of the counter as though he's afraid we're contagious.

"Yeah, you do."

Savannah bites her lip, and I run my hand down her back to her ass then squeeze it. We share a look. I'm pretty sure she's thinking what I was moments ago. Why the hell doesn't Denver have somewhere to be on a Friday night?

"So you two made up?" I ask.

Savannah pinches Denver's cheek. "He's just too lovable, I suppose."

I inspect the kitchen, looking for alcohol, but I don't even see a beer bottle. They're sober?

"I think she felt bad for me."

"It was the orange chicken from Wok For U," Savannah tells him.

"What's with the cake?" I ask.

"Well..." She looks at her brother and they laugh. "I was watching a baking show and Denver said he could do better than the lady, so I bet him he couldn't. We found this old mix tape in your desk over there." She points at Denver as though he was the snoop. "And we're wondering why you have a mix tape and a tape player?" She waves me off like I can answer that another time. "And we decided to make an ugly masterpiece together. Lucky for us, you had all the ingredients." She runs her finger down my chest. "Are you a secret baker?"

I laugh. "I'm not a baker."

"Neither are we." She picks up their lopsided cake, which has one piece missing.

I wish I could watch her all night. She's so free and living in the moment. Did all those things I made her do really make a difference? "And the missing piece of cake?"

They both laugh again.

"We had to taste-test," Denver admits.

Not surprising for him, but I am surprised Savannah's not annoyed by the less-than-perfect creation they made.

"Now we're going to frost."

Right after she says that, Pat Benatar's "Hit Me with Your Best Shot" begins. Savannah screams. As she dances around us, pretending to punch us, Denver's eyes meet mine. There's an apology there. I nod in acceptance and take a seat at the breakfast bar.

"You created a monster," he says, his gaze zeroing in on Savannah.

I don't say anything because I'm loving how comfortable she looks right now.

"Where did you get this anyway?" She falls into my lap and wraps her arms around my neck. I'm happy to see that she's growing more comfortable with showing me affection in front of her brother.

If I'm honest with them, I might put a screeching halt to this fun night, but then again, both of them might appreciate the truth. "Your parents. Austin shoved a crate at me with a bunch of your dad's music after... I found this in there, and I bought a tape player to play it."

Denver sits on a breakfast stool. "This was Dad's?"

"I think it was your mom's actually."

Savannah goes limp in my arms, then she straightens, stands, and frosts the cake.

"Why do you think that?" Denver asks, but my eyes are on Savannah. She's checked out of the conversation now. "I'm Free" by Kenny Loggins comes on, and Denver's foot taps. "This is from that *Footloose* movie, right?"

I want to agree, but Denver's gaze is on Savannah and

her gaze is on the spatula moving the frosting around the cake.

"Remember your mom and her eighties movies? That red-haired actress was in almost all of them."

"Molly Ringwald," Savannah says.

"Yeah." Denver's voice softens.

Yep, I killed their good time.

"Want to watch one?" I ask.

Savannah finishes frosting the cake, and yeah, she might need a little more practice with this cake decorating thing. She dumps the bowl and spatula in the sink. "I have to do the dishes."

Denver swipes his finger through the frosting and licks it off his finger. "It might look like shit, but it tastes grrrreat." He does the whole Tony the Tiger from Frosted Flakes impression for the word great.

I laugh while Savannah keeps her back to me.

Silently, I ask Denver to give me a little time with her, and he nods.

"I gotta go take a piss," he says and stands.

"Ugh, can't you just say use the restroom?" Savannah snips.

Once Denver is gone, I run my hands around her middle and place my chin on her shoulder. She continues washing the dishes as though I'm not there.

"You know it's okay to remember them," I say.

"I remember them all day, every day."

"You can smile at memories. Like I remember coming over during the Christmas break right before their accident and seeing you, Brooklyn, and your mom having an eighties movie marathon. You had all this food. Your hair was teased high and sprayed different colors, and you had on bright blue eye shadow and pink lipstick. Your mom bragged that you and Brooklyn were wearing her clothes from that era. Don't you remember those times?"

She violently scrubs the cake pan. "They're over now."

I nod. "True, but you don't have to pretend like they never happened. Come." I lightly tug on her middle to pull her away from the sink. "We can do this later."

"Then it will dry and it's even harder to get clean."

"I'll do it. Come on. I worked all day and I want to eat your cake."

"It's not going to be very good. It's dry and lumpy." Her voice sounds gravelly, and I worry that she's trying to hide her emotions again.

"Ah, it can't be that bad. Plus I get pie later, right?"

She turns to me, apparently questioning my meaning, and rolls her eyes when it clicks. She elbows me and I pretend it didn't hurt, but damn she's boney. "Has anyone told you that you push too hard?"

I take a moment to stare at the ceiling. "No, I'm not sure I've ever gotten that complaint."

I slide my hand down her arm to grab her hand and pull her toward the family room. She tries fighting me but eventually relents.

"Denver!" I yell.

He barrels down the stairs. "I'm ready."

He runs into the kitchen, grabs the entire cake, three forks, three waters, and joins us on the couch. The cake ends up in Savannah's lap as we all dive in while we watch *Footloose.* It takes Savannah a little while to settle in, but I take it as a good sign when she asks to watch *The Breakfast Club* after the first movie is finished.

She wasn't waiting for me naked in my bed when I got home, but somehow, I think we made more progress toward the end goal. Tonight was exactly what she needed.

THIRTY-THREE

Liam

Saturday is pretty busy at the shop, so I end up having to go in for a while. I told Denver yesterday he needed to sleep somewhere else tonight, and he stops by at one point to let me know that he's going to Brooklyn's.

When we're finally closed, I come home, and again, Savannah's in the kitchen. She smiles at me over her shoulder from where she is at the stove.

"In the kitchen two nights in a row?"

She laughs. "Well, you said whatever we're doing tonight is my last task, so I figured a celebration and a thank you are in order."

I snag her chin to kiss her, and I slide my tongue into her hot mouth, spurring her to turn around and wrap her arms around my neck. I don't want to draw the kiss to a close, but I'm also starving after missing lunch. That's mostly because I couldn't eat because of how nervous I am over what I'm about to do.

"I have some really good news," she says as she stirs

whatever she's cooking. Savannah knows her way around a kitchen. I've been eating her cooking since before Mr. and Mrs. Bailey passed away.

I slide up on the counter, grabbing a cracker and cheese she has set out. "What's that?"

"My house is ready. I went over there today, and everything is finished."

"Really?" *That sucks.* "That's awesome."

She turns off the burner and sets a timer on the microwave, then she comes to stand between my legs. Her hands run up my thighs. "I know. I'm not sure I'll like sleeping by myself anymore, but it does allow us to have more freedom from Denver."

I place my hands on either side of her face and stare into her eyes. "How about Denver moves into your house and you move in here?"

She laughs.

I wasn't joking.

"Funny you say that. When Austin came to the office, he suggested Phoenix and Denver move into my place."

"He is your older brother, and you should always listen to your elders."

"Can you imagine if I always listened to Grandma Dori? She's the eldest of the elders." She shakes her head. "It's only been a few weeks for us. Moving in together permanently seems to be rushing it."

I jump down from the counter and grab her hand. "How much longer before dinner?"

She checks the microwave. "Twenty minutes."

"Good. Come with me."

"Where? What about the oven?"

I tug on her arm. "It's fine. We'll only be in the barn. Set the timer on your phone."

"Barn?" Her eyes light up as if I told her N'Sync is outside waiting to do a private concert for her.

"Yeah, but hey, if you don't want to know..."

"Oh no." She takes off her apron and tosses it on the counter, heading toward the back door. "Let's go."

I open the door for her and laugh. The sound locks in my throat. The more I try to swallow, the drier my mouth gets from the anxiety hijacking my body. She's shared so much with me. I owe her this.

We walk along the brick path, and I think that this must be what a person feels like when they're going to go bungee jumping or skydiving. With every step I take, an impending doom bears down on my shoulders. Once she sees this, she'll never be able to unsee it. What will she think of me? That I suck? That all of it should be kept in the barn and never see the light of day? My biggest fear is that she'll think I'm weak. I'll no longer be Liam Kelly, the tattoo artist, the one who finishes the Bailey twin's fights. This will change her view of me. As my hand rests on the doorknob, I take one last deep breath.

"Hey." She stops me before I turn the knob. Her warm hand lands on my chest and she rises up on her tiptoes. "If you're not comfortable with this, you don't have to do it. You don't have to show me. It's okay."

"Why do you say that?"

Her hand covers my heart. "Because your heart is beating like a stampede of elephants is running through your chest."

I chuckle, taking her hand. "I'm usually an open book, but what's behind this door, I haven't shared with anyone... ever. But you're a part of my life and I want to share it with you."

"Okay." She nods.

I turn the metal doorknob, pushing the door open. We step into darkness, but I flick the light on. The barn isn't really a barn. I've refurbished it to suit my needs.

"Liam!" She gasps in awe.

She steps into my private space where all my easels are set up and paintings are hanging, some stacked up in the corners. The tables dotting the space are full of paint and brushes. The floors are covered in cloths to protect them, and there's a full fridge in the corner and a couch and chair for the late nights when I find myself blocked.

She turns away from a painting of Lake Starlight at dusk. "You painted all these?"

I nod, stuffing my hands into my pockets and feeling my cheeks heat.

She walks to another pair of easels. One has a painting of Calista at Brooklyn and Wyatt's wedding. The other has a painting of the gazebo in the town's center, all decorated for Austin and Holly's wedding. She says nothing as she takes them in.

I crack my neck, watching her gaze move up the walls. The pictures I've hung up are mostly ones of Lake Starlight. One when Terra and Mare opened. Wyatt's hotel from the backside with the lake in front of it.

"Say something," I urge.

She glances at me, then her hands run over the completed canvases stacked in the corner. "They're all so beautiful. So realistic."

I rock back on my heels.

"Why are you hiding all these?" She goes through my stack of paintings leaning in the corner and I fight the urge to stop her. Some of my first paintings are in that stack, including some that will probably sadden her.

"Because they're just for me."

She nods, but she stops perusing. I slowly walk over and see that she's looking at one of her parents' caskets side by side. Before bringing her in here, I thought about getting rid of those, but I couldn't.

"I did that from memory."

She studies it for a second. I'm sure she sees the nine Bailey siblings, all years younger than they are now, sitting in the first row of the church.

"It's everything I remember from that day," she says in a quiet voice.

"Remember Phoenix and Sedona wouldn't leave you alone?" I brush the backside of my hand along her arm.

She nods, then rummages through the pile again.

"I should warn you—"

But her gasp says she's there. The picture of my mother and her mother laughing on the couch. She's not ready to see all the ones I've done of us as kids at cookouts and fishing trips.

"You do look just like her."

She turns around and the pictures land back in place. "Why?"

"Why what?"

"Why do you do this?"

I shrug. "It helps me process, I guess."

"Process what?" She steps toward me, and I wonder whether she's going to slap me for bringing her in here.

"Their death. My parents leaving. Life."

She turns away from me, glancing at the one of Calista in her flower girl dress. She's looking at the front of the aisle, at Rome, while placing flowers on the ground. They're smiling at one another.

Savannah sits on the stool and just stares. A tear slowly

falls off her cheek. She brings her knees to her chest as another tear races down her face.

"I didn't bring you in here to make you sad." I come alongside her, and she leans into my chest.

"I know. They're all so beautiful and life-like. It hurts that my parents never got to meet Calista or Dion or Holly or Wyatt or Harley." She turns and looks at me. "What do you think they would think of us?"

I swivel the stool around and bend down to her level. "I like to think they'd be happy. Probably surprised like the rest of your family, but happy for us."

A small smile graces her face. "Thank you for sharing this with me. Here I thought you just had cars or some giant beetle collection in here."

I laugh, gripping her hands and helping her stand. I wipe away the tears that have stained her cheeks. "Beetle collection as in cars?"

She shakes her head. "No, I thought, like, insects or something."

"Why would you think that?"

She shrugs. "I have no idea. But I never would've imagined this." Her gaze circles around and rests once again on the stack in the back. "Are all of those from before?"

"Yeah, there're some of just my parents, my childhood home, my bike."

"So they're not all so emotional?"

I chuckle and pull her into me. "No. It's just whatever captures me, and I want to recreate."

"Liam?" she says into my shirt.

"Yeah?"

When she draws back, her blue hues meet mine. "Why don't you share these? People would buy these, they're that good. I'm sure Rome would love the one of him and Calista. Your mom would love that one of our moms laughing with coffee mugs in their hands. You should be proud of your talent."

I shake my head. "I'm not ready for that step. I'm not sure I ever will be. I'm sharing this with you because you need to know that when I'm in here, I'm not watching porn or, like you thought, playing with my beetles."

She laughs and her forehead hits my chest. "Okay." I hold her even tighter. "Thank you for sharing."

I bend down and kiss her lips. "Thank you for not freaking out too badly."

"Am I allowed in here?" she asks, biting her lip as though her mind is working overtime.

"Yes. Whenever you want, but I have to warn you, there are some pictures that might be painful to see."

She nods. "Thanks for the disclaimer." The buzzer on her phone goes off. "Time to eat." We're on the brick path outside when she looks over her shoulder. "Maybe you could paint me like in *Titanic*?"

"I'm not sure I have Jack's self-control." I pick her up by her waist and swivel her around so that her legs are wrapped around me. "Want to paint with me tonight?"

Her face pales. "I'm not like that, Liam. I'm not creative."

"You don't have to be. The fifth step is for you to paint whatever you want. Just sit there for an hour or longer. Believe me, it's calming. You could paint a rainbow or a flower or a tree. It doesn't have to be people." Her face twists in an *I'm not sure about that* motion, so I change topics for the time being. "Let's just eat first."

There will be plenty of time for me to convince her of a lot of things.

THIRTY-FOUR

Savannah

After dinner, Liam convinces me to paint with him. Now he has me dressed in an oversized button-down shirt that was his once upon a time.

"I better be the first girl to do this with you." I point at the paint splatters on the shirt.

He bends down and kisses my lips. "I promise."

"Then care to explain how a nice shirt like this got ruined?"

"I came in here and painted without changing my clothes. Had the picture in my mind and didn't want to lose it so..."

I look down at the blue dress shirt, but I can't remember him wearing it. "What was the picture in your head?"

He chuckles. "You trying to catch me in a lie?"

"Just curious." I shrug.

He's setting up my easel with a fresh white canvas, paints, and brushes at the side. This is insane. My picture will look like a five-year-old's. I'm not saying a five-year-old's picture is bad. They're just five. I'm thirty-one. Big difference.

"If you have to know, it was after Brooklyn and Wyatt's reception."

I narrow my eyes. "When you yelled at me?"

He shakes his head. "When you yelled at me, you mean."

He kisses my forehead. I know it's just to appease me, but the man knows how to use his lips to distract me.

I focus on the white canvas as my gut twists and turns. The last thing I want to be doing is this.

"Okay, you're all set. Any specific music you wanna listen to?" He heads over to his stereo, which I missed my first time in here.

I can't stop checking out every painting he's done. He's so talented. I don't understand why he doesn't have a gallery on Main Street. The landscape paintings would fly off the shelves because they capture our small town perfectly.

"Then I'll decide." His thumb presses and slides around his phone. Through the speakers, Lewis Capaldi plays.

"Are you trying to pull sadness *out* of me? And put your shirt on. It's distracting."

He chuckles, sitting down at his own easel. "We could skip the canvas and paint each other and roll around the floor."

"I think I'd do just about anything not to have to paint right now. This is so unfair. What if I put you in front of a computer with an Excel spreadsheet and a P & L statement?"

He laughs and leans to the side of his easel to look at me again. "You forget, I'm a business owner."

I growl and fling a brush at him.

"I'm sure there's something you can make me try that I wouldn't feel comfortable doing."

His words sound good, but he's so easygoing that I know he wouldn't care whether he sucked. I'm not used to sucking at anything because I shy away from anything outside of my comfort zone.

"Just relax and let it come to you."

I sulk on the chair for a bit, hearing his paintbrush swooshing across the canvas.

The song changes. In the pause between songs, he must hear me sighing because he comes over to me, picks up my hand, and puts a paintbrush in it. "Let's start with your favorite color."

"I don't have one."

He sighs. "I already know you do."

I think back to the journal he gave me as he dips my brush into the red. Guiding my hand onto the canvas, he puts a swirly line across it.

"What is that?"

"What's it to you?"

"A swirly line."

"Use your imagination." He leaves me and goes back to his easel.

I stare at the line. "I don't think I'm an imagination kind of person. You use pictures. Can't I use pictures?"

"Maybe I should make you do a paint-by-numbers," he says, not getting up from his stool.

"That would be perfect."

He leans over again, shooting me that look that teeters between annoyance and humor.

"Fine." I blow out a breath. "But I'm not showing you after."

"Okay. You don't have to."

Ugh. Mr. All The Right Answers. I swear.

With my paintbrush on the canvas, I continue the swirly line in a circle to make a flower. Dipping another paintbrush in yellow, I do the center of the flower, then green for leaves and stem.

Once I figured out what I'm going to paint, I do enjoy the process. I continue with another flower, then more green and yellow. The music switches to a more upbeat track, which makes me bounce in my seat as I flick little dots of blue on the canvas for water droplets.

Liam checks me out a few times, but I put my two fingers to my eyes and back at him. "Keep your eyes on your own work, Kelly."

He laughs and his foot taps on the floor to the beat of the music.

A half hour later, I spin around on my stool. That did feel awesome. I got lost in the process of painting and the time flew by. "Done!"

"It's not a race, babe." He's still dipping and stroking, dipping and stroking.

I watch his forearm muscles shift and flex. I've grown used to seeing him without a shirt, but I'm positive I'll always get hot and tingly from looking at him.

"Stop staring," he says without even glancing my way.

"Are you almost done?"

"Almost." He dips his paintbrush again.

I tilt my head back, looking at the ceiling. Jumping off the stool, I head back to the pictures stacked in the corner. The squeak of Liam's stool says he's watching me.

I can't say finding that picture of my mom wasn't like a gut punch by Floyd Mayweather. I've seen pictures of my parents. I pass one every morning when I enter the Bailey Timber Corporation building. My dad's picture is beside my grandfather's in the executive hallway, but I never stop and truly look. I glance, never fixating on it. That's how I've survived these years.

Flipping through the paintings, I smile at some, skip over others—like the one from the funeral—and stop cold at the last one in the stack. It's my parents' wedding.

I shift all the other ones to pull it out. "They were such a beautiful couple."

"Like Ken and Barbie," Liam says from behind me.

I stare at the picture of my parents on their wedding day. We capture this scene every year in the Founder's Day parade.

"The picture is kind of iconic. That's why I had to do it."

I stare at my parents. My mom's in a sleek white dress, and my dad's wearing a suit instead of a tuxedo. "I do look like her."

"Mostly, but you have some of your dad in you too. It's the blonde hair that makes people only see your mom. But you have your dad's nose, and see how his upper lip almost disappears when he smiles? You have that too."

"How would you know? I never smile," I deadpan.

"You smile a lot more than you think."

I place the picture down. "I've always kept their memory tucked into a box, you know? It's too painful to fully remember them."

"I know." He kisses my forehead.

"Show me your painting?" I ask.

"I'll show you mine if you show me yours."

"You're just going to make fun of me."

He tugs me forward. "Never."

We walk over to my easel and stare at the painting for a minute.

"I swear it was a bundle of flowers a moment ago. Did you switch it out as a joke?"

He laughs. "It's good, babe."

He ignores my question, which says he didn't. I just suck at painting. "No, it's not. It looks more like rotten apples."

"It's your first. Give yourself a break." I pick it up to throw it away, but he takes it from my hands. "Nope."

Instead of fighting him—because he'll win anyway—I run over to his picture. Again, I'm in awe. "I'm beautiful."

He laughs, not shy about sharing his work with me. He painted me in his button-down shirt with no pants on. "You are."

I cover my mouth when I register what I said. "I didn't mean it like that. I meant you make me beautiful."

He bends down and kisses my neck. "You've always been beautiful, but I like to think it's me who brings that glow to your cheeks."

I touch my messy bun. "If I'd known you were going to paint me, I'd have done my hair or something."

"This is how I like you." His chest hits my back and his fingers land on the top button of his shirt. "Except without the shirt."

I barely blink before his shirt is open with all buttons intact. "How did you get so good at unbuttoning things?"

"When I was little, my mom had one of those blankets with the snaps, buttons, and Velcro? She said I loved the button one. Who would've guessed it would pay off when I got older?"

He pulls the shirt over my shoulders until it falls into a pile on the floor. His warm hands unclasp my bra, guiding it down my arms until it's on the floor in front of us. Bending, he hooks his fingers into the sides of my panties and slides them down my legs. I step out of them and he tosses them somewhere.

"Remind me to thank your mom the next time I see her."

His lips land on my shoulder, one hand running down my side and the other up my torso. With his body over mine, sheltering me with his bare chest, I never want to leave. Being with Liam, seeing myself through his eyes is enough to bring a fresh set of tears to my eyes.

"Congratulations, you've graduated from Find Yourself University. Your professor would like to give you your reward now."

Goose bumps rise on every inch of my skin as his fingers slide through my folds at the same time he pinches my nipple. As much as I'd love to stay in this position, there's something I've been wanting to do, and there's no better time than now.

"Actually, Professor Kelly, I'd like to give you a thank you gift." I turn and fall to my knees, unbuttoning and unzipping his jeans. Pushing them down his legs, I take his boxer briefs with them and watch how his hard, thick length springs out and strains toward his belly button.

He helps me get him out of his clothes and releases my hair tie so that my hair falls around my shoulders. "Sav," he sighs when my hand wraps around him.

I cut our game of professor and student short, licking up his length and twirling my tongue around the crown. His fingers dive into my hair, twisting the strands. He watches me with a heated gaze that only makes me wetter. I close my mouth over him and pump him at the same time.

"Tell me you watched a YouTube video to be this good?"

I chuckle, my lips still wrapped around him, and stare

up at him, not answering his question because he's not listening anyway. His eyes roll back, and I thank him in my own way for helping me find myself again. I might not be that same nineteen-year-old girl anymore, but I'm enjoying my life again as the woman I am.

His fingers grip my hair harder, so I bob faster, suck harder, and pump tighter. Every moan and groan and growl that falls from his lips spurs me to keep going. The fact that I can get him to where he is right now elates me. He bucks into my mouth, and I moan. He looks so hot from down here. His eyes fly open and I stare at him, not wanting to miss a second of his reaction.

"Sav, I'm going to—"

I keep going, not relenting until he pushes into my mouth and finishes down my throat.

"Fuck," he whispers.

I lick him clean before rising from my knees, and he wastes no time picking me up and taking me over to the stool I was painting on earlier.

"Leg on either side, babe. It's my turn to feast."

This time it's him who falls to his knees.

THIRTY-FIVE

Liam

I've been to Bailey Timber because of this library fundraising gala so often that Carrie keeps my name tag on the corner of her desk now.

I slide it off her desk as I walk by. "Hey, Carrie."

"Mr. Kelly."

I hop into the elevator. Phoenix no longer waits to direct me where to go. Lucky for me, Savannah's fridge didn't come in on time, so she's still living with me until it arrives this weekend. Sunday after the gala dinner, I'll sadly take her back home, but my plan is to spend the night. She doesn't know that yet, but I doubt I'll hear a complaint.

The conference room is empty, so I head down the hall and stop at Samara's small desk.

"You can go in, Liam. She's just finishing something. Dori's running a little late," Samara says.

"Thanks."

I knock, and Savannah waves me in. She's at her desk in

her big office. I can't imagine my entire day being spent in front of a computer.

"Hey, you," she says, sliding her chair out from behind her desk. She presses a button and her blinds draw closed.

"I better be the only guy you've done that for."

"I promise." She rises up on her tiptoes and kisses me.

After working late last night, I crawled into bed with her but didn't get up this morning before she left for work. Shame, because now I see she's wearing her wrap dress again. "Are we trying the two-second trick?"

She laughs. "Not unless we want Grandma Dori to catch us."

I tug on the strand of fabric and find the button. She gasps, but I splay my hand wide and run it up her stomach to cover her breast. The dress falls away from her body as I capture her lips.

"You don't play fair," she mumbles against my lips.

I tweak her nipple, pushing her to the edge of her desk. She follows my non-verbal command and spreads her legs to make room for my hips.

"I never said I did."

Her lips are soft, and I slide my tongue into her mouth to meet hers. Having her in my arms, with my lips and my hands on her, I'm not sure I'll ever tire of this. Nor can I really believe it's happening. It still feels surreal sometimes. My lips cascade down her neck and my hand pulls down the cup of her bra. I'm shocked she hasn't stopped me yet.

"Guess what?" she says, and I look up at her, taking her nipple into my mouth. "We got two contracts, so we're going to be okay. I mean, we have to get more, but this will keep us in the black for a while."

My mouth comes off her tit with a pop and I capture

her lips again. When I draw our kiss to a close, I say, "Congratulations. Let's celebrate."

"Tonight?"

"Yeah, at Terra and Mare. Not to brag, but I know the owner." I wink and her face falls.

"About that..."

My dick deflates just as things were getting good. I step back. "What?"

"Just listen for a second, okay?"

I'm already annoyed. I've given her time, but this is ridiculous. I stand silent, waiting.

"I figure it's only a few days. Let's wait until after the gala. We don't want to overshadow the event. So many questions will come up about us, and the focus should be the charity. Right after—Sunday, if you want—we'll go to dinner and I'll give you the biggest kiss on the mouth right in the middle of the gazebo in the town square."

I blow out a breath. Seeing my reaction to her shitty news, she puts her breast back into her bra and fastens her dress in less time than it took for me to get it open.

I sit on the couch and put my head in my hands. "I can't pretend to be cool with this. I was hoping to go to the gala *with* you. To hold your hand and get your drink. Hell, I'll hold your purse for you. I'm done with this hiding shit."

She rushes over and sits next to me, putting her hand on my thigh. "Me too. You think I don't want the same thing?"

"Truthfully... I don't think you do."

She grips my thigh and presses her lips to my jaw. "I do. I really do. It's just the timing is off. But we're at the finish line."

Finish line being that we can announce our relationship on the same day she moves out of my house. Stellar.

But I nod because what choice do I have? We've gone weeks. I can go a few more days. "Okay, but I expect a quickie in the coatroom."

"Done." She smiles at me and her lips meet mine. This time it's her tongue sliding into my mouth and pushing the physical relationship.

I know my anger is transparent right now, but I can't help but think she's embarrassed to be dating me. If that's the case, what the hell do I do with that?

Her office door opens, and I'm relieved we're actually dressed. Dori and Phoenix stand at the door, staring at us.

Dori beams while Phoenix rolls her eyes. "Heard you two were doing the nasty."

Dori shakes her head. "Don't mind Phoenix. She's in a mood."

"Yeah, because you fired me this morning but gave me two weeks' notice. The two-weeks thing is supposed to be the other way around."

Dori sits in a chair, her overjoyed eyes on Savannah and me. "How about a thank you?"

"You want me to thank you for firing me?" Phoenix puts her feet on the table. "And I'm not getting any drinks today. I read my job description, and it never said anything about waitressing during meetings."

Her indignant behavior pulls a laugh out of me, even in my sour mood.

"The day is almost here, so let's get all our ducks in a row and make sure this event goes off with a bang." Dori's excitement doesn't entice anyone else to slide to the edge of their seat.

I'm pissed, Phoenix is pissed, and Savannah can't stop touching me. It's a welcome change from her usual hands-off approach around her family but I can't help but think it's because she's afraid I'm going to cut off whatever this is between us. I use the word whatever, because if we were in a relationship, I'd be sure that everyone in Lake Starlight knew.

THIRTY-SIX

Savannah

It's finally the night of the charity gala. Since Liam and I couldn't arrive together, I chose to get ready at home instead of at his house. I want to catch his eye from across the room when he sees me in my red dress for the first time. Plus, I had to sneak in his big surprise.

The venue we chose is the Lakeside Grill. It's in Lake Starlight and big enough that we can fit all the tables that sold. I'm organizing the silent auction items while the wait-staff finishes setting the tables and filling water glasses.

"This is so cute. This was our best idea ever," Grandma Dori coos. "*The Cat in the Hat* table is my favorite. Oh, but the *Goodnight Moon* one is adorable too."

I face her as she's walking from table to table. "They turned out great, right?"

"If this doesn't get us enough for the addition, I'll be shocked."

We're both happier now that Bailey Timber has the new contracts we obtained this week.

"I'm partial to *Charlotte's Web* myself. And did you see the dessert tables with each theme? Greta outdid herself."

Grandma Dori shifts her attention to the back wall where the dessert tables are lined up. Each one has a cake to go with the theme, along with bite-sized sweet treats. "She sure did."

Silence fills the room, other than the clinking of silverware. I straighten the pads of paper and make sure there's a pen at every station. I double-check the silent auction for a one-of-a-kind painting by a new Lake Starlight artist and bite my lip while staring at the easel I placed it on. Liam did an amazing job of capturing the town of Lake Starlight—the gazebo is lit up with twinkle lights, and the changing trees surrounding the square have the most vibrant colors. Even down to the miniscule details of each storefront. I question whether I'm doing the right thing, but he won't be upset once he sees how high the bids reach.

"Whoa! It's gorgeous in here," Brooklyn says. Her gold dress and Wyatt's black suit make them look as if they just flew in from New York City. Wyatt bought a table but put it in the name of Brooklyn's company. He could've used the resort, but he said Brooklyn's business needed the advertising more. He's a keeper. "Heard about you and Liam. You cougar, you."

I smile tightly.

She sighs since she knows my body language. "It's a joke. I'm kidding."

"I know." But I hold up my hands to say we're not talking about it here.

"It's a good thing. I'm sure all that anger is good for your sex life."

"Brook." Wyatt shakes his head but slides his arm

around her back. "We said we weren't going to say anything."

"She's my sister. She's secretly dating the town bad boy. Come on."

"We're going to look around. You did a great job." Wyatt whisks an arguing Brooklyn away.

Her remark about my anger throws me off-kilter. I haven't fought with Liam for weeks. Unless you consider this semi-silent toddler treatment he's been giving me since I said we'd be open about our relationship after tonight. But Brooklyn hasn't seen us together lately. All she remembers is how much we nitpicked one another.

I help the manager put up the barriers for the silent auction since I'm going to announce each item and describe it right after dinner.

More guests arrive, and I make the rounds. Austin and Holly look as though they've spray-tanned themselves because no one gets that dark during the summer in Alaska. Rome and Harley already have drinks in their hands by the time I catch them.

"No kids!" They clink their glasses together.

Denver comes with Phoenix, and they sit at the Lifetime Adventures table. Juno and Colton come to represent the veterinarian's office. Kingston got called to a fire, and Sedona isn't coming back from New York for this.

The Baileys in attendance appear to be doing their own thing. The one person I don't spot while greeting and thanking everyone is the man who bought the Smokin' Guns Tattoos table.

I walk over to Rhys, who's sitting at the table with four girls I don't recognize and two guys. The guys work at Smokin' Guns. The girls don't. And why are there four of them? I repeat in my head how much I trust Liam. I just don't like that I'll be at the Bailey Timber Corporation table at the front while he'll be in the back, but I chose this.

"Hey, do you know if Liam is here?" I ask.

One girl turns to me and looks me up and down, but I ignore her.

Rhys bites his lip. "I haven't seen him yet, but he told me to secure *The Cat in the Hat* table." He fidgets with a red-and-blue bowtie left on the table for photo ops.

I nod. "Thanks."

The one girl asks who I am as I walk away, and Rhys tells her I'm the organizer. Great. That doesn't grate on my nerves at all.

As I walk out of the room, Greta stops me. She and a few other smaller businesses went in together to purchase a table. Sweet of them. It tells me my original idea to include more than just the wealthy businesses in this town would've been nice.

"Greta, it all looks great. We're in love with them," I say.

She carries on about the molding of the pigs' figures and how her air conditioning went out and she had to make room in her fridge. I feel horrible for what she had to go through to get it all done, especially with six different themes. I'm grateful, but mid-conversation, Liam appears at the door. I want to give him a small wave, but Rhys raises his hand at him and Liam nods, walking across the room to him.

My gut and heart plummet.

"Are you okay, Savannah?" Greta's hand touches mine.

I plaster on a smile. "Great. I have to cut you short though. I have to make sure everything is set for dinner."

"Of course. Go."

I walk past Liam's table, noticing the girl who appraised me earlier is making Liam the center of her attention. He doesn't stop me, and I don't glance his way because what's the point? Obviously we're going for the we-still-hate-one-another vibe tonight.

The manager tells me that dinner will be served shortly, so I head to the microphone, not feeling as confident as I usually do. I purposely ignore the back left side of the room and clear my throat.

"Excuse me," I say into the microphone. "If you could all find your seats, dinner is about to be served."

Rome sits with Denver and Phoenix because Terra and Mare couldn't afford a table and Denver said Chip and Nancy couldn't come. Bailey Timber has two tables with employees seated at them, except for Austin and Holly since Austin sits on the board he sits with us.

Once everyone sits, Grandma Dori gives me a thumbs-up. She's been doing that since I was twenty and she made me take over these thank you speeches at all the charity functions.

"On behalf of Bailey Timber and the Lake Starlight Library, we'd like to thank all of you for joining us tonight. The extension for the library..." I continue my speech, not having the nerve to look at Liam's table. "After dinner, I'll fill everyone in on the silent auction prizes. The businesses have been very generous this year."

When I finish, Holly's eagerly tapping the chair next to her, but I signal that I'll be right there. I head toward the bathroom but decide to get some fresh air instead to calm my nerves. The valet guy glances at me as I stand by the side of the brick building, inhaling and closing my eyes.

"Great speech." Liam slow-claps while he walks toward me.

"Hi."

"Hi." He tucks his hands into his pockets and stands

feet away from me. God, I miss him. Why did I get ready at my house? His gaze takes me in from head to toe. "You look breathtaking."

I could say the same about him. He's wearing a black suit, white shirt, and black tie. His hair is gelled, and the tattoos sneaking out from under his cuffs and collar only increase his sex appeal.

"Are we okay?" I signal between us, purposely not acting like a jealous girlfriend by asking about the girl at his table.

He shrugs. "Yeah."

"Then why are you all the way over there?" My voice is shallow, and I hate it.

"I thought we were still in the closet. Don't want to tip anyone off, right?" His malicious tone says we're having a fight but not admitting it. Passive-aggressiveness at its finest.

"All right then. I can see you're still mad." I walk away, but he performs his signature move by grasping my elbow. The valet guy steps forward and Liam digs into his pocket then hands him some money. "Go find a car to attend to."

The kid's fearful eyes say he'd go jump off the pier as long as Liam doesn't kick his ass. Unsurprisingly, he runs off.

"Way to intimidate a kid," I grumble.

"I just gave him twenty bucks, pretty sure he's good." He lets go of my arm. "I'm playing by your rules, so what exactly is your problem?"

"Nothing. It's just... you're mad. I know you are."

He blows out a breath. "I'm annoyed. I'm not going to lie and pretend I'm not."

I touch his tie, but he makes no move to touch me back. It stings. "After tonight, we're done hiding."

"Until something else comes up."

"No." I tug on his tie. "Nothing will. I promise. We're alone right now. Are we going to keep fighting?"

"We're not fighting."

I tug on his tie once more. "Kiss me."

He smirks. "Because you want it so bad, I kind of wanna punish you and say no."

"But?"

His hand comes out of his pocket, his arms wrap around my waist, and he lifts me off the ground. "I have a hard time saying no to you."

I lower my lips to his, and finally my world rights itself. The melancholy feeling overtaking me leaves with a swipe of Liam's tongue against mine.

He slowly sets me down and kisses me one last time. "We're leaving early."

"No complaints from me."

I catch the valet peeking out from behind the bushes.

I push Liam toward the door. "You go first."

He inhales a deep breath but smacks my ass and walks through the entrance. I wait a few minutes then return to the room where everyone is already eating. I slide into my chair. Holly, being too observant for her own good, flutters her eyelashes at me.

I ignore her and eat two bites of my salad. We talk about the overly hot summer, and I ask her about the honeymoon, though my gaze keeps wandering to Liam's table. His eyes always seem to be on me too. Did I make a mistake by not coming out beforehand?

Midway through dinner, Grandma Dori clears her throat. "Savannah, time to tell everyone about the auction items."

"Let her eat," Austin says.

"We're the hosts, and there are certain expectations."

Austin says nothing but gives me the classic *I'm sorry* look.

I wipe my mouth and place my napkin on my chair, grabbing my list of items to announce.

When I stand at the microphone, I wave. "Hello everyone. Me again."

This time, I do look at Liam. He's smiling brightly at me, and I smile back. My dinner isn't sitting well in my stomach from being so nervous about outing Liam, but I'm so proud of him. He's going to see how well his paintings are received by everyone, then he'll be able to live a free life just like he wants me to.

"In a few minutes, these barriers will be removed for you to cast your silent bids and try to win an array of generous donations. To start, we have a survival excursion from Lifetime Adventures. A six-tier cake from Sweet Suga Things. There's a toolbox filled with every tool man's dream, donated by Hammer Time. Terra and Mare has donated a six-course chef's table meal. And Lard Have Mercy has donated a two-hundred-fifty dollar gift certificate. And our bigger prizes include a Harley-Davidson motorcycle, and an all-inclusive trip to New York City on a private jet."

Everyone 'ohhs' and 'ahhs.' Thank you, Wyatt Whitmore. Brooklyn smiles at her husband.

"But there's one item I want to talk about in particular, and I'm going to unveil this one first." I take the microphone off the pole, my gaze glued to Liam, who tilts his head as though he wonders what I'm talking about. I can't stop smiling because I'm so happy to share his talent with everyone. I move the barrier and take the cloth off Liam's painting. "This is an original piece of art by a local artist. It features the gazebo in fall with a lot of the businesses in downtown."

"Gorgeous," Grandma Dori says.

There's another course of 'ohhs' and 'ahhs'.

"I see Terra and Mare." Harley nudges Rome.

"And there's the diner on the corner. Is that Karen inside?" someone else points out.

"Who did it?" Holly asks, leaning forward.

"You might be surprised to hear that it's our very own Liam Kelly." I put my hand out toward his table.

Everyone turns around, but my eyes land on a vacant chair.

"You got mad talent, dude..." Denver's words fade when everyone searches for Liam.

But he's gone.

THIRTY-SEVEN

Savannah

"I'll be right back. Please everyone bid away and enjoy the dessert." When I toss the microphone on the table, its loud screech echoes through the room.

I get outside and find Liam already halfway to his car.

"Liam!" I call, but he keeps walking. "Liam!" When I run after him, his shoulders slump but he stops. "Where are you going? Everyone loves it!"

"You overstepped this time, Savannah."

I stumble back as if he slapped me, but he turns his back to me and stalks toward his car.

Oh hell no, we are clearing the air now.

Liam reaches his car but turns around. "What gave you the right? That was my business."

"Because you shouldn't hide it. I bet it's one of the biggest purchases tonight. If you would've stayed and heard everyone, you'd see that. They loved it."

"It's not theirs to love."

"I thought you'd be happy. Now you don't have to feel

like you have to keep your work all cooped up in the barn. You can share your talent with people."

He shoves his hands into his pockets and looks toward the lake for a moment before fixing his gaze on me. I've never seen this expression on his face before. Through all the fights and disagreements he's had with me and others in town, never has he looked so raging mad. "So that's why."

I shake my head, not following. "Why what?"

We're sandwiched between two cars and his volume continues to escalate. "Why you wanted to wait until tonight. Wanted to tell the town, 'Look, he's not some schmuck who just gives people tats, he's a painter.' You probably want me to close down Smokin' Guns and open some gallery on Main Street. Would I be good enough for you then?"

What the hell is he talking about? "No, I told you why. I didn't want our relationship to overshadow the fundraiser. I was already second-guessing that decision during dinner. I missed you." I blow out a breath. "I showed that painting because I wanted to do the same for you that you did for me." I run my hands down my body as if he could outwardly see how different I am. "I laugh now, Liam. I'm happy, and it's because of you. I wanted you to feel how amazing I do." I step forward, pleading with him. "I wanted you to be open about your painting because it would make you whole."

"I was whole." He draws away from me, his stance rigid. "I'm not like you. I don't give a shit what people think of me. Was it hard sharing that with you? Hell yes! Because there are pictures I've painted that would affect you. But I don't want to share my art with everyone. It's mine and mine only." He points at himself.

Tears prick my eyes, but I blink them back. "I was trying to help."

He blows out a breath and runs a hand down the back of his neck. "Just admit it. I'm a big boy. I can take it. But I'm worth more than being your dirty little secret, your plaything, and because I fucking love you, I let you string me along, thinking we were on our way somewhere, but you want a suit. You want a guy who's flashy and shows off his money. News flash, I'm never gonna be that guy."

"I don't want that. Why do you think that?"

A hollow laugh escapes him. "Look what you did tonight. 'Oh, we can't tell anyone because of the family business. Oh, not yet, Liam, we don't want to overshadow the fundraiser.' You conveniently left out the part where you decided to share my biggest secret with the town, so they'll see me as a person worthy of a person like you. Well, I'm out of this ridiculous game you're playing."

"Why aren't you listening to me?" I grab his arm, but he yanks it out of my grip, going for the handle of his car door.

"Rethink these past weeks. I've done everything to get you to love yourself. To find peace with who you are and discover who you want to be moving forward, not who those people want you to be. You're both the strongest and weakest person I know. And I loved you for every bad and good quality you possess, but that's not enough for you." He opens his car door, but I stand in front so he can't shut it. "Let me go."

"No! You're not listening to me."

His eyes lock with mine. "You want to know what's funny? I just told you I loved you—twice—and you never even addressed it. You only hear yourself and never anyone else."

I'm stunned speechless. He told me he loved me? Surely I would've stopped in my tracks. No way he did.

His large palm lands on my hip. He slides me out of the way, gets in, and shuts his car door. Before I can go over his words in my head, his taillights are the only thing left of him.

THIRTY-EIGHT

Savannah

I head back inside, smile through my pain, and put on the happy face I'm expected to. I lie and tell anyone who cares that Liam wasn't feeling well. Then I bid an exorbitant amount of money on his painting under a different name.

As the evening draws on and my sporadic calls to Liam go unanswered, my skin itches. All the conversations fade into background noise. Scanning the room, my gaze lands on Brooklyn and Wyatt strolling from table to table of the silent auction. I watch his hand rest on the small of her back, dangerously close to her ass but not causing a scene, and the ease with which my sister follows his lead. She's so comfortable with him and with showing affection, regardless of anyone's eyes on her. She laughs and he leans forward, his lips landing on her neck. They share a look to say, 'if we were alone.'

I sip my wine and sit at the table alone, my mind

wandering to when Denver was in the room and Liam snuck touches or kisses. Was what Liam said right? Maybe I am uncomfortable with people seeing me doing anything other than dictating what needs to happen. But it has nothing to do with Liam himself. Sure, it's a little weird to date someone younger than me, but he seems more mature at times.

Picking up my phone, I bury my head in the land of Instagram, scrolling through all the pictures of everyone attending tonight. Harley and Rome outside by the lake, all dressed up, the sun at their backs. Austin and Holly at the table with champagne glasses in their hands. There's even one of Denver and Phoenix at the bar, saying cheers to single life.

Someone slides into the seat next to me, and I turn off Instagram and put my phone face-down on the table. Turning to my side, I find Grandma Dori.

"Do you need something?" I ask, because usually at these events, she's busy bossing me around and not really up for conversation.

"No. Just wondering how the night is going?" She's looking around the room and not at me.

"Fine."

"Except for Liam walking out?"

"I don't want to get into this. Your meddling antics aren't working on me."

She laughs. "Oh, you're so smart, but you do realize the reason you're running a movie reel in your head right now is because of my meddling. Imagine if you hadn't moved in with Liam. Or didn't have to do the charity event planning."

I think about it, and she's wrong. Those reasons aren't why I'm sitting here with an ache the size of the Pacific in my heart. It's the bet we made. How he made me feel as though there isn't anything wrong with me, except that maybe I lost myself for a while.

"Excuse me," the manager of the Lakeside Grill interrupts. "Can we chat, Miss Bailey?"

I've been called Miss Bailey my entire life, but this time, it sounds like nails on a chalkboard.

"I'll be back," I say to Dori and follow the manager to his office to finalize all the details.

An hour later, I'm leaving the event when Brooklyn pushes off the wall.

"Hey sis," she says, putting her arm through mine. "Let's go for a walk."

"I want to go home."

"Humor me. Wyatt and I have been so busy with the house, he's driving me crazy. I need some girl time."

She's lying through her teeth, but we'll pretend she can fool me.

"Okay."

She leans her head on my shoulder. "Thanks."

Leading me down the sidewalk, she rounds the bend. I should've known who would be here. Every one of my siblings is sitting on Adirondack chairs, shooting the shit. The only people missing are Holly, Wyatt, and Harley. Part of me wonders if they're seeking out Liam.

"Great event, Sav!" Denver holds up a bottle of wine and downs a gulp before handing the bottle to Rome.

"Thanks."

Austin pats the chair next to him. I slide into it as graciously as I can in an evening gown.

"Liam's got some skills, huh?" Phoenix says. "It raised the most money, behind the Harley."

"Where's Grandma Dori?" I ask. Usually she'd be the first one to be here.

"I sent her home. This is for us to handle." Austin looks at me.

Tears build so fast, I can't pretend they aren't there.

"Aw, Sav." Austin pulls me into a hug.

Sobs erupt out of me. "I was trying to get him to be happy. He made me so happy and now he's mad."

"Slow down." Austin runs his hand over my back.

Brooklyn and Juno each take a spot at my feet, hovering at my knees.

"It's okay," Brooklyn says.

"It's Liam, he doesn't stay mad," Juno says.

"I'll beat his ass if he doesn't forgive you," Denver says.

We all take a time out from "cheer up Savannah" to give him a look that says he can try, but it's probably not gonna happen. I lean back in the chair and swipe at the tears on my cheeks.

"You like him?" Rome asks. "I mean, Denver told us you guys were sleeping with each other, but you like him, right?"

I wipe a tear and nod. "I do."

"You've changed so much since you got together," Denver says. "I barely recognize you anymore."

Austin shoots me a soft smile. I can tell he thinks I should be honest with my family.

"Liam and I did this stupid thing about finding the real Savannah Bailey. The one I was before the accident."

They all go quiet, and no one makes direct eye contact with one another. The slow waves on the lake make the only noise.

"What do you mean?" Juno asks.

Austin sits up and clears his throat. He'd be happy to

take this one, explain it to the siblings who didn't have to take on the responsibilities we did after our parents died, but I put my hand on his knee to stop him.

"I've lost myself over the years. Having to take over Bailey Timber so young changed me."

They look at each other as though they need someone to fill in the blanks. Austin and I took the weight so they wouldn't have to bear it, and I wouldn't have it any other way, but I can't expect them to understand when they still got to fulfill whatever dream they wanted. Yeah, we all lost our parents and that changed us, but Austin and I are the ones who agreed to take on the roles of pseudo mom and dad.

"Guys, Savannah and I, we wouldn't change our decision," Austin says. "When Mom and Dad died, we talked and made the plan. I think I speak for both of us when I say that we're happy it all worked out, and we're thrilled you all got to live your lives, but both of us did lose ourselves a little because of it. Savannah more than me because she's the face of Bailey Timber. She's the one employees look to as their leader. With that role comes responsibility and a presence she has to uphold."

"Wait. What does this have to do with Liam and you?" Denver asks.

Rome, Austin, and Brooklyn give me a soft smile. They understand that when you get into a relationship, you find out things about yourself. The good and the bad.

"I'm just explaining what we did." I wave it off and look at Austin to ask him to keep that part out of it. "Liam thinks I don't want anyone to know about us because he's a tattoo artist and I want a businessman. And he keeps referencing me wanting a suit. I have no clue why."

Denver and Rome look at one another. I catch their

matching expressions that say, 'Do we say something or keep this to ourselves?'

"What?" I point at them.

They draw back, seeming shocked that I saw it. Just like when they got in trouble when they were little, they try to read each other's minds as to what story to give.

"Do you guys know something?" Austin asks.

Denver shakes his head, but Rome opens his mouth, shutting it immediately.

"Come on, you guys. Tell me?"

Rome pleads with Denver non-verbally. Sometimes I find their ability to have a complete conversation with only their eyes and mannerisms scary.

"I think Liam is self-conscious," Rome says as if it's only his opinion.

"Why? All the women want him in this town," Phoenix adds her unhelpful two cents.

"Not all," Austin chimes in.

"Yeah, I'm sure Holly's repulsed by him." Phoenix rolls her eyes and props her feet on the small footstool. Why is that girl always so relaxed?

"Everyone loves him," Juno adds.

"This event wouldn't have been a success without him," I add.

Rome looks at Denver again then turns to us. "Exactly. Why do you think that is? He wants this town to like him, and I never really understood it until just now."

"What?"

Denver shakes his head like *don't share anymore, we're betraying our friend*, but thankfully Rome disagrees.

"We always knew he had something for you, Sav. If you were in the house when we were younger, he'd be like, 'Let's go bother your sister,' or 'Let's look for her diary.'"

I swear he told me it wasn't his idea. Hmm.

"When you went to college and he started dating Rachel, we figured it was done, but after Mom and Dad's accident and you returned, he dumped her right away. We thought..." He looks at Denver. "They were really serious. We were shocked when he told us." Rome shrugs. "It just always seemed like he was trying to get you to notice him, whether it was in a good light or a bad one, with you two bickering."

"Oh, my God." Juno covers her mouth, and Denver nods as if she's figured it out.

Since when can she speak twin telepathy?

"What Rome's trying to say is that he's been trying to be an upstanding citizen of Lake Starlight, so he'd be good enough for *you*." Phoenix stops scrolling on her phone and looks at me as though I'm stupid.

"But I..."

Brooklyn and Austin sigh because I've been the most honest with them.

I say, "I mean, yeah, the age thing scared me. Him being your best friend." I signal to Rome and Denver. "But I never thought he wasn't good enough for me."

"I think you guys have to have a long heart-to-heart," Rome says.

I bolt to my feet as fast as my dress will allow. "I need to find him. Where would he go?"

Rome looks at Denver and they both shrug.

"Lucky's?" I say.

"Honestly, I don't have a clue anymore. You'd probably know before us now." Rome looks at his twin.

Denver stands. "Come on. I'll take you to all his favs." He shakes his head. "I can't believe you're in love with Liam."

"I never said love," I say on the way to his truck.

He opens the door for me, and I climb in. "You didn't have to."

THIRTY-NINE

Liam

Poppy's is the only place no one would think to find me. My phone rings with calls and texts messages, but I'm done with Savannah Bailey. She thinks I'm not worthy of her. Maybe it's time for me to show her exactly how unworthy of her I am. She does love to be right. But that's not my style.

All I wanted was somewhere to be able to gather my thoughts but sitting at a table in the back with a water isn't allowing me to blend in well. The waitresses have side-glanced me, probably wondering why I'm not drinking. Why I'm in a suit.

This is the kind of place Savannah sees me at, right? Who she thinks I am? That I'm like Slim and his crew. A deviant to society. I'm exhausted and I've tried everything with this woman only to still get shot down.

Selling my painting because she thinks it will free me?

I hate that she thought there was ever something wrong with herself. That she needed me to make up a stupid bet and do bullshit things. I told her from the beginning that pieces of the old her were there, she just had to let them out.

I figured at the end of five weeks when she said I'd failed, I'd have to show her what was in the barn, but for five weeks, I would've had her attention. That was my only goal. Maybe it was selfish and bastardly. Shit, maybe I'm not good enough for her. I practically manipulated her for a month.

"Hey, stranger." The body belonging to the voice slides into the chair next to me.

I know the voice and I down the rest of my water, crushing the bottle while I stand.

"Where are you going?" she asks.

"Leaving," I tell Nina.

She leans back, wearing an outfit similar to what Savannah had on when we were here except Nina's skirt is black leather instead of Catholic school girl plaid. She twirls her hair around her finger. "Going back to your sugar momma?"

"Slim okay with you talking to me?" I ignore her comment about Savannah. How she figured out who Savannah is doesn't surprise me. Nina's a stalker by trade. She legit gets hired to find people.

"We broke up."

I nod. "Good luck. I gotta go."

"Hey, Liam?" she calls after me, and I stop but don't turn around. "You'll never be able to keep her. Girls like that might think they want the bad boy, but that's who they fuck, not who they marry."

I close my eyes. Her words hit a little too close to the reason I'm at Poppy's tonight. But knowing better than to engage with Nina, I walk out of Poppy's and get into my car. My phone vibrates in the glove compartment, but I ignore it, starting the engine.

Driving has always cleared my head. After my parents left me to move to Florida the first chance they got after I graduated high school, I drove down to Seattle just to escape.

After the Baileys passed away, my mom wasn't mentally stable. One day she'd be happy, then the next, she'd cry uncontrollably. She could barely stand to be around the Bailey kids, so the majority of my time was spent over at Rome and Denver's.

So now when I feel the need to escape, I pull onto the interstate and drive. Put Savannah behind me. Though not having my passport puts me at a disadvantage.

I head to Glenwall and Sunrise Bay and drive around the towns. They're not half as nice as Lake Starlight. Savannah's face when she finally registered that I'd said I loved her occupies most of my thoughts. Her shock and awe. How did she not know? I've been wearing my heart all over my tattoo sleeves these past weeks.

The night replays in my head. I saw her when I arrived, and I purposely gave her the cold shoulder because I was hurt she didn't want to announce we were seeing each other. Maybe I saw her as more of a prize than I'd like to think.

I shake my head. No. That wasn't it. I just wanted everyone to know.

The devil sits on my shoulder and replays my words back differently and with a sneer. *You wanted everyone to know you were good enough. That she saw value in you.*

Fuck, where did that come from? I did not create this entire thing in my head. She was ashamed of me.

The angel appears again. *Why would she run after you for any witnesses to see?*

Shit. That's a good point. But no one came. At least not that I saw. How would I have seen though when she was my sole focus by the cars?

Admit it, it's you who thinks you're not good enough for her.

I yank the steering wheel and do a U-turn in the middle of the interstate. The one truck on the road honks.

Speeding, I drive back into Lake Starlight, but am greeted with sirens and flashing lights.

Fuck. As I pull over, I hit the steering wheel with my fist. I wait for Sheriff Miller to walk up to my car. He knows it's me. We're way too familiar with one another.

"Liam Kelly!"

Oh shit. It's not Sheriff Miller. I mean, I'm sure he's in the car. And I think he needs a lecture when it comes to this woman.

"Dori," I say. The lights from Sheriff Miller's squad car shine through her thin blue hair. "Doing some meet-and-greets tonight?"

"I'm not in the mood for your jokes tonight. Unlock your doors." She rounds the hood of my car and waves back to Sheriff Miller.

I unlock the door, and she slides into my car before putting on her seatbelt. "Am I giving you a ride home?"

"You're giving me a ride to Savannah's so you two can kiss and make up."

After Sheriff Miller honks and drives past, I pull out into traffic. "I was just on my way."

"You were?"

The surprise in her tone makes me smile. "What? Upset that you can't talk me into it?"

I know her MO. She's the one who talks sense into her grandchildren when they've made a mistake. She meddles in all their love affairs, and she seems to be on some quest to get all her grandkids married. That includes Savannah and me.

She pouts. "A little."

"Shouldn't you be talking to Savannah?"

"You're my grandson too, and I think you need to hear what I'm going to say more than Savannah. I left her in capable hands though."

Austin, I presume. "You don't have to lecture me. I'm on my way to her. I know I misconstrued the entire thing."

"You really didn't."

Say what?

We get stopped at a light. Sheriff Miller turns on his lights and siren to run it. Nice.

"What?" I ask.

"I want you to know, you're a Bailey. Maybe not by blood, but I've always thought of you as my grandchild. Which makes it slightly incest with you and Savannah."

"Um. No, no it doesn't."

"Kind of," she says matter-of-factly.

"No. Not at all."

She shrugs. "You loved Tim and Beth like parents. Didn't you?"

"Yeah, but that doesn't make Savannah my sister."

She laughs. "I meant that you lost them too."

I say nothing until I'm five minutes away from Savannah's. "I can drop you off at Northern Lights."

She shoos me with her hand. "I like to watch the making up."

"No offense, Dori, but that sounds creepy."

She laughs. "Not the sexy-time make up. Just when you guys finally get your heads out of your asses make up."

"My head is out of my ass."

"So we're good, you're saying? You want to hear a story about Mr. Bailey and me? I was a poor girl and Mr. Bailey's family had a lot of money. I never would have dreamed he'd love me—"

"Yeah, thanks and all, but I'm good. You can save your wisdom for the next Bailey."

She slouches.

In a moment of weakness, and because I owe her a lot—Savannah never would have moved in with me if not for Dori pushing her—I say, "Actually, I'd love to hear it."

"Really?" She doesn't wait for me to agree before she starts out about her ice skating on the pond where the elementary school is now. She goes off on a couple tangents about Mr. Bailey being a fisherman, but she felt like she wasn't what Mr. Bailey's parents would have hoped for because she didn't come from much.

I get what she's saying, but as egotistical as it sounds, I think her son and daughter-in-law would have liked me being with Savannah. It's me who has to believe I'm good enough for her.

We arrive at Savannah's, and it's dark.

"No one's home," I say.

"She's probably up in her room." Dori digs through her purse and holds up a keychain with a bunch of keys. "I have a key."

"What are all those keys for?" We climb out of my car and walk up the path to the front door.

"All the houses, but that's a little secret between you and me."

"As long as my key isn't on that ring, your secret is safe."

She mocks offense. "Sure, let's pretend it's not."

For some reason, it warms my heart that she actually might, but I'll still be changing my locks come tomorrow.

We enter the house, and it's quiet and dark.

"They did a great job. She practically redecorated it herself," I say as we enter.

I haven't been here in a few weeks, but my vision is only to find her, so I walk around, looking in rooms, climbing the stairs to check bedrooms. I lose track of Dori at some point. I'm in the master bathroom when Dori's scream rings out.

I run down the stairs, paranoid because she's screaming, and follow the glow of a light to find her in a doorway.

"You found her?" I ask.

"No, but look." She steps back, and I smile at the same orange, yellow, and green floral wallpaper that Austin and Holly tore out of the family house. "Why would she put that in here? It doesn't go with her gray-and-blue pallet."

I put my arm around Dori's shoulders. "Because she wants to remember her childhood."

Dori seems confused, but I'm not.

"Let me drive you back home. I'll find her on my own," I say.

"Thanks, Liam."

She locks up Savannah's house and is quiet for most of the ride to Northern Lights. "You're a good egg."

I chuckle. "Thanks?"

"Like when you crack one open and you get double yolk. That kind of an egg."

I nod a few times. "Thanks, Dori."

She pats my cheek. "Now go get my granddaughter."

"That's the plan."

She gets out of the car, and I watch her go through the

front door, the night person approaching her. They'll make sure she gets home.

After pulling my phone from my glove compartment, I run through my texts, ignoring all the ones from anyone but Savannah. She's messaged me a million times but never said where she is. I'm fairly sure I know where she is though.

Ten minutes later—thankful that the Northern Lights residents are fast asleep and I wasn't stuck behind any slow drivers—I pull down my driveway and am slightly disappointed when I don't see her SUV. Climbing out of my car, I decide to go in, grab a water, and change my clothes, then I'll go to every Bailey house to find her.

I put the key in my lock and open the door, finding a shadow in the dark.

"Are you here to murder me?" I ask.

The light flicks on. "That depends. Are you going to hear me out this time?"

FORTY

Savannah

"I'm here to listen. Denver home?"

Liam looks horrible. His jacket's long gone, his tie in his hand.

"No. We looked everywhere for you, and I decided to wait here. You're lucky you're alone." I can't lie and say I wasn't worried he'd be drunk with some girl in his arms when he stumbled in. Maybe I've watched way too many movies.

"I almost wasn't."

I narrow my eyes at him. "Nice."

"No." He throws his keys on his table. "Dori. She was riding with the sheriff when they pulled me over. We were at your house looking for you. Nice wallpaper by the way."

I smile. He might be the only person who appreciates that wallpaper, and it took me way too long to realize it's because he misses my parents too. He's more to my family than just my brothers' best friend. "I have an extra roll if you want it."

"That depends." He sits on the far side of the couch from me. I wish he'd sat beside me.

"On what?"

"Whose house are we moving into?"

I laugh. I wish it was as easy as brushing our spat under the rug, but I need him to be certain of my feelings. "Maybe we can talk first?"

He releases a breath, but his eyes stay steady with mine. "I'm sorry. I overreacted."

I climb over to him on my knees. "No, you didn't. I shouldn't have done what I did, and you wouldn't have drawn the conclusion that I was doing it to try and make you something you aren't if I hadn't kept insisting our relationship be kept a secret. It was all so stupid to keep waiting. In my head, I just thought..." I stop because I was trying to make everyone happy rather than making the most important person in my life happy. How shitty is that?

"First of all, get up." He pats his lap, which I'm really hoping means this isn't a break-up conversation but a make-up conversation. I want it to be, but I'd never seen him so mad.

I climb into his lap and wrap my arms around his neck.

"I've been a selfish prick. I have to admit something before we even get into all that 'I'm not good enough' stuff. I tricked you into thinking I could pull out an old version of yourself just so I could spend five weeks with you."

I smile. "It helped. I'm cured."

"I think you just allowed yourself to come out."

I straddle his legs because I need to look into his eyes so he believes me. "I had a lot of time to think in the dark because you must have been driving around all of Alaska before returning home. But I think the only reason I was happier was because you gave me a safe place to be myself.

Sure, the bet was like permission to show sides of myself I had kept hidden for way too long. When we were within these walls, I felt safe and secure that I wouldn't be judged. That's because of you." I point at his chest. "I think when you wanted to come out, I was scared. Scared that I'd disappoint you because when I walk around Lake Starlight, sometimes I feel like there's this huge microscope above me and everyone's examining everything I do."

His face softens. "You can't live like that."

"I know. I know that now. When you drove off and I thought I'd lost you, I didn't think of anything but how to get you back. It's then that I realized the entire world wouldn't fall apart if I started living for myself rather than everyone else."

He smiles and leans forward, but I put my finger to his lips, and he shoots me a look to say touché. How many times has he done that exact move to me?

"I have more fear I want to put out there so you can refute it," I say.

"Yeah?"

"I was scared you'd hurt me, but I know now you won't. Someone who does what you did—take time to meditate and research ways to help someone find themselves again—isn't going to disappoint me. You're in this for the long haul, and I'm sorry for doubting you."

He grips the sides of my head. "I feel the same. I'm sorry for doubting you. I should never have thought you were embarrassed of me. I guess I have to work on myself a little bit too."

"I think it'll help if we show one another how much the other means to us."

"Can I show you right now?" He leans forward, but I put my finger to his lips again.

"Hold on one second."

I grab my cell phone from the table. Terra and Mare isn't open, but I have to do this before I let him carry me upstairs and make us both forget this fight.

"Sav?" Rome answers groggily.

"I need a reservation tomorrow, by the window, for two."

"Go to hell. You just woke Dion." Crying rings out through the receiver as Harley groans.

"Thank you. See you tomorrow at six-thirty."

"Dumbass, we're closed on Sunday nights." *Click*. The line dies.

Liam laughs and pulls me into him. "It's the effort that counts. A Sunday hand-in-hand stroll down Main Street is enough for me."

He leans forward, and when I put my finger to his lips again, he growls.

"Just one more thing."

"Sav..." He's losing patience and I kind of like it.

"I love you, Liam Kelly."

He smiles and locks my hands behind my back, capturing my lips in a belly-dancing, heartbeat-pounding, lady-parts-having-a-party kiss.

I lean back. "Don't you have anything to say?"

That classic smirk that only Liam can pull off lights up my insides. "You forget so soon? I said it first."

I stand to get off him, but in one move he stands, picking me up and holding me. "No running away."

I press my lips to his. "Oh, you're stuck with me."

"About time you realized."

He locks the door, turns off the lights, and carries me upstairs, where we spend the next two days wrapped in his navy sheets.

Well… except for the Sunday hand-in-hand stroll down Main Street.

Surprisingly, no one looked horrified as we bought donuts from Sweet Suga Things, coffee from Brewed Awakenings, and pie from Lard Have Mercy. We even sat on a park bench in the square while he read the paper and I ate the donuts. The world did not fall apart, and no one said anything.

That's not true. Rome opened the window of his apartment and screamed for us to get a room when we started making out. We quickly figured out we might not be ready for the outside world just yet. There are still more erogenous zones to find and sexual positions to discover, after all.

EPILOGUE

Savannah

Six months later

I'm setting out neon slitted sunglasses, plastic bracelets, and fingerless fishnet gloves on the kitchen island when the door opens and whoosh of cold air runs up my short jean skirt. These hot pink tights are not keeping me warm.

"Hey, babe," Liam says, hanging up his coat and toeing out of his boots. "It's getting bad, maybe we should reschedule this." As usual, he comes up behind me, wrapping his cold arms around my waist and putting his freezing nose in the crook of my neck.

"You're lucky I love you." I lean my head to the side to kiss him. "And it's Alaska. The majority of my family owns trucks. They can make it here."

"If you say so." He rests his chin on my shoulder. "Where's my mullet?"

"On the bed. Along with your mesh tank top and cut-off jean shorts."

"Thanks." He kisses my cheek.

"I still think you should've taken my advice and gone with the George Michael lookalike."

He scoffs, stealing a chip and popping it into his mouth. "My outfit is the best."

"I wouldn't say it screams eighties."

"Good thing we're not one of those couples where you pick out my clothes," he says.

I arrange all food from Wok For U and the rest of the goodies, because after a full week at Bailey Timber, I wasn't going to cook. Plus, it's supposed to be junk food with eighties movies. Mom was always so specific on that part.

My eyes focus on the wall in front of me. The painting of my mom and Liam's mom laughing uncontrollably is there for anyone to see. Liam's graciously let go of some paintings. He gave Rome the one of Calista, and Austin and Holly got the one of their wedding. And he gave the town library the one of Lake Starlight. That was after a lot of apologizing on my part and a lot of casual conversations where I brought up what a nice thing it would be to do.

"Hey, did you stop at the store like I asked?"

He stops on the staircase, and even with his back turned to me, I know he's swearing up a storm right now. "I forgot. The weather distracted me and I—"

"Fine. I should be good until the morning, but I guess you're not sleeping in."

He groans. He acts as if picking up tampons is the worst thing ever. Never did I imagine a guy like Liam would have a problem with it. He doesn't ever care what anyone thinks about him, except me. Eventually he usually caves, so I'm not sure if the weather was an excuse or not.

He heads upstairs and I finish getting everything ready.

We moved into Liam's house. It just made more sense to live here since Liam has a bigger house and it's out of town a little, giving us the privacy we prefer. I graciously gave mine to Phoenix and Denver. They're supposed to pay me rent, but so far, I'm O for five in months I've received it. And I gave them the first month free.

I hear engines outside. A knock sounds and then the doorbell and then a knock again.

"I'm coming."

I open the front door, and six of my family members trample in, complaining about how cold it is.

"You might be having a lot of guests spend the night," Harley says, shedding her coat and handing it to me.

"I'll take everything upstairs," Holly says. "Denver's old room, right?"

"Thanks, Holly."

She collects the coats and purses before walking upstairs. A second later, she shrieks. "Liam! Is that eighties?"

"No, it's not," I yell up the stairs.

"It is," I hear Liam say.

"Maybe lose the cut-off shorts. I'm with you on the mullet and mesh tank top though." Holly always finds something nice to say. Probably how she handles being a principal.

"What's to eat? I'm starving." Rome heads toward the kitchen.

Liam appears at the bottom of the stairs as the door-knocking starts again. "I'll just stand here until everyone comes."

"Good idea." I kiss his cheek.

He opens the door, and Grandma Dori and Ethel come in. In order for me to stop the knitting classes, I had to agree to let Ethel join our eighties theme parties where we eat junk food and watch movies all night. Plus, she's a decent driver and it keeps Grandma off the road.

"Love the Sophia lookalike!" I say.

Ethel straightens her glasses and pushes up her already white hair, the spitting image of Sophia from *Golden Girls*.

"Dori, are you supposed to be Blanche?" Harley asks, noticing Grandma Dori's low-cut silk pajama set with jewelry and a lot of makeup.

"That's a lot of skin," Brooklyn says.

"Maybe too much skin," Austin comments.

Liam doesn't so much as shut the door before Phoenix, Juno, and Colton arrive.

"Kingston's right behind us," Phoenix says.

"Where's Denver?" I ask, slapping Austin's hands when he tries to pick up a piece of orange chicken.

"Here, I'll take them." Holly grabs all their things and runs back upstairs. The woman never calms down.

"He said he'll be a little late." Phoenix sits in the middle of the couch, putting her feet up and burying her head in her phone.

"My mom and Uncle Brian are coming for the movie too," Holly informs me, panting.

"Why don't you take a break now?"

She sits on a breakfast stool. "Thanks. I have a lot of nervous energy I can't get rid of."

Austin goes over to her and puts his arm around her back. She leans into him, smiling.

"Okay, everyone, dig in. As it was voted, we're watching *Weekend at Bernie's* and *St. Elmo's Fire*." I don't even finish before Austin grabs the serving spoon and serves himself a huge helping. "Maybe serve your wife first."

"I am."

"That's a lot for Holly?" Not that I want to food shame her or anything.

"She's hungry, like me." His snappy attitude says *leave the topic alone*, so I move away and let our guests fill their plates.

Brooklyn stands with me.

"Eat," I say, gesturing to the spread.

She grabs her stomach. "I'm not feeling the best. I'll pick at it later."

"Do you have the flu?" I ask.

"The flu?" She scrunches up her face.

Everyone stops and zeroes in on Brooklyn as though they want to tell her that if she has the flu, she better get the hell out of here.

"We've got Calista and Dion to worry about. You can't go around bringing in diseases, Brook." Rome goes berserk because that's what he does if he feels his kids are threatened.

"I don't have the flu," she says. "I just don't feel great. I ate a little candy this afternoon."

"A little?" Wyatt says. "Try the entire stocking I filled for you at Christmas."

She sticks out her tongue and makes faces at his back in true toddler fashion.

"Well, I'm starving," Harley says. "Chasing around two kids all day and only eating a half-eaten waffle and a couple spoonfuls of mac and cheese just isn't enough."

"No one would think you're engaged to a chef," Rome says, shaking his head.

"Well, the chef doesn't cook for his beautiful wife or his kids." She gives him a saccharine smile.

"I told you to bring them down to the restaurant."

"And you also said you refuse to make them boxed macaroni and cheese."

Harley's voice is snippy, and I laugh. Rome shoots me a glare and I bite my lip to stop.

"That stuff is crap. I made them mac and cheese."

Harley looks around the room. "They don't want the real cheese. They want the powder." Harley's on edge too.

I think we should change topics. "Well, I ordered plenty. We have two more trays in the oven on warm just in case."

Liam pulls me against him and kisses the top of my head. I can't wait to be with him tonight. Then the light bulb goes off and I panic because with all the running around, I forgot.

"I'll be right back," I whisper and sneak out of the room to the bathroom upstairs.

Opening the drawer, I reach for my box of tampons, and there's definitely a problem. It's very light and there's nothing moving around inside.

Sure enough, I'm holding an empty box.

Shit.

My purse is downstairs, which is probably where I put the last one. Damn Liam for forgetting to stop and get them on his way home.

After pulling up my pants, I wash my hands and look down the hall at my old bedroom. I almost feel as though it wasn't me who lived in there. But Denver's door is open, and I remember that's where Holly was putting all the purses. Surely one of them has a tampon in there.

I scramble across the hallway, hearing all the laughter and jokes downstairs. We're all in a good place. I mean, some of us are still finding ourselves, like Phoenix and

Denver, but all in all, we've survived. I smile, thinking about how close we all are.

I open the first purse and move around the wallet and the keys and the makeup bag. Nothing. Obviously this person expects everyone else to be prepared.

The second purse might have a tampon, but it's overfilled with receipts and papers. Is that an uneaten Snickers bar? Yeah, I'm not taking my chance that an animal has burrowed a home in here.

"Is there something you need to tell me?"

I look up and find Liam leaning along the doorframe, his ankles crossed, his arms across his chest. He's so damn hot. How did I ever lock him down? He's sweet and caring... but he didn't buy me tampons, and now I look like a klepto stealing from my family.

"A hidden drug problem or just a snooper?" He cracks a smile.

"I'm looking for a tampon because you didn't go to the store."

"It makes me feel weird," he admits. "You refuse to buy condoms."

"I don't refuse. I just don't think of them until—"

"We're half undressed. I know. We're kind of lucky that you're looking for a tampon right now."

We've agreed not to go on the pill or anything else because having kids isn't that far off. I'm already thirty-one. I give him the "exactly" look.

Looking back inside the purse—because there is no way none of these women own a tampon—my eyes zero in on a bottle instead. I pull it out. "Look!"

"That's not a tampon, babe," Liam says, sitting on the edge of the bed.

"No, they're prenatal vitamins."

"So?"

"So someone downstairs is taking them."

"Maybe they're old. Harley has been pregnant twice."

The bottle feels pretty full, so I unscrew the top and there's a seal over the bottle. "They're brand new."

"Whose purse is it?"

We both look at it then look at one another with our mouths hanging open.

TEN MINUTES LATER....

AFTER I FIND a tampon in another purse, go to the bathroom, and ramble on to Liam about the prenatal vitamins, we head downstairs. Denver's finally arrived, but with a ghost-white face. He's at the kitchen table. No one ever sits at the kitchen table. Everyone's around him. Grandma Dori is at his side with her hand on his forearm.

"What is it?" I ask.

Liam grabs my hand as though I'll need his support.

"Chip Dawson passed away," Austin says.

I gasp. "I'm sorry, Denver. I know how close you two were."

Denver nods, and Rome sits next to him. We're all close, but those two are far closer to each other than any of us. He'll know what to do in this situation.

"I'm sorry, man. You should feel good that you helped him out these last six months though. I'm sure it meant the world to him," Rome says.

Denver shakes his head. "I can't believe he's gone. It feels so surreal."

We all lean forward because Denver's voice is so low.

"Were you with him when it happened?" Rome asks.

The doorbell rings and we all look around, almost like we're counting everyone who's here.

Liam walks to the door, and I follow. Cleo Dawson stands on the other side, her teeth chattering and snow covering her blonde hair. She stomps in and scans the room until she sees Rome who's now standing in front of the kitchen table.

Storming past Liam, she pokes her finger into Rome's chest. "I want the key for Lifetime Adventures! If you think you're gonna steal that away from me now that my dad's gone, you're crazy!"

Rome holds up his hands and steps aside.

Cleo's eyes shift from him to Denver. "Ugh... who pissed off who to procreate two of you?"

The End

COCKAMAMIE UNICORN RAMBLINGS

We have to admit, whether it was the six-month break between the Bailey books or all the teasing we did through books one through three, the anticipation for Liam and Savannah's story made us nervous. We had our doubts whether we could deliver the story everyone was so eager to get their hands on.

In the end, we're happy with the story and feel it's true to Liam and Savannah's characters. Savannah wouldn't just lie down and admit she had fallen for someone five years younger than he—and her brothers' best friend at that. Savannah holds the weight of the entire Bailey family on her shoulders and she struggled to carve out a life of her own.

We knew Liam having already reformed some of his playboy ways before ever pursuing Savannah, would find a way to fight for Savannah without her realizing he was. That he was patient for all these years, no matter how hard he wanted her, he wouldn't rush a few months.

A little bit of insight on one of us...

Rayne is four years older than her husband (five for two months out of the year, but who's counting? Oh yeah, Rayne is). When she first met her husband, it was a hard thing to get over. He was perfect in every way, but the social stigma of a woman being older than the man was still alive. It is even now. So much so that she warned Piper that readers might be turned off by the age difference between the two. Being married for almost thirteen years now, they still receive shocked faces that she's older than him. It's just not the norm in our society. She could list comments she gets like cougar, cradle robber, or people do the math—when you were sixteen, he was twelve. Everyone is joking, which Rayne knows. Surely no one loses sleep over it. But it was a hiccup she had to overcome for their relationship to last. Her kids thank her for her ability to adapt every day (totally joking).

Many thanks to our team who if not for them, we'd never be able to give you these books!

- Danielle Sanchez and the entire Wildfire Marketing Solutions!
- Cassie from Joy Editing for line edits.
- Ellie from My Brother's Editor for line edits.
- Shawna from Behind the Writer for proofreading.
- Sarah from Okay Creations for the cover and branding for the entire series.
- Sara from Sara Eirew Photography for the sexy and steamy Liam and Savannah.
- Bloggers who consistently carve out time to read, review and/or promote us.

- Piper Rayne Unicorns who shout from the rooftops about our new releases and love our characters like we do.
- Readers who took a chance on our book with so many choices out there.

And we're on to Denver Bailey next. Boy oh boy, the biggest playboy is going down by the hands of Cleo Dawson and we're quite sure he won't know what hit him!

Hugs to everyone!

Xo
Piper & Rayne

ABOUT PIPER & RAYNE

Piper Rayne is a USA Today Bestselling Author duo who write "heartwarming humor with a side of sizzle" about families, whether that be blood or found. They both have e-readers full of one-clickable books, they're married to husbands who drive them to drink, and they're both chauffeurs to their kids. Most of all, they love hot heroes and quirky heroines who make them laugh, and they hope you do, too!

ALSO BY PIPER RAYNE

The Baileys

Lessons from a One-Night Stand

Advice from a Jilted Bride

Birth of a Baby Daddy

Operation Bailey Wedding (Novella)

Falling for My Brother's Best Friend

Demise of a Self-Centered Playboy

Confessions of a Naughty Nanny

Operation Bailey Babies (Novella)

Secrets of the World's Worst Matchmaker

Winning My Best Friend's Girl

Rules for Dating your Ex

Operation Bailey Birthday (Novella)

The Greenes

My Twist of Fortune (FREE)

My Beautiful Neighbor

My Almost Ex

My Vegas Groom

The Greene Family Summer Bash

My Sister's Flirty Friend

My Unexpected Surprise

My Famous Frenemy

The Greene Family Vacation

My Scorned Best Friend

My Fake Fiancé

My Brother's Forbidden Friend

The Modern Love World

Charmed by the Bartender

Hooked by the Boxer

Mad about the Banker

Complete Set (all 3 books)

The Single Dad's Club

Real Deal

Dirty Talker

Sexy Beast

Complete Set (all 3 books)

Hollywood Hearts

Mister Mom

Animal Attraction

Domestic Bliss

Bedroom Games

Cold as Ice

On Thin Ice

Break the Ice

Complete Set (all 3 books +)

Charity Case

Manic Monday

Afternoon Delight

Happy Hour

Complete Set (all 3 books)

Blue Collar Brothers

Flirting with Fire

Crushing on the Cop

Engaged to the EMT

Complete Set (All 3 books)

White Collar Brothers

Sexy Filthy Boss

Dirty Flirty Enemy

Wild Steamy Hook-up

The Rooftop Crew

My Bestie's Ex

A Royal Mistake

The Rival Roomies

Our Star-Crossed Kiss

The Do-Over

A Co-Workers Crush

Hockey Hotties

Countdown to a Kiss (Free Novella)

My Lucky #13

The Trouble with #9

Faking it with #41

Sneaking around with #34

Second Shot with #76

Offside with #55

Printed in Great Britain
by Amazon

83742013R00192